Mistletoe

Also by Alison Littlewood

Mistletoe

ALISON LITTLEWOOD

Jo Fletcher
BOOKS

First published in Great Britain in 2019 by
Jo Fletcher Books

an imprint of Quercus Editions Ltd
Carmelite House
50 Victoria Embankment
London EC4Y 0DZ

An Hachette UK Company

A CIP catalogue record for this book is available
from the British Library.

HB ISBN 978 1 78747 587 8
TPB ISBN 978 1 78747 588 5
EBOOK ISBN 978 1 78747 590 8

10 9 8 7 6 5 4 3 2 1

Typeset by CC Book Production Ltd
Printed and bound in Great Britain by Clays Ltd, Elcograf S.p.A.

MIX
Paper from
responsible sources
FSC   FSC® C104740
www.fsc.org

Papers used by Quercus Editions Ltd are from well-managed forests
and other responsible sources.

For Ann, Trevor and Ian
For all the Christmases past

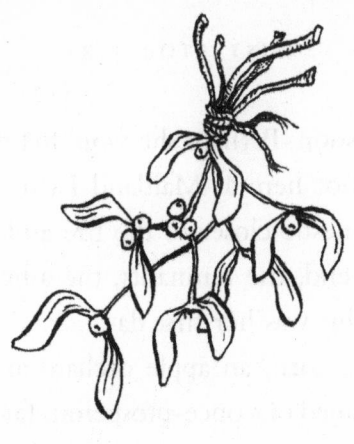

Chapter One

There was something in the snow. Leah sensed it even before she shifted her eyes from the sagging wreck of her barn and scanned the white fields. She didn't know what it was, but she felt it waiting, almost recognised it – life, as she wanted to live it? The future, or something else? It was hidden in the spaces between snowflakes, almost visible through their flicker and dance. She couldn't reach it, not yet, so instead she tilted her head back and relished the snow's cold kisses on her face, the numbness that spread across her skin.

It was almost Christmas. She had escaped the city, the gaudy shop windows, the ever-repeating chirp of carols, the cheerfulness of her colleagues that faded when they saw her watching. She couldn't bear the constant advice: *you shouldn't, mustn't, can't, not when you're . . . You'll regret it.* The standing-room-only trains and jostling pavements. The nights that drew in too soon. Perhaps she wouldn't mind those long nights, though, not here at Maitland Farm. When it grew dark, she would nestle closer to the fire and tell herself that this was not the end, the remnants, the ashes; it was a new beginning, and this was her first day.

A farmhouse, a barn, an apple orchard and a single field were all that remained of a once-prosperous farm. The original boundaries had suited the land, but they had stopped suiting the people who lived within them and the fields had been sold off, piece by piece, to other farms, those who could still make them pay. Eventually even the house was lost to the family, at least until now. Leah smiled with satisfaction. The place might be a shadow of what it had been, but it would suit her. A dry-stone wall enclosed the pasture that stretched away from the yard up an undulating slope. She could see no other buildings from within her little hollow and that sense of being alone, cut off from everyone and everything, met some need within her. She even liked that it didn't look like a home, not really. The darkened stone was dour and unwelcoming and there was no garden, no frivolous bright colours to suggest loitering and leisure. It was businesslike. It would keep her focused. She wanted to create something new, and she would; the farm would rise again, becoming the living, lovely image of a perfect country life.

She turned towards the farmhouse with its narrow leaded casements, all of them dark, except for the lowering sun glaring redly from their panes. Despite its two storeys, the house looked low and hulking, crouching under the cleanness of the falling snow. The roof was already blanketed, hiding the prized slate the estate agent had been quick to point out. Leah's incongruously bright red car, parked on one side of the yard with the haulage trailer unhitched next to it, was also in the process of being buried. *Forgotten*, she thought, without quite knowing why.

She tried to picture the farm in the light of summer, the fields turned to green, the sky an innocent blue with little scuds of cloud, and as if conscious that she was trying to banish it, a breath of cold wrapped itself about her. She felt the silence rising at her back like an exhalation from the land. It had been farmed for centuries and was now in abeyance. Was it too waiting to see what it would become? She had intended to walk around her land, beating the bounds, as they might once have called it, planning for that future, but now she couldn't bear to do it, didn't want to step into the empty field and mar the pristine glistening surface.

It was growing late. The sun would soon sink below the horizon, taking any vestiges of heat and life with it. Chill water had seeped into her boots and tomb-cold air snaked down the back of her neck. Her coat was speckled with white and she imagined it accumulating until she too was covered.

Telling herself that there was no rush, she had plenty of time to review this place she had bought, Leah made her way back across the narrow yard, her feet slipping on the irregular cobbled surface beneath the snow.

She tried to ignore the feeling that something was watching her leave.

Inside, once she'd pulled off her boots and wet socks, she found the stone-flagged floor was hard as iron and just as cold. The chill was radiating upwards, making her shiver, so she hurried to don some slippers before going into the living room – or just 'the room', as the estate agent had called it. It was the largest space in the house, the ceiling high and crossed with beams rife with woodworm holes – an old infestation, the surveyor had assured her, long since dead. The dark grey flags continued in here, mottled by years of use, chipped paler in places, stained darker in others. Someone had once papered the walls in dull hues of mustard and olive green, although thankfully great swathes of it had peeled off, revealing plaster that was in turn crumbling away from the laths beneath. Leah envisaged exposed stone and whitewashed walls, generous sofas and warm rugs, a blazing fire on the hearth – which for now was empty, without even a supply of logs for burning.

The room was largely bare of furniture, with nothing to make it feel cosy. An ugly coffee table had been left by the previous residents, along with a wing-back seat in a light brown velour that made her think of mice. The nap had worn bare along its arms, while the back was darkened with grease, or perhaps hair oil. Leah already knew she wouldn't be able to sit there without wondering what was happening behind her, what shadows were gathering in those empty corners. Instead, she perched uncomfortably on the only decent piece in the room: an ancient wooden settle that looked like it had always been there. The seat was barely softened by a long, threadbare cushion.

If there was little to make it comfortable, there was less to make it hers, but in time it would be both. In the New

Year, Leah planned to have her own furniture brought over from Manchester; she had brought only the bare essentials for now, along with tools, clothing and food supplies. She had told herself this was deliberate, that she wanted to live with the place for a while before filling its empty spaces, although she would admit that it had been a relief not to have to deal with removal men. She didn't think she was ready to face their questions and curious glances.

And there had been a kind of satisfaction in packing up her life and letting it all go. In the end she'd done it quickly, as she had with Josh and Finn's things – as if their clothes and shoes and books and toys had belonged to people only remotely connected with her. But each item still summoned such memories, and she had been clinging to too many of them: Josh's warm woollen sweater; Finn's teddy bear, the first they ever bought for him; his fire engine, though the siren supplied by his voice was now for ever silent; the tattered plush puppy he had chosen himself.

When Leah had packed up her own things there were no such feelings, nothing she could connect with anything else, and when she'd finished she stared at the sealed boxes as if they belonged to a stranger. And perhaps that was what she'd wanted. She couldn't even remember what half of them contained, but that was all right; she was here to look forward, not back.

Now, catching sight of the fireplace again, she shifted on the hard settle. It was cavernous, edged by stone slabs and topped by a broad wooden beam greyed by time and cracked by centuries of heat. There were scratches in the surface, patterns she couldn't quite make out: witch marks, intended to keep evil at bay, maybe, or some other message from the past – or nothing at all? When she went over to examine them, peering as if they were a language she couldn't read, she realised they were only notches where some hard object had repeatedly struck the wood. She ran her finger over them, deliberately not raising her eyes to the objects she had placed on top of the beam, the first things she had brought into her new house. She could still see their shapes at the edge of her vision. The two urns were of carved marble, one a little larger than the other, just objects, and yet the voice at the back of her mind started up again with the question she couldn't bring herself to answer: didn't she understand what was in there? Didn't she *know*?

She shook herself, shifting her gaze to the mirror above the mantelpiece, something else left by the previous occupants. Its face had been left turned to the wall, a mark of respect when someone died, or maybe just superstition. It was apparently supposed to prevent the spirit of the deceased from being trapped in the house.

It was time to let that go too. Leah reached up and grasped the frame so she could free the creaking wire from the solid brass hook on the picture rail, then turn it and rehang it mirror side out. She peered around the frame at the foxed and clouded glass, seeing in its reflection the blank wall – and something else; a pale shape that glimmered, there and then gone.

She started back with a cry, letting the mirror crash back into place and sending fragments pattering to the mantelpiece.

Leah examined it in dismay, expecting to find shards of broken glass everywhere, but there were only crumbs of plaster.

She put a hand to her heart and let out a dry laugh. What was wrong with her, spooked by what must have been her own reflection? She turned to look around the room, trying to push away the thought that it couldn't have been, that the angle hadn't been right, and instead she replayed the words her friend Trish had said to her when she'd waved her off.

'Lots of luck, Leah – not that you'll need it. You'll smash it!'

Well, at least she hadn't smashed the mirror; she certainly didn't need *that* kind of luck. She left it as it was, facing the wall, and sat down again. To distract herself, she reached out and grabbed the estate agent's pack from the table. As she started flipping through the pages, the phrases lingered: *A rare opportunity . . . historical Yorkshire farmhouse, parts dating back to the seventeenth century . . . secluded position along a private track, unspoiled view. Solid timber doors and staircase . . . A stone-built barn, ripe for conversion.*

They made it sound like a story she'd once been told – but then, it always had been, hadn't it? A fairy-tale spun by the man she loved, a dream she could almost step into . . .

No matter how desirable the agent had made it sound, the reality was very different. The farmhouse had been a vacant possession – indeed, on that first viewing, it had looked abandoned, its rooms scattered with a miscellany of furniture, as if the occupants had up and left at a moment's notice and might suddenly return and reclaim it all. But no one had lived there in months. It had lingered on the market for a long time until Leah had come along. *Lucky for you,* the agent had crowed, although it hadn't felt so much like luck as Fate: the house had still been there for her when she'd needed it; when she was ready. And why not? After all, her ancestors had once owned this farm and the land surrounding it.

Leah closed her eyes, remembering the day she'd first seen it.

Josh had been at home, on the laptop, although she didn't know when he'd stopped working – since he'd been made partner he'd grown sick of running the business, juggling problems with staff or the office or some other crisis and rarely able to spend time on the legal work he loved. He'd kept hinting that he wanted to *make* something instead, to withdraw the money he'd invested in the firm to buy bricks and mortar, to do up a property and turn it into a living.

'Oh my God – I've seen the future, Leah . . . Look at this!'

She'd grinned at his excitement. 'Are you a soothsayer now?' she'd said, and laughing, leaned over his shoulder. Her smile had faded at the sight of a neglected room, everything dark and cast into shadow.

'It's just the other side of the Pennines. Isn't it *perfect?*'

She hadn't understood what was so wonderful. He scrolled down, exclaiming over the potential, pointing out the period features. He was even enthused by the acres and acres of space all around it – acres and acres of *nothing*, as Leah privately thought.

'And this – see, Leah? Can't you just see Finn playing there?' He called up an image of a rough field and placed his fingertip on the screen before trailing it downwards, as if describing their son's haphazard route as he ran through the meadow.

He turned and grinned at her, bubbling over with excitement at the picture he was painting, his story of the future for the three of them, but she had felt only a growing dismay.

'It's perfect – isn't it perfect, Leah? Just imagine . . .'

She hadn't wanted to imagine. It was all too much work – it was too remote, too far from home. She had her job, her friends. She even remembered thinking, *I have my life*. She had not known then how easily it could all be snatched away.

She reached over his shoulder and scrolled back up, looking for the asking price. Surely the cost would be too high? It must be . . .

And instead she'd seen the name: Maitland Farm.

Josh had let out a whoop of triumph as the cursor lingered on the title. 'You see? It was meant to be!'

What would the estate agent have said if he'd known? She imagined he'd barely have been able to contain his excitement if they'd told him that Maitland was her maiden name, or that her family had hailed from this very part of Yorkshire, that they'd been landowners who'd lost their birthright . . .

Her mother had told her something of it once, although Leah hadn't really been paying attention. Her mother always did love to tell her stories . . . but it had all seemed to fit. In response to the questions she'd tried to present as idle curiosity, the agent informed her that the farm had been in the Maitland family for years before they'd lost it, and after that, no one had ever settled here long enough to make a real go of it.

When she'd first seen the name at the top of the computer screen, however, Leah had given a dismissive laugh, declaring it a coincidence, distancing herself from the idea that it might mean anything at all.

Now she was a landowner, and she'd done it in spite of her friends' well-intentioned warnings: that she shouldn't leave her job, shouldn't leave her home and everything she knew, shouldn't make any big changes, not while she was grieving. They'd been so certain that this was no time for her to be alone, no time to take on the biggest challenge of her life.

She didn't care for any of that. This was what Josh had wanted, something Finn would have loved. They couldn't be part of the story any more but she could finish it for them, couldn't she? Leah could no longer build the perfect family, but she could build the perfect house for a family to live in. After Josh's death she'd taken the money from the business and ploughed it into his bricks and mortar, and it had felt right. There would be clean air, good hard work and the satisfaction of making something better.

And after all, she was a Maitland.

Trish was the first person Leah had told, but to her surprise, her closest friend hadn't told her, '*You'll smash it!*', not then. Instead she'd wailed, 'But you can't! It's almost *Christmas . . .*'

And that immediately triggered images of laden plates, piles of presents, paper hats and crackers and happy children, *living* children with ruddy cheeks and brightened eyes; pictures that came around every year and yet depicted a reality she knew was as fragile as tissue paper ripped from a parcel. She'd scarcely thought about it – she hadn't wanted to – so it had come as a relief when Trish's husband announced he wanted to escape Christmas too. Although in their case, it wasn't so much escaping it as running headlong towards it. Curt wanted to take Trish and their daughter Becca to Lapland, to see Father Christmas and Rudolph and ride on a real sleigh over real snow.

When Trish remembered she wouldn't be there for Leah, she had been stricken, insisting in a quavering voice that she would stay – or even better, that Leah must join them.

'Of course you have to go – it's going to be brilliant,' Leah said. 'I'm thrilled for you – you'll love every second of it! And I'll think of you when I'm slaving away on the farm.' She'd winked at this last and laughed before insisting that she really would be too busy. She would spend the winter clearing the house, making a clean sweep and deciding what to do with it next, planning the new start she would make in the New Year.

'Seriously, it'll be good for me,' she'd added, and when she picked out a gift for Becca, she chose a toy farm, complete with wooden sheep and cows and horses.

Leah smiled, thinking of Trish and Curt and Becca having fun in Lapland, and set aside the papers. The bright prose – *a rare opportunity* – belonged to the future, while the farmhouse lingered in the past. Still, the place echoed something inside her, right down to that turned mirror, the windows that had been shuttered against the light.

She made her way up the creaking staircase – *beautifully carved, fine workmanship* – to her bedroom. She had not chosen the largest, the one at the back of the house overlooking the orchard; that's the one that she would have shared with Josh. Nor did she take any of the smaller rooms that might have been claimed by Finn. She'd decided on the second double room, which also might have been meant to be, since it was already furnished with another remnant, a heavy old wooden bedstead. Her possessions were stacked in a corner, largely still in their boxes. They looked a little like Christmas presents, but instead of the new, they held only the old.

She ran her hand across the closed lids, thinking of unpacking, and opened the first, pulling out T-shirts and old jumpers and ripped jeans, all the clothing she'd need for the dirty work ahead of her. She hung the clothes neatly on the cheap clothes rail she'd set up to keep her going until she furnished the place properly. Outside, it was full dark. The window casements were framed in stone, the glass leaded into diamonds, and if it hadn't been for the snowflakes stroking the panes, brightening momentarily in the light of the room's single naked bulb, she would have seen nothing at all.

Leah put her face up close to the glass, noticing the flaws in the panes. There was an icy aura, as if the air outside was leaking straight through the imperfect glazing. When she'd looked around earlier she'd heard distant traffic on the road, every sound reaching her easily, the thin window glass providing no barrier, but now there was nothing. There was no trace of another house, not even a light, but when she peered through one of the clearer diamonds she realised it was not entirely dark after all. She could make out the field in the gleam of the moon, ending in the suggestion of a stone wall with trees jutting from it. Indeed, the sky was strangely pale, pregnant with snow, made of snow, and flakes hung in the air, motionless as the picture on a Christmas card. Each one was fat and white, a child's idea of what snow should be.

For the first time, Leah felt a thread of disquiet. This snow wasn't going to stop any time soon. It wouldn't be melted by the heat pulsing from a city's tightly packed buildings or scattered by numerous tyres on busy streets, turning filthy grey before it vanished. This snow would cover everything, pushing it all deeper and deeper, like memories; like secrets. It would soften detail and steal away colour, changing the world into something new and strange.

Leah told herself again that it was magical and beautiful, trying to shake off another, more insistent thought: that this was her new start and it was already in a shroud.

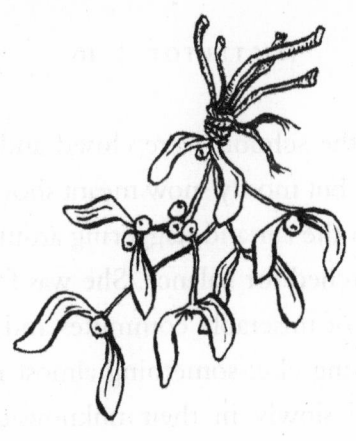

Chapter Two

When Leah awoke the light was strange, the room still half dark but with a peculiar luminosity that flickered in an ever-changing pattern. She wondered whether that was what had roused her; the house was otherwise motionless and perfectly silent, as if nothing had changed here for centuries and never would.

When she sat up, she saw the source of the light. Outside the window, the snow was glowing as if lit from within. She pushed the duvet aside and cold air took its place like a mantle about her neck as she padded across the exposed floorboards to the window.

The silken edge of dawn was just colouring the field, though the moon still rode high, turning the snow into a glory of silver light. Leah stared into it, frozen by the vision. In her old life she'd never really enjoyed winter. There had been rare days when the schools were closed and she'd stayed at home with Finn, but mostly snow meant shovelling the drive, scraping ice from the car and staggering around like a drunk, her arms outstretched for balance. She was familiar with the filthy, wet snow of miserable commutes and aching fingers. This was something else: something almost miraculous.

The flakes fell slowly in their unknowable pattern and she focused upon a single one, trying to trace its descent. She quickly lost sight of it and another took its place, then another, almost making her dizzy.

Finn would have loved this. He wouldn't have been silent before its mystery, though, and she smiled at the thought of him flying through the house, clamouring for snowmen and sledging. He would have been out in that field with his dad all day, hurling handfuls of snow in each other's faces, shrieking as they pushed it down each other's necks.

As if in answer to the images in her head, Leah heard a sound.

Her forehead creased and she leaned towards the cold glass. She expected to hear nothing – *it was only imagination, not even a memory* – but the noise came again, quite clear through the thin pane: a dull *whoomph*, the sound of snow shattering against a wall.

Leah bit her lip. She wasn't sleeping; she hadn't imagined it. She remained motionless, listening, but heard only the blood rushing through her veins. It had sounded so real . . . perhaps a clump of snow or an icicle had fallen from the roof, that was all. Who could possibly be there? Her friends were miles away, in another life. Perhaps it was a trespasser, then, or a poacher – but what could they expect to find out here, at this time of year?

And why throw snowballs at her house?

She peered out, already persuading herself there would be nothing to see, that she had been half dreaming, and she heard another sound: the distinct dry scrape of a hand delving into layers of crisp snow, the kind that would make a perfect snowball. Surely she must have imagined hearing that – but it was followed by a high, clear giggle.

She froze. *It's not real.* Still the sound hung in her ears, unmistakeable: a child's bright cry of happiness coming out of the dark, as if from the heart of the snow itself. For one crazy moment she wondered if that was exactly what she had heard – the sound of the snow, its true nature – until the fantasy was dispelled by the hollow rattle of something striking the front door.

Leah held her breath. Was it a snowball striking wood – or someone knocking to come in?

On the edge of hearing, so faint she wasn't certain if it was real or only the memory of another sound, came the echo of laughter – a child's voice, silvery and clear, and yet fading, as if they were walking away across the field, passing beyond her.

She swiped at the breath-damp window, clearing it almost as if she could clear her vision, and peered out, but she could see nothing. Snow moved and shifted across the field, obscuring her view, hiding everything.

When the laugh came again, she knew that *someone* was there. She rushed from the room and across the landing, down the stairs and through the hall. The key was in the front door; she let out a frustrated cry as the latch stuck, but at last it clanked open and she pulled the door wide – to be enveloped by a whirl of icy air and feathery snowflakes. They clung to her, and blinded, she struck out as if she could push them aside. They danced away but there were more, always more of them, so many that she couldn't see the field any longer. The world was full of swarming snow and the only thing she could make out was the moon's cold disc, shining through it all and showing her nothing.

'Hello?'

Her voice came as a shock to her, too little used and with a quaver in it, but she didn't care. She called out again, louder, though the word uppermost in her mind was her son's name; as if, having begun to build the home Josh had envisaged for the three of them, he could possibly have come to find her here. She pictured the sound weaving its way through the cascade and into the field, crossing any barrier the snow tried to place between them, but her cry quickly died away.

All that answered her was silence. The laughter had faded; the snow muffled everything. Without thinking, Leah stepped outside, and when her bare feet sank into the snow, she almost welcomed the numbness it brought, ignoring the bitter chill, moving into it, away from the light spilling from the house. She did not call out again. She realised she was shivering with cold – or was it something else? For a moment the only sound was her teeth chattering. Beneath that was dead silence and she knew it was hopeless. The child she'd heard wasn't about to show himself. She wouldn't find out who they were, not tonight. Possibly there hadn't been a child at all. Perhaps she had only dreamed of walking to the window, of hearing a voice. Or maybe the trickster snowflakes had confused her hearing just as they had deceived her vision.

They were still swirling madly around her, flurrying against her as if to push her away from whatever she had seen. Another shiver shook her in its grip. It was too cold out here for the living; she didn't belong in this world – but nor did she belong in Finn's, not now. She couldn't follow where he had gone.

Opening her mouth as if to call out, although she had no idea what she wanted to say, she tasted the snow on her tongue.

Defeated, she turned back towards the house – and saw the mark that must have been on the door the whole time she'd been standing there looking out at the field.

White clumps clung to the wood, forming a broken circle where a snowball had shattered against the door. Leah glanced at the ground, searching for further traces, but all she could see was her trampling footprints.

She took another step and realised she was freezing. Her feet were red and throbbing, her fingers icy, her limbs leaden. Pain, waking at last, flared and she hurried inside, quickly closing the door behind her to cut off the bitter air.

As she went back upstairs, she was conscious of the horrid intimacy of her damp feet on the dry boards. The play of snow at the window mocked her as she climbed back into bed, the grime of the house still clinging to her skin. She curled into a ball under the duvet and closing her eyes, thought, *I am going mad.*

The cold wrapped itself around her bones; the image of snowflakes dancing in front of her eyes wouldn't leave her. It didn't help to know that she should have dried her feet and changed her clothing before getting into bed.

She steeled herself to emerge into the draughty room once more, wriggled from under the covers and went to the light switch, blinking as the sudden glare asserted reality around her. That was what she needed, to stop her from entertaining thoughts she surely never would have allowed herself in the light of day. Half dreaming, her imagination had escaped her control. It couldn't happen again; she had to be able to trust herself.

She turned to the pile of boxes and yanked open the nearest, hoping to find some warm jumpers. Softness met her touch; her fingertips sank in and she pulled out the top one, and another, and then she stared at the objects spilling across the floor.

They were Finn's toys. She peered into the box and saw more inside, all piled together: everything she hadn't been able to bear throwing away when she'd cleared his room.

The cold forgotten, she picked through them. Here was the cuddly puppy that had grown ragged from her son's love; his first grown-up cricket ball, the leather worn by summers of play; the model Spitfire Josh helped him make; the bright red plastic of his favourite fire engine. *Woo, woo* . . .

And on the floor, staring up at her with bright black eyes, was his old teddy bear.

She stooped and picked it up. Bear had been Finn's from babyhood. It had always been Bear, never Teddy. A lot of its fur had fallen out, though it was still soft and golden at the seams, where little hands and rough games couldn't wear it away. The texture was at once familiar and strange. She'd always insisted Finn keep it, this toy he'd had the longest, even when it had only been her favourite, no longer his. She pulled Bear's ears straight and adjusted his arms so they were held outwards, awaiting a hug, or offering one.

Leah blinked. She had no recollection of bringing the toys with her – in fact, she was quite sure she remembered deciding *not* to bring them to the farm. She'd thought it would be better for her, a step towards facing the future rather than surrounding herself with the past. She hadn't been able to bring herself to give them away, so the toys had been destined for storage along with the rest of her old life, ready to be picked up again when she was ready.

So it was just a mistake, then. After all, she'd packed quickly, automatically, without thought – and yet maybe a part of her had known what she was doing all along? Maybe her subconscious hadn't been able to let them go – or *something* hadn't let her. She shook away yet another fanciful idea, a wild idea that it was her son who had guided her hand, making sure she brought all his precious things along, so that when he came to visit her they would already be waiting for him.

She sat on the edge of the bed, cradling the little bear in her arms, holding him close. Why *should* she let go? His presence warmed her. It felt right in her arms, meant to be. She rested her cheek against Bear's head, no longer shivering, no longer cold. She should perhaps be afraid, but what she mostly felt was wonder. Had the snow given her a glimpse of some kind of miracle? It was the right time of year for that, though it struck her that it wasn't even Christmas yet – it wouldn't be for days – and she started to laugh, though her cheeks were wet, with melted snow or with tears, she could not have said.

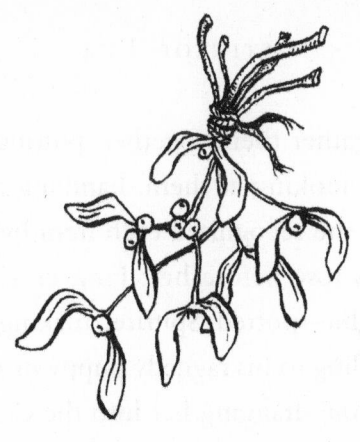

Chapter Three

When Leah woke again, she knew by the quality of the light that it was morning, though not how early. It was pleasant to be roused by the movements of the sun instead of shutting it out with curtains or blinds, or to have a clock tell her when to sleep and when to rise. The events of the previous night were at once as unreal and as present as a dream. Vivid moments came back to her – a child's bright laughter, the feel of ice under her feet, soft fur in her hands, and something else: hope, perhaps.

But what had she seen, after all? Nothing. The sounds she'd heard could have been the play of wind against stone, the sigh and creak of ancient wood, the settling of a house she wasn't yet familiar with. She had brought Finn's toys here herself. Had she really thought it might be a miracle? The notion dissolved as she looked at the toys scattered across the floor in the light of a new day.

She began to gather them together, putting them back in their box. Barely looking at them, handling them as briefly as she could, still she recognised each item by touch. A succession of images rose before her: Finn chasing around the room with his glue-spotted Spitfire, making machine-gun noises. Finn snuffling to his raggedy puppy in a language only he understood. Finn dragging her into the garden, clutching his cricket ball, pretending to be a champion spin bowler. He had always been so full of stories, full of vivid imaginings, and she had loved them, but she had always known where they had ended.

Then only the teddy bear remained. She retrieved Bear from her bed, intending to return him to the box too, and instead raised the toy to her face. Any trace of the scent of Finn's skin or his hair had long since faded, but she could not bring herself to shut this part of him away again, leaving Bear in the dark. Perhaps he *had* been brought to this place by some sort of magic – if only the human kind.

Leah went to the window and placed Bear on the sill, facing away from her, looking out into the snow. It was only when she turned again that she noticed something on the wall behind her pile of boxes. The plaster had already been partly exposed when she'd moved in, the dull, browned wallpaper peeling away and hanging loose in great swathes. Now she saw that its hanging weight had dragged it down further, revealing more of the wall.

She stared at the shape outlined there, wondering if it was mould or damp, but when she went closer, she saw that it was neither. The plaster itself had discoloured, forming a figure that looked a little like a child. His hair was a shadow and his eyes were uneven holes in his face. There were his head and shoulders and torso, one arm raised as if he were waving. She grimaced. It looked like a boy but it was old and fallen into decay and she didn't like to see it there, a part of this house. She wished she could wipe the figure away and promised herself that soon, she would. It meant nothing; it was an unfortunate suggestion of a shape and nothing more.

She realised she had raised a hand to peel off more of the wallpaper and snatched it back. Why should she want to see more of the old plaster now, before she was ready to resurface and paper it? Better to leave it covered.

Shaking her head at herself, Leah grabbed her jeans and a shirt and crossed the landing, moving quickly past the silent stairs. In the bathroom, plumbing creaked and whistled before a gush of water emerged from the bell-shaped, lime-scaled tap, more air than liquid. Pipes clanked and juddered against the wall and holes gaped where they vanished into the floor, the boards black with rot. The bath, a heavy affair of chipped enamel, had a greenish stain from the dripping tap. Leah imagined it refinished and restored, lying there in a room made cosy by candlelight. She would change it all; and she would be changed along with it. She'd not often been the one to take up a hammer and put up a shelf, but when she had tried, she'd always enjoyed the satisfaction of knowing she could do anything, if she only took the right steps, one after the next. She'd prepared herself as much as she could, packing a pile of instruction manuals and downloading dozens of TV programmes and YouTube videos; now she reminded herself that the further the distance to go, the greater her sense of achievement would be.

The water was as cold as ice-melt. She splashed it over her face, the initial shock quickly giving way to tingling, making her feel suddenly and brightly awake. It occurred to her that she could have boiled a kettle – her ancestors had doubtless heated water on the range for washing – but she'd be getting the heating fixed as soon as possible. She'd find someone qualified to take a look, although with the snow already drifting deeply across the much-lauded private track, she didn't suppose that would be any time soon.

Anyway, she'd soon get used to a little privation. First on the agenda this morning would be to finish her tour. She would walk the boundaries of the farm as she'd planned, surveying it afresh, and this time without an irritating estate agent talking the place up incessantly as he peered over her shoulder. It would help to make it hers, to claim it. And she'd start drawing up her list of everything she'd need to transform it, imposing her will on the old stone, the rotting wood, the chipped enamel, the leaking pipes and crumbling walls.

Everything, she thought. *This place will have everything.*

She visualised the rooms around her, warm and glowing and full of comfort instead of empty and grey, smelling of neglect and must and time.

A short while later, Leah stepped out into the raw chill. There was no colour in the land, but the sky was a glorious azure, fading to the palest hint of blue at the horizon. The sun's glare was merciless, the snow a blinding brilliance that made her squint against it. The wall edging the field was turned to silhouette, the outlines of the jutting trees as sharp as knives. She told herself the firs were ready-made Christmas trees, a jolly sight, though snow clung to their forms, rendering them lumpen and troglodytic. The prevailing wind had swept it from one side, leaving dark profiles a little like faces half turned away.

She focused on the glitter before her and a memory came: of her skipping along at her mother's side, her fingers encased in mittens, a scarf drawn up to her chin and her mother's words: 'Look, Leah! The snow shines brighter than any diamond.'

She smiled wistfully. Her mother had passed away some years ago, but Leah remembered her stories, fairy-tales that always ended in marriages and diamond rings. Her mother had always seemed so wise, almost as if she had been envisioning a life *after* the happily-ever-after. Leah pictured her with Finn as a newborn: the way she'd fitted his whole face into the span of her thumb and forefinger and laughed at how tiny he was. She imagined her own mother that small, her great-grandmother doing the same thing, and *her* mother, going back and back . . . perhaps even leading to this very place, this field, this farm.

She reached the gate that divided the pasture from the yard. 'Just enough land for a family,' the estate agent had said. Loops of frayed twine secured the gate to the post, but Leah could find no way to untie the knot and anyway, the bottom rungs were buried in a drift. She brushed snow from the top and, testing her weight on the sagging bars to ensure they wouldn't break, climbed over. Before jumping down, she hesitated. This was where Josh had pictured their son, running haphazardly down the meadow. The word that came to her was *pristine* – something perfect so easily spoiled – but then it wasn't, was it?

The snow shattered like spun sugar when her boots broke the surface. *Deep and crisp and even*, she thought, and it was: beautiful and smooth, save for where marks had been gouged into the surface a short distance away.

Disquiet stirring inside her, Leah walked towards it. The snow was deeper here, reaching the top of her boots, and she heard nothing but the crunch and creak of her steps. She felt like the only living person for miles around, and perhaps she was.

She stopped and stared. Here, the surface was scored with lines – almost like writing, though they spelled no message, yielded no secret. Leah could picture how they had been made: a little hand sweeping through the crust to reach the softer snow beneath, the kind that would clump into the best kind of snowball, one that would fly fast and keep its form until it shattered against a back or a wall or a door.

There was nothing strange about the marks except that they were here, in the middle of her field.

Leah looked back at the house. The white flecks still clung to the front door like a miniature wreath. She imagined a boy drawing back his arm and throwing his missile as hard as he could. A child could have thrown a snowball from here, couldn't he? She told herself that Finn could have. For all it had taken her a while to walk here, that was because of the deepness of the snow . . . it wasn't so very distant, was it?

The snow. There was something about the snow.

She shook the thought from her. It must have been local boys trespassing, having a snowball fight, not knowing that someone now owned the place – after all, how could they? But there was no sign that whoever had made these marks had been snowballed in turn, by *return fire*, as Finn would have put it. And when Leah searched the field again, she realised something else, finally facing the thing that had been nagging at her since she first stepped out: there had been no footprints leading to this place. The snow had been so perfect, such a lovely picture, until she had walked on it. And still there was not the trace of a footprint to mar its surface except her own.

The cold ached in her throat. There should be more – there must be some message or meaning she could understand – but she stood there and waited and nothing happened. The traces remained as they were, nothing more or less than they had been a moment ago, and she could not read them. She did not know who had made them. But there must be some simple explanation; there had to be.

She let out a long breath, which hung on the air in front of her before it vanished. She brushed at her eyes, chilling her skin with her damp gloves. Then she bent and plunged her hands into the snow. Defying herself, logic, and all the sane world around her, just for a moment that belonged to her and her son, she pressed a handful together and threw it into the centre of the field.

'There,' she whispered. '*I'll* play with you.'

Feeling that she had made an irrevocable promise, Leah turned and followed her own trail back to the gate. After a final glance behind her, she strode into the yard, past her car, now engulfed in snow to the top of the wheels, its windows glazed blind, white with frost. A thread of concern passed through her, then was gone. What did it matter? It wasn't as if she needed to go anywhere, and in any case, the village wasn't far. She could walk there if she wanted, all the while breathing clean fresh air instead of polluting exhaust fumes.

When the barn came into sight, built of the same darkened stone as the house, the estate agent's words rang in her ears: 'What a find, what an opportunity. Everybody wants converted barns these days, don't they?' Leah wasn't thinking of that yet, though. First, she was focusing on the land; she was going to see the orchard.

Finn would have loved that. She smiled, remembering a wonderful day they'd once spent in Sherwood Forest, pretending to be Robin Hood, firing arrows as they'd raced along. Josh had lifted Finn onto the lower branches of a tree – he did so love to climb them – and they'd cheered as Finn pulled himself higher, punching the air in triumph.

Suddenly tired – *time to leave the fairy-tale behind* – Leah leaned against the wall marking the boundary between Maitland Farm and the fields that had once belonged to it. According to her surveyor, who'd told her what he knew of the history of the farm and its decline, they'd been parcelled off and sold piecemeal to pay various debts.

'It's suffered over the years from falling yields,' he'd said on the phone. 'It would have made for a poor living. The soil's exhausted and that's no good if you're trying to make a farm pay its way. And the more land the owners sold off, the less they'd have been able to rotate crops and livestock, so things would have got worse and worse. It's a good thing you're not really interested in anything but the house, otherwise I'd have to advise against the purchase.'

It had all sounded so much worse than the estate agent's talk of previous owners 'failing to make a go of it' – especially as he'd couched it as a real opportunity for her, even though she'd never even had an allotment before, let alone a farmyard. But Leah wasn't bound by the past and not everyone could be a farmer: the fields would provide the perfect view, regardless of yields or fertility. Once she'd breathed life back into the buildings she'd have buyers lining up for a slice of rural life, the kind with dried flowers in the hearth, top-of-the-range Hunter wellies by the door, Land Rovers still bearing that showroom gleam and bouncing hypoallergenic labradoodles. Okay, so it might be a city person's idea of the country – but she was a city girl herself, and what was wrong with that? It needn't stop someone being happy here.

The path to the orchard was almost concealed between the side of the barn and the sold-off land. She could feel the uneven footing as she started down it, frozen hard as rock beneath the snow. It narrowed where the stone wall gave way to a leafless hedgerow of what she thought might be spindly hawthorn. She leaned in closer to the barn to avoid the spiked black twigs grasping at her coat.

Leah saw at once that the trees in the orchard couldn't be

climbed. They were planted haphazardly; indeed, they made her think of figures bowing their heads together, drawn into different groups and allegiances. Narrow limbs sprouted from thin, contorted trunks, some grizzled with clusters of twigs resembling bunched fists. Most of them were growing too close together. When the breeze shifted their branches, they clacked against one another with a hollow, hungry sound. She realised she had been hearing it for some time, the background to her thoughts.

Leah stared in dismay. The trees were so withered, they must be dead. Surely they hadn't been so forlorn when she'd first seen them? Distracted by the agent's forceful chatter, she had tasted the word *orchard* on her tongue: its cheerful, sweet, domesticated savour. The agent had told her knowledgeably they were native trees and she had liked the sound of that.

'They're likely Yorkshire Beauties or perhaps Greenings,' he'd said, as if he knew what he was talking about. 'Both varieties are good cookers, and even better, they keep well over the winter. Exactly what you'd want from your orchard.'

But that had been in the autumn – shouldn't fruit have been hanging from the boughs then, ready for picking? She hadn't really thought about it then, too caught up in a vision of baked apples and pies turning golden in the oven, but now she realised she hadn't seen any apples. She told herself it made no difference: she hadn't come here for apples, much less cookers that would need to be picked and preserved, or sold, maybe – to whom? She'd have enjoyed trying out the occasional crumble, getting her arms floury, sharing her produce with the neighbours maybe, but how many apples would one person need in any case? Her vision of country life didn't extend to self-sufficiency; she was more accustomed to picking food off supermarket shelves.

Still, she couldn't help feeling melancholy at the sight of the place, drained of vitality and colour, everything turned sour; as if life had not just retreated beneath the ground for a season but forsaken it altogether.

Clack, clack. The mournful sound came again and Leah narrowed her eyes. Was that a hint of green she'd glimpsed through the stirring branches?

She left the path and walked under the trees, pulling away from the twigs catching at her hair, and she caught herself imagining being entangled here, imprisoned by the branches until she was discovered in the spring, leaves wrapping her upraised arms. She blinked the peculiar vision away and found herself in a wider space between the trunks, in what must be the orchard's heart.

Leah realised she had been right, but also wrong. There was greenery, though not of a tree in leaf: mistletoe was wrapped around the branches, creeping over the trees. Here and there it had grown heavy, forming thick clusters as if in mockery of the foliage long since dropped away. The curved leaves were fresh and pale, the cream-coloured berries gleaming where they caught the sunlight. They looked like a gift; they looked like Christmas.

A smile touched her lips. Had the plant been cultivated here to provide some colour in this colourless season, so that it could be cut and brought indoors for the big day? But then she remembered that mistletoe was a parasite. It forced roots down into its host. If her trees were dead, maybe this was the reason.

Wasn't it poisonous, too?

She reached up to rip it from the branch, but was caught by the sudden memory of holding a sprig of mistletoe over Josh's head. She felt his bear-hug, his arms wrapping around her like vines about a tree, him kissing the dimple in her cheek and then her lips, until she couldn't breathe.

She closed her eyes and let her hand fall. At least some trace of life remained in this place. Let it stay.

As the memory faded, a noise cut through the air: the crystalline sound of a child's giggle.

Leah froze, thinking of a pristine field, no tracks leading to its centre; a child standing there, delving into the snow, and the promise she'd made.

I'll play with you.

She fought her way free of the trees, batting their low branches away from her face. When she emerged she saw nothing, no child and no one else, but she was still sure she could not have imagined that sound.

Without making any conscious decision, she found herself running back up the path, clawing her way along the side of the barn. When she burst into the yard, she found herself searching it for the form she knew better than her own – would he be wearing his red coat? Would he have found Bear, be dragging him along by one arm, as he had when he was a toddler? Shaking her head, she stumbled to a halt – and saw the fresh marks in the snow in front of her, not footprints or the remnants of a snowball fight, but something else.

There was a snow angel in her yard. Leah stared at it. Someone *had* been here, a child lying in the snow, and she couldn't help herself; she pictured her son. *I can fly, Mum!* Finn grinning, waving his arms and legs to form wings and robes, just as his dad had shown him. Finn, leaving behind an impression of his own dear self so that she could see he hadn't gone, that he hadn't left her entirely alone; leaving a message for her after all.

She was doing what she'd promised herself she wouldn't. Mist plumed from her mouth, a long exhalation. She continued to stare at the shape in the snow even while some treacherous voice whispered, *No.*

Whoever had done this was real; they had weight. It wasn't even the right size to have been made by her son's body, was it?

Finn's voice echoed in her mind: 'Five-and-three-quarters, Mum! Six-and-five-eighths!' He had always been racing towards the next birthday, wanting so badly to grow up, to be taller. Perhaps, wherever he was, he had been granted his wish.

She shook away the wild flow of thoughts. Her little boy was gone. He could not have come to find her, couldn't have left this imprint as a sign for her.

A sound came from behind her – was it the scrape of a boot on a rough surface? Leah spun towards the barn. The door was hanging open, sagging and settled into place like an old man by the fire, the wood so fissured and cracked she wasn't sure it would ever close again. The sun cut a sharp triangle into the interior, where snow had swept inside, thinning as it went to reveal patches of scuffed concrete, still bearing traces of dirt and straw. Was that a trail of footprints leading inside?

'Hello?' Just like the night before, her voice was hesitant.

A shadow re-formed, changing shape, and Leah edged forward. Was that the sound of another footstep, muffled by her own? Then came the unmistakeable ring of metal as something fell or was knocked over in the barn.

Leah stepped forward. In another moment, she might see her visitor. For now, all she could make out was the tangle of rusting farm implements heaped within. There was an old harrow, its rows of spikes opening like jaws, and what might have been a horse-drawn plough, though it was thoroughly rusted away. Pieces of harness lay rotting where they'd been thrown: the remains of collars and bridles, reins and straps. Old tools were stacked against the wall and next to those was an ancient chopping block, with an axe still leaning at its side. The blade, turned upwards, was the only thing in the barn that remained bright and sharp.

An explosion of movement sent spades and hoes and garden forks clattering across the pitted concrete. A shadow separated itself from the darkness by the door and Leah glimpsed a white, pinched face; a dirty coat with stuffing or straw protruding from the sleeves like a scarecrow; and something small, a teddy bear perhaps, clutched under one arm.

Leah leaped without thinking as the boy tried to slip past her. He gave a thin cry as she grabbed his arm and tried to whip his sleeve from her grasp, but she held on, calling out a name that she knew was not his, had never been his.

This boy's hair was red. He wasn't a ghost; of course he

wasn't Finn. She could see his breath, puffing from his mouth in clouds, and feel his bones even through her gloves and the padding of his coat. Still she found herself repeating, 'Finn?', the name slipping from her before she could gather herself, as if by saying it she could impose his shape on this boy who was nothing like her son. He was too tall, his face too round, his snub nose scattered with freckles, and he was older than Finn, eleven or twelve, maybe. His clothes were not Finn's clothes. The stuff jutting from his coat sleeves was not straw but wool, fraying from the jumper beneath. His dull blue coat was dirty. She would never have dressed her boy that way. She had loved to see Finn in bright, clean colours which set off the fine blond locks that were so like his father's, so much paler than her own nut-brown hair.

The boy stopped struggling and turned to face her. His hazel eyes stared at her. Not Finn's eyes; Finn's eyes had been blue.

Finn hadn't got his wish; he hadn't grown up and he never would. Finn was gone and Leah was going mad.

What on earth had come over her? What was she doing, terrifying this boy? He was only a child and his eyes were wide with fear and still she hadn't said a word to him except a dead boy's name.

'Who are you?' She spoke gently, but he only shook his head. And words spilled from her – she couldn't stop herself – as she demanded, 'Were you here last night? Did you think it was clever, playing a trick on the new neighbour? How did you—'

Only then, when she glanced down, did she see the thing

he was holding. It wasn't a teddy bear – it wasn't a furry toy at all, but something dark and misshapen and it took her a moment to realise what it was. A head, too large, lolled on its neck. Old straw spilled from the heavy body through holes in the filthy sacking, and its *face*—

In that moment the boy tugged free of her grasp. He threw the horrid object to the ground and backed away before turning to run. Leah didn't follow but watched as he scrambled over the wall, yanking his arms free of the grasping hawthorns, and headed across the field, his strides sending up plumes of white powder, obscuring his form.

She wondered where he had come from. Maitland Farm had been empty so long, he probably came here all the time to play or snoop around. He must know this place better than she did. She was the one who had just appeared out of nowhere.

She looked down and a jolt went through her at the sight of the doll. She had to force herself to pick it up. It was heavier than it looked; for a moment it felt as if it was made of flesh and blood and she recoiled from its touch, even though she was wearing gloves. Sacking arms, too long and slender for an infant's, protruded from a waistcoat that might once have been yellow but was now muddy brown, thoroughly ingrained with dirt. When she tilted the doll, sand trickled from a split in the seam and settled on the clean snow. That's what made it so heavy, almost the weight of a real child. The back of its head wasn't right, though: it was flat, as if part had been cut away. Between the few strands of wiry hair still clinging to the head she saw that the cranium was made of

ALISON LITTLEWOOD | 39

stained wood, although the face was some softer material. Whatever colour it had started, it was now every hue of a bruise, the surface crazed and contorted and chipped. The eyes were nothing but hollows, though when she stared into them she could make out little curves that might have been painted lashes resting on its cheek: the closed eyes of a doll meant to be sleeping.

What was it made of? Was it wax, moulded over a wooden base? Leah turned it and, where the light caught, it glowed a paler colour, almost translucent. For an instant she could almost see how it might have been when it was new, looking like real, healthful, smooth skin.

Mesmerised, she brought it closer to her face. There was a scent: dust and spice, pepper, and something greener, sharper – fermenting apples? And, yes, beeswax. That must be what it was made of. It would explain the distorted features. Perhaps it had been left outside, softening in the sun's heat, then cracking with cold. But another scent reached her, growing more pervasive by the moment: the suggestion of something animal.

She held the doll at arm's length, but couldn't bring herself to drop it. She wondered if it had a name – and, belatedly, what the boy's had been. Whatever had he been doing with such a thing? He was surely too old for dolls, and, anyway, this couldn't have been sold by any shop. Had someone close to the boy made it for him, or had he found it?

She thought of the boy's dirty coat and frayed clothes. *Perhaps you are his toy, after all.* She wondered if he regretted leaving it behind. After the way she'd surprised him, she didn't suppose he'd come back again, which made her feel a pang of guilt. She wished she could just throw it away, but instead, she carried it back to the house.

She kicked off her wet boots in the hall, but kept her gloves on; it might be stupid, but she still didn't want to touch the doll without them. Without really thinking, she went upstairs and into her bedroom, to see Finn's worn but clean little teddy bear sitting on the windowsill.

The air grew colder as Leah went over to it and looked at the two toys, the one in her hand staring up at her, the one on the sill with his back turned. They surely couldn't exist in the same world. She couldn't think why on earth she'd brought the horrid doll here, as if such a thing could ever have had anything to do with her son.

She pictured them sitting side by side and her focus shifted to the field. An image rose: a candle placed in a window, a signal to call the master home. Was that what she'd been trying to do when she placed Bear here – sending some message to her son? And now she had brought the doll here too. What might it summon, to visit her?

She pushed the fanciful thought away, telling herself she'd had far too many of those already. Still wondering why she had brought it to *this* room, she turned and saw the wall behind the pile of boxes, where the figure outlined in the stained plaster even now appeared to be watching her.

Moving as if in a dream, she went towards it and set the doll down – not on her bed or touching anything of hers, but on the floor. She reached out to the discolouration on the wall. 'That's all it is, isn't it?' she murmured. The human mind, trained by evolution to spot faces, could be fooled into seeing them anywhere.

Leah caught hold of the swathe of wallpaper and pulled. It came away from the plaster in little fits and starts, sending dust pattering to the floor, revealing the torso. Was the child waving, or curling an arm over its head in protection? The other hand was hanging at its side, until the wallpaper eased down and she saw it was holding something.

Suddenly short of breath, tasting plaster dust at the back of her throat, she stopped. This was ridiculous. *She* was being ridiculous.

With one hurried movement she yanked the wallpaper away. The shape was definitely a child, no one could mistake it for anything else, and in its hand . . .

She blinked, but the image did not vanish or resolve itself into anything else. A doll – or a teddy bear? Was this why she had brought the doll here, to discover an image of itself in her house? But how could it be?

It was a coincidence – an odd one, but nothing more. She pushed away the impression that the house had brought her here, had wanted to show her this thing, that it was the source of her strange thoughts. This behaviour wasn't like her. She'd been feeling so optimistic when she'd awakened that morning, looking to the future, only for it to end in her mad flight from the orchard. And she thought back further still, to her first sight of the old Yorkshire farmhouse on a computer screen, and how determined she'd been *not* to come here.

Yet here she was.

Had this place been influencing her somehow even then? She shook her head. *No.* It simply wasn't possible.

Leah thought of Trish's confidence in her, her assurance that she'd *smash it.* And she recalled something else she'd said, quiet, more heartfelt words:

Are you really sure you want to be alone just now?

She was no longer certain. But she couldn't afford doubt: not her friend's, not her own. She bent and grabbed hold of the doll, turned her back on the stain on the wall – it was just a pattern, no more than that, not a message meant for her or anyone – and hurried from the room, ignoring the unpleasant looseness of the doll's arms as they swung about its body, the weight of that body in her gloved hands.

She couldn't bring herself to throw it away, but she didn't want it anywhere near her.

She wasn't planning on using the master bedroom any time soon and there was an old wardrobe built into one wall. It had heavy, carved doors and was lined with shelves and hooks. She pulled open the creaking door, shoved the doll onto one of the shelves and closed it again.

There, she thought. *Forgotten.*

But it was not forgotten. And she was glad, when she left the room, that she wouldn't be sleeping in there; that she wouldn't have to lie awake in the dark and think of it sitting nearby, endlessly facing the closed door with its blind and empty eyes.

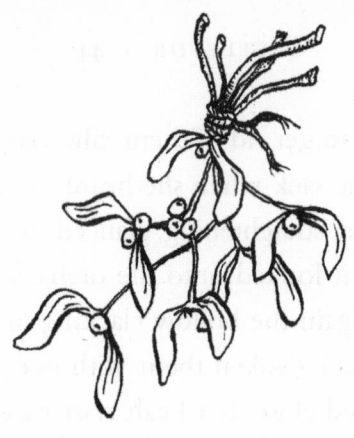

Chapter Four

When they arrived, Leah was working in the kitchen, breath misting from her mouth. The room was surprisingly small, so she was considering knocking through the scullery and pantry to make it bigger, more suitable for a family. When she'd first come in she'd had to boil a kettle to unstiffen her cleaning cloths, frozen where she'd left them hanging over the taps, before she could get started. Now she was exploring the kitchen cupboards, collecting all the things that had been left behind. The old deal table, much scarred with knife cuts, was soon covered with a miscellany of items – not so much interesting relics from the distant past but tat from more recent times: chipped china plates with faded flowers about their rims, cracked mugs, a broken plastic colander, knives and forks with fake silver finishes peeling away from cheap plastic handles. They never could have belonged here and she couldn't wait to get rid of them. She was throwing them into a black plastic sack when she heard the rumble of a car engine outside and, straightening, glanced automatically at the window, though it looked onto the orchard rather than the yard. She heard again the hollow clacking of dead branches, almost as if she had awoken them with her gaze.

The car sounded close, but Leah wasn't expecting visitors – she wasn't yet ready for them, and besides, her friends were no doubt rushing round, trying to get everything done in time for the big day, all that last-minute shopping and baking of mince pies – or at least warming Marks & Sparks' finest – wrapping presents, decorating Christmas trees. It must be out on the road then, some acoustical anomaly making it sound closer than it was . . .

But no, the high-pitched squeal of a handbrake being yanked on told her that someone was here.

Leah dusted down her jeans, in equal parts apprehensive and excited. The house might feel isolated, but it wasn't alone. The village was close enough to walk to; she'd taken a look before she bought the place, envisioning evenings in the pub chatting with new acquaintances, exploring the area with friends-to-be, people who couldn't remind her of the past. Maybe she could make herself useful, baking crumbles for charity or watching out for older neighbours in the winter weather, fetching groceries for them or changing library books.

She realised she was holding her breath and exhaled, then let out a dry laugh. What was the matter with her? Had she become so averse to human company that she panicked at the first sound? She really needed to get a grip.

A car door slammed and a woman's bright voice rang out, the words indecipherable but her tone encouraging. Leah rubbed her hands on her jeans again, conscious of how grimy she was, and went through into the hall. Taking a deep breath, she opened the door.

A battered crimson Land Rover stood in the yard and two figures were walking towards her. The first was a woman with a frizz of sandy hair tending towards red, her softly rounded face bare of makeup. The other was a boy, maybe eleven or twelve years old, his hair several shades warmer than his mother's. He was wearing a blue coat that was none too clean and a sulky scowl.

It was the boy she'd seen yesterday, Leah realised, biting her lip, remembering how she'd grabbed his arm, then, hanging onto him, had started demanding answers. She wished she could duck out of sight before they noticed her and hide until they went away – then it struck her that perhaps the boy had come back for his nasty toy. Thank goodness she hadn't thrown it away. What kind of person would destroy a child's toy anyway, even such an ugly one?

'Well 'urry up then, lad.' The woman sounded bluff and exasperated, but it was a playful cuff about the ear she gave him as he slouched over to her side. 'Straighten your face, eh? Tha looks like a wet weekend.'

The boy, wrinkling his nose, saw Leah watching and his eyes widened. His mother turned too. Despite the softness of her features – her nose rounded, her cheeks like apples, ruddy with health, or perhaps days spent outdoors in the cold – her gaze was as forthright as her words had been.

'Ah, there you are.' She moderated her accent a little when she addressed Leah, though her tone was just as decided. She stuck out her hand. 'You're our new neighbour. Welcoming committee.'

Leah held out her own hand, felt it taken and pumped and then dropped again. 'So good of you to come,' she began, but the woman cut in.

'We've an apology to make,' she said. 'Haven't you, Charlie?'

The boy looked sulky again, then thought better of it and adjusted his expression before nodding. His mum looked expectantly at Leah.

Leah gathered herself. 'It's really nice to meet you – please, come in. It's a bit of a mess, I'm afraid. I'm doing it up.' She indicated the hall, which looked worse than it had when she'd moved in, now strewn with bags of rubbish and discarded cleaning things.

They followed her inside, stepping around the mess, then kicking off their boots and shucking their coats. Leah held out a hand for them just as the woman tossed them over the acorn carved atop the newel post. They caught each other's eye and smiled. Leah felt better about her own dishevelled state when she saw the mother's checked shirt had a rip in the hem. She recognised Charlie's hand-knitted woolly jumper, a much-loved garment, perhaps, by the frayed sleeves.

She led the way into the kitchen, apologising again when she realised it was too cluttered for visitors, but they protested that they didn't mind. She busied herself with the kettle, then searched through the boxes in the corner for mugs. As she washed and dried them, her guest started talking.

'I'm Cath, by the way,' she said. 'Sorry, should have started with that. Cath-er-ynne.' She sputtered with laughter as she spelled it out, as if Leah was about to write it down. 'My parents couldn't spell. I think they liked confusing everybody. Mind, it was hell for me at school – the teachers hated it.'

'At least they didn't think you were a boy. Being Leah, I always got called *Lee*.' She laughed in turn.

'We're at Ingleby Nook – just think of inglenook, like a fireplace, and you'll not forget. It's the farm over the next hill. If you look out your upstairs windows past your barn, you'll likely see our chimney-pots. You're welcome any time. It's right nice to see this place with a family in it.'

'I understand it's been empty for a while. Looks like it too, I'm afraid.' Leah gave a wry smile. 'I imagine you might know something about the place?'

'There's three of us,' Cath replied, almost as if she hadn't heard. 'Me, my brother Andrew – only I call him Drew, 'cos it annoys him – and this here is Charlie, of course. Got summat to say, an't you, Charlie?'

He screwed up his nose.

'Don't mind him. Practisin' for his teens, aren't you, lad?' She looked stern despite her words and nudged him in the back. 'Well, cat got your tongue?'

He caught Leah's eye and glanced away again. 'Sorry.'

'Louder,' Cath said, her voice quiet but determined.

'Sorry,' he repeated, raising his head, and this time he held Leah's gaze. 'For trespassin'.'

Leah opened her mouth to say it was all right, of course it was, and that she was sorry too, for frightening him, but Cath was off again, her haste broadening her accent once more.

'He'd always wanderin' ower t' fields, that one. I've towd him but he don't listen – and no one's been at Maitland in years so he treats it like his own, don't you, lad?' Her countenance softened as she looked at the boy, but it hardened again when she turned back to Leah, as if she was coming to the point. 'Scared him off good and proper, you did. Still, I suppose that's best, you not knowing anyone round here, an' all.'

'Oh – no, I'm sorry,' Leah jumped in. 'I really didn't mean to scare him. I – I love children. It was just that he took me by surprise, and I thought—'

But what had she thought? Nothing she could explain, nothing that wouldn't have her neighbours thinking they were living next door to a madwoman. She closed her mouth again while Cath waited, trying desperately to think of something else to say, because she liked this woman with her sure way and bluff manner. There was warmth beneath the bluntness, something that reminded her of family dinners where everyone talked at once, chattering and arguing and bragging and telling well-worn jokes only they would understand.

In the end she repeated, 'I'm sorry, Charlie. You startled me, that's all. You can play here whenever you like, if that's all right with your mum, of course. I'll know it's you next time, won't I?'

She smiled at him and his shoulders relaxed, although he still didn't speak, despite another nudge from Cath.

She didn't want them to leave, not yet. 'Why don't we take

our tea into the living room? We can all sit down there. It's comfier—' She paused. 'Well, maybe not comfy, exactly – I haven't got the heating going yet and I'm afraid I haven't even got biscuits or cake to offer you. I'm a rubbish hostess . . .'

'Don't you worry about that,' Cath said as they followed Leah and perched themselves gingerly on the edge of the settle.

They didn't look in the least bit comfortable, Leah thought, watching as they took in the beamed ceiling, the massy fireplace, the empty walls, the mirror turned back to front.

'You've a job on, with this place,' Cath said. 'I've never been inside before, though we've lived next door for donkey's years.'

Her face closed up and Leah remembered the way she'd ignored her question about the farm. Had she been running on, or was it something else? Maybe she hadn't wanted to answer. Leah's curiosity was piqued. 'Did you know the people who had the place before me?'

Cath looked around as if searching for another subject, but then she did answer the question. 'The last owners didn't even live here, love. I heard they bought the place for their son, so's he could continue in the life, but they didn't even bother askin' if he wanted to farm, from what I heard. Any road, it were put up for sale soon after, not that there were any takers, mind. It was up for a long old time . . .'

That was what Leah had been told too. She'd never had any direct contact with the sellers; any information she had needed had always been filtered through the estate agent or the solicitors, not like when she and Josh had bought their house in Manchester. 'What a shame, to leave it empty,' she said. 'There would have been a family in it before that, I suppose? It's such a big place . . .'

'Well, going back a good bit, there was an owd couple for a while, but they kept themselves to themselves, never said nowt to anybody. Didn't do owt with the place neither, from what I heard. You're right about it being a fair old size, so mebbe it were too much for them. Then it were empty, like I said – oh, I don't know how long. People who owned it then had more money than sense, I reckon – well, that, or they just couldn't get shot of it.' She cast a glance at Leah as if realising what she'd said.

Leah smiled. 'They definitely had no sense, taking all this on.'

That made Cath laugh and she looked more at ease.

'And have you lived here a long time?' Leah asked. 'It must be nice, being part of the place. Do you farm it?'

'Aye, love, we do. Arable, mostly, some barley and oilseed – you going to get this place going again, then? People do say the soil's not so good this side of the hill, though I don't see why not. It gets the same rain and sun as we do.'

'No, I'm not quite that brave. I'm just going to renovate the house.'

'Ah,' said Cath, drawing out the word as if it was what she had expected to hear, and she sipped at her tea. 'Wouldn't say that.' She didn't elaborate, just turned to Charlie, who was swinging his legs and humming tunelessly under his breath as he tilted his head, first to look at the ceiling, then around again to study the room. 'Hush now, lad.' Then she added, 'It'll look nice in here, once you've got it trimmed up.'

At first Leah thought she was talking about new wallpaper, then she remembered that it was almost Christmas and she hadn't even considered putting up a tree or hanging a shred of tinsel: she had left all that behind as something separate from her. Now she saw the room through a stranger's eyes. It was cold and bare and unwelcoming, with none of the good cheer she ought to have been able to offer a neighbour, none of the colour, none of the life, especially in this festive season.

Was it only last year that Trish and Curt had brought their daughter round to theirs? Becca had immediately run off to play with Finn and it hadn't been long before the kids, high on sugar and excitement, had been pounding around the place like mad things. For once, the adults had been too contented to tell them off. The mulled wine had been richly scented with cinnamon and cloves and orange and their plates piled high with mince pies, shop-bought, maybe, but heavy with alcohol-soaked fruit and each one round and perfect. That was the year Josh had got ambitious and bought far too many lights – he'd had to rush around at the last minute tapping nails into walls and window frames to get them all up.

He'd taken Finn to choose the tree, like he always did, letting him pick the one he wanted, even though it would be far too tall for their house and he'd have to dig out the saw and cut the bottom off the trunk as soon as they got home. It didn't matter: that was as much a part of the season as stockings and carols and cards. Later that night, they'd all stood around the tree and belted out *Jingle Bells*, making up their own words and laughing uproariously.

'Are you married, love?'

The memory faded and the cold, bare room took its place. Had Cath read her mind?

'I'm a widow,' she said, the word still feeling strange on her lips. Then she smiled. She would not bring the pitying glances and the silences with her to this place; she had left them behind.

'Sorry, love – me and my big mouth.' Cath laughed, as if to wave away the uncomfortable moment, then powered on, 'Me, I'm divorced. I was Mrs Wilkinson then, but I've gone back to Slater now. He buggered off down south years ago.'

She stopped suddenly and glanced at Charlie with concern, but he didn't appear to have noticed his mother's words. Leah guessed he didn't see much of his dad.

As if he'd felt her eyes resting on him, his head swivelled towards her. 'Have you got a boy?' he asked, his voice loud in the bare room.

For a moment Leah couldn't speak. The word 'widow' was bad enough; she couldn't talk about Finn. Why had he asked such a thing?

'Charlie!' Cath cut in. 'There, he's got his mum's big mouth, love – runs in the family, it does. Don't mind him, will you. You don't have to tell us owt.'

Leah swallowed hard. 'No, it's all right. I don't – I don't mind.' She took a breath to steady herself, then looking at Charlie, she forced a smile. 'Yes, Charlie, I did have a son, but he's gone now. I'm sorry that you won't have anyone to play with.'

He looked puzzled. 'But I thought I'd seen . . . I mean, I thought he'd been here.'

Leah stared at him. Of course someone had been here: *she* had. He must have seen her footprints in the yard, her car sinking into the snow. He must have heard her calling her son's name. She thought of the marks in the otherwise pristine field, the snowball thrown at her front door – but that couldn't be it, could it? Surely those had been made by Charlie himself?

He said, 'I thought it must've been him who made that snow angel outside your barn.' His eyes were innocently wide as he waited for Leah to reply; he didn't look like he was trying to trick her, or playing some game. In fact, he seemed as forthright and straightforward as his mother. But might this be some childish way of paying her back for scaring him?

She thought about the impression in the snow. Hadn't it been Charlie's size, rather than Finn's? She only realised she was still staring silently when Cath rose to her feet and set down her mug, breaking the moment.

'That's quite enough questions, Charlie. Right, love, why don't you come over and see us one day? You know where we are now. If you can't dig your car out, you can walk round, no problem – down the road and up the next lane from yours. There's a sign at the bottom says Ingleby. Or walk ower the fields, the same as Charlie does, if you fancy it. It's quicker that way.'

'I would like that, thank you.' Leah was already envisioning starting her visit with a trip to the village to pick up some mince pies to take with her, showing that she wasn't mad after all, that she was a friendly neighbour, that she was *normal*. Then she remembered the doll – surely that was normal too, not as bad as she'd first thought? Someone had probably made it for the boy, just like someone had knitted his jumper by hand, not bought it off the peg.

'Charlie, hold on – you forgot something the other day. Just a minute.' She left them in the living room and hurried up the stairs. Perhaps Charlie had been using the doll as target practice for his snowballing. It wouldn't explain the lack of footprints in her field or the presence of the snow angel, but there could be other reasons for those: Charlie might have made the angel on a previous visit and forgotten about it and she had simply failed to notice it before. And if he really hadn't made the angel himself, it must have been some other child from the village – probably someone older, since they'd also been creeping about at night.

Leah hurried into the bedroom and pulled open the wardrobe. The doll was just as she remembered it and her brightness faded. It really did look hideous. It looked *haunted* – and she still didn't want to touch it.

She reached into her back pocket for the duster she'd tucked in there and wrapped it around the doll's body before picking it up. As it hung loosely in her hands, head lolling, arms swinging, she heard the patter of sand scattering across the floor. She pulled a face.

Downstairs, she found Cath and Charlie in the hall, already booted and putting on their coats.

'Here, Charlie,' she said, as their expressions began to change. 'You left this behind.' She held it out.

He didn't say a word, but Cath stepped in front of him, almost as if she was trying to block the doll from his view, looking as disgusted as if Leah had presented him with something dead.

'What on God's good earth is that?' she said.

Leah faltered. Even as she stood there, dismay creeping over her, she realised she could smell it again, that scent redolent of passing time, the hint of something animal, growing stronger by the moment: a *butchered* smell.

'I thought you dropped it, Charlie,' she said. 'You did, didn't you? You had it in your hand.'

'I found it.' He shot an apologetic glance at his mother. 'Sorry, Mum.'

'You found that thing?' Cath didn't bother to disguise her repulsion. 'Ugh. I don't know what that is, love, but it's not my boy's. I'd burn it if I were you. Take it out and burn it.' Her nose wrinkled. She still hadn't taken her eyes off it. 'Did you really think that was my Charlie's?'

'Well, he was holding it,' she said. She wanted to protest that she didn't like the thing either, but the distrustful look that had been in Cath's eye when they'd first met had returned. They weren't a neighbourhood welcoming committee. Cath had come here to see the woman who'd scared her boy.

And this thing? Of course it hadn't been Charlie's. It came from here, a part of Maitland Farm, just as Leah was now. It was *hers*; she couldn't pass it on to anyone else. She shook away the thought, wishing she'd flung the thing in the bin when she'd found it.

She felt a hand on her arm, a reassuring squeeze, and blinked. Her eyes focused on Cath, whose face was full of concern.

'Why don't you show me, love?' she said. 'Let's see where he found it. We'll all have a quick look, shall we?'

And so she pulled on her own coat and gloves and boots and the three of them stepped outside, Charlie leading the way as if he were the proprietor and they his visitors. He skipped across the snow in the yard, only stopping to wait for Leah and Cath when he reached the doorway of the barn. The fear of his last visit was clearly forgotten for he was grinning, a boy showing off his playground, as he gestured inside.

His mother peered in at the heaps of tools, the old harrow with its wicked spikes, the tangle of rusting metal. She pursed her lips. 'Bit of a death-trap in here.'

Leah glanced at her – was Cath blaming her? But no, Cath was looking reproachfully at her son. Still, Leah had told him he could play here whenever he liked. She opened her mouth to rescind her permission, at least where the barn was concerned, just as Cath said, 'You're not to come here again, you hear, Charlie? Not on your own. Never again.'

The two women glanced at each other, understanding passing between them, although Charlie's scowl gave Leah a pang; she had liked the idea of children playing on the farm, making use of the space. Then Cath added, 'Only in the field. And then, only if it's still all right with Mrs—'

'Allonby.' Leah smiled. 'Yes, of course it is.'

'Aye. Right, so where did you find that thing, Charlie?'

He didn't tell her, just turned and held out an arm. As he pointed, they twisted to stare at the far side of the barn. There was the chopping block Leah had glimpsed previously, the old wood of the long sturdy bench gnarled and darkened and pitted with cut-marks. Next to it, leaning against the wall, was the axe, its blade keen and gleaming.

'You found it by the chopping block?' Leah exclaimed. 'Charlie, you might have cut yourself.'

Cath shook her head at Leah's words. 'No, that's not a chopping block, love. That's next to it, see?' She indicated an old tree stump sitting a bit further away, similarly scarred. 'This here's an old pig bench. They would've used it for slaughtering the animals.' Her tone was musing. 'Probably worth a bit if you scrubbed it up, polished it, like, and took it down to an antiques shop. Some folk – city folk, you know – they like that sort of thing.' She straightened and turning to her son, repeated, 'You don't go nowhere near it, lad, do you hear me?'

'Mu-um,' Charlie protested, 'I *didn't*. That doll thing? It weren't there. It was in that 'ole.' He pointed again and Leah realised he hadn't meant the pig bench or the chopping block or even the axe, but the wall behind it, where there was a fissure in the rough stone.

They walked over and when they got close enough to see it properly, Leah frowned, peering at the fragments of crumbling render that had spilled to the floor. Why was there a hole here? The rest of the wall looked solid enough, and she didn't recall the surveyor mentioning it in his report, although it would surely have been his business to do so – after all, he'd been thorough enough about everything else. But then, she thought, she hadn't been, had she? She'd done little more than cast her eyes over the documents, skimming the text, half in a daze, so certain this was where her future lay that she wasn't about to be put off by mention of damp or woodworm.

Still, she was sure that dark hollow in the stone hadn't been there before. Had the doll been walled up in there – and for how long – and why? Leah had heard of offerings being built into old structures, for good luck or to ward off witches, but she didn't think the farm was old enough for anything like that. And why a doll? Why would anyone leave such an ugly thing for some unsuspecting soul to uncover, years and years away?

She could almost feel the accumulated past of the place creeping over her: seasons passing by, previous occupants and all their efforts falling into death and decay, rot setting in beneath the earth she stood upon. Why had the doll surfaced now, just when she had arrived? Had it taken a Maitland returning to Maitland Farm to reveal its secret?

She opened her mouth to ask if Charlie hadn't thought it nasty, even been afraid of it, just as Cath put her hand on her son's shoulder and pulled him towards the door.

'Well, Charlie,' she said, 'I think we'd best be going.'

Leah couldn't blame her. For a moment she wished she too could walk away from the farm, but it was too late for that.

Cath leaned in towards her and, her voice low and full of meaning, said, 'Don't you forget to call by, now. Walk across the field, you hear?' She gestured towards the white expanse in the distance, at the line of footprints left by her son showing her the way.

Leah promised that of course she would, she was already looking forward to it. Then they were making their goodbyes, searching for car keys, clambering into the battered old vehicle. She waved after them as the Land Rover jolted its way across the drifts and into the lane.

Cath rolled down her window and stuck out her arm. 'Don't forget!'

Leah found herself grinning. Cath hadn't minded the mess in the house, her unpreparedness or, worst of all, that awful doll. It really had sounded like she meant the invitation. Perhaps she wouldn't just be a nodding acquaintance – she might even become a proper friend.

She waved until the Land Rover passed out of sight, the roar of its engine faded from hearing and silence surrounded her once more. The wind lifted fine white powder from the fields, forming strange shapes in the spindrift before letting it fall again.

Leah drew her hands up into her sleeves, her fingers already clumsy with cold, and turned to go back inside. She was thinking of what the place would look like once she'd effaced the past, erasing all trace of it from every room, so it startled her when she stepped across the threshold and saw the doll sitting at the foot of the stairs.

She tried to remember putting it down on the floor and couldn't, but she must have. She supposed she'd left the thing there when they'd been putting on their coats and boots, all bustling together, preparing to go and see where Charlie had found the horrid toy.

At least she could get rid of it now. *Burn it*, Cath had said, but she hadn't got any logs for the fire and in any case, the hardwood of the doll's frame – its *bones*, she thought

– might resist the flame; the sand it was stuffed with would stifle it. And in any case, the thought of that wax face, slowly softening, then melting away, gave her pause. A year from now she might still be finding traces of it on the grate, what was left of its translucent skin gleaming from the blackened ironwork.

She remembered a news story from a few years before: a mummified cat had been found within the walls of an excavated cottage on the Lancashire moors, where the infamous Pendle witches had once lived. Walling up a cat, often a live one, had been a mediaeval precaution against evil spirits. Leah supposed she should be grateful they'd only found a doll. She looked at it again, picturing it trapped in its dark prison, loose limbs scratching at the wall, trying to get out. Of course, if it really had been meant for such a purpose, it might be filled with animal hair – or human hair . . . or even blood. Would that explain the odd feeling it gave her, of something that lay *beneath*?

A child, she thought. *It was supposed to be a child.*

And if it was meant to protect against evil, to ensure the farm's prosperity, she wondered what might happen now that it had been removed? That was a discomfiting idea. She told herself she was being ridiculous, and that someone like Cath would never countenance such silly notions. A child had hidden their horrible toy in a cracked wall; there was nothing more to it than that. And if she put it back where it had come from, at least it wouldn't be in the house.

Telling herself that was the only reason for her actions, Leah rewrapped the duster around the doll, determinedly not thinking about why she didn't want to touch it, and carried it outside.

Her neighbours' visit had left the yard cross-hatched with footprints and tyre tracks that made the place look more lived-in. The barn, however, did not. As she picked her way through it, she realised there weren't even any birds' nests high among the beams, no tracks left by animals, not even foxes or mice, marking the snow that had blown inside. She paused by the old pig bench, trying not to imagine the squeals and struggles it must have witnessed over the years. How could anyone want such a thing in their living room? Polishing it up wouldn't polish away its past, would it? All that slaughter wouldn't be erased. The wood could never be made gleaming and smooth; it was hopelessly stained. It even looked, when she tilted her head, as if it was wet with what looked like blood. *But that's stupid; it's just the damp*, Leah thought, yet again shaking her head at herself. After all, the barn was open to the elements, so it was only to be expected.

She knew she would feel better once she was rid of the doll. She thrust it back into the gap in the wall, trying to position it with its back turned, but it kept falling over so that its blank sockets were staring accusingly up at her, looking like a sleeping child. A *dead* child.

She tried to pull the duster up to cover its face, but the cloth slipped from her hand and as her fingers touched the doll's grimy waistcoat, something came over her. Without conscious thought, she found she had pulled the doll out of the hole and was cradling it like a baby, and it was a baby's weight she felt in her arms, though its face was a mockery of that. Here was no smooth pink cheek, no blue-grey eyes, no soft young flesh glowing with life. And its face was not a baby's face, despite the suggestion of peacefully closed eyes. The proportions were different, the features those of an older boy. Fascinated, Leah ran a finger down its skin, lingering over each crack and crevice. The texture was at once brittle and yielding. This close, she could see there were traces of colour in the cheeks and lips. Had it been so before?

Leah hugged it closer, not knowing why – and was interrupted by a voice in the yard. Was it Cath and Charlie, come back again? She couldn't see anyone, but she was certain she had heard a boy's voice. Perhaps Charlie had decided he wanted to play in the field already. Or he'd decided the doll should be his after all, since he'd found it, and had come to claim it.

But no, it wasn't Charlie. She felt it in the way her heart knocked against her ribs, the way her breath caught in her throat.

'Finn?'

She walked towards the door, seeing more of the yard with each step, and at last the speaker came into view. It was a boy, but not Charlie, and it was not her son.

Of course it's not Finn. He's dead.

The boy, a stranger to her, was wearing peculiar clothing, which made her think that it must be some kind of costume – perhaps he had been carolling and wanted to look like a Dickensian character. His jacket and cap might have been Victorian, like the high-buttoned yellow waistcoat he wore over his shirt. His back was very straight, his stance formal. His dark, wiry hair was slicked neatly over his ears.

Leah opened her mouth to call out to him – then stopped herself, although she wasn't sure why. He looked so out of place it made her feel odd, as if it was she, rather than the boy, who didn't belong here.

As she stood there in silence, he spoke again. 'That is so very kind. But you did not need to get me a Christmas present.'

Leah glanced at the doll still cradled in her arms and frowned. She was certain he couldn't see her, and she couldn't see anyone else he might be addressing. She stepped closer to the entrance, towards the light.

'Hello?' Her voice was nothing but a croak.

The boy didn't reply; he didn't even turn towards her. Had he heard her? But his voice had carried quite clearly on the cold air, so surely hers would too.

Then he said, 'Did you make it for me yourself – a *doll*?'

With a shock, Leah realised that he too was holding a doll in his hands, its head lolling towards her, revealing a smooth face with cheeks and lips touched by pink. Its wiry black hair was just like his, and long, fine eyelashes were painted onto its cheeks, giving it an expression of peace. It too wore a bright yellow waistcoat.

The clothing on Leah's doll was so dirty its original colour could barely be seen, but when she hooked a finger into the little waistcoat at the neck and pulled it away from the sacking, she could see that the original shade had been a strong, bright yellow. Somehow the boy in front of her was not just holding a similar doll, he was holding *her* doll, though it was clean and new. And somehow Leah knew that he wasn't really here; not in the same way she was.

'Ah – it's a kind of portrait, then?' The boy smiled. 'How clever! Thank you. I shall keep it safe for the big day.'

There was no concern in his voice, no awareness that someone else might be listening. Despite his youth, he was full of the natural assurance of one accustomed to being in charge, or maybe with the expectation of being so at some future date.

'Oh, but his back is flat, Jack, and his eyes are closed – I hope it is not meant for my burial doll.' His laughter rang out across the yard.

A burial doll? Leah gripped the one in her hands tighter. Its blood-scent was all around her now. *When I open my eyes*, she thought, *he will be gone. All of this will.* But when she straightened, the boy remained standing there. He had turned a little so that he was now facing Leah, but still he didn't see her.

He tucked the doll under one arm and, raising the other to point in her direction, asked, 'Were you cutting wood for the winter, Jack?'

He wasn't looking at her; he couldn't see her, could he? He was pointing at the barn and in another moment he might walk towards it. If he did that, what would happen when they met? Would he see her then?

But of course he wouldn't; he wasn't even real. Leah's mind had slipped, somehow: she had been disturbed and her thoughts had run wild and now she was seeing and hearing things that couldn't possibly be there. It was nothing but a dream: a *hallucination*.

'Mama said we shall need plenty of logs to keep away the

chill this season. And she said most particularly that you must not forget the party, Jack, since you and Martha shall come too.'

He did walk towards her then, although only a few steps, and Leah shuffled forward before she could stop herself. She wanted to see this mysterious Jack. The boy wouldn't notice her. He was – well, what *was* he? An echo of the past that had seeped into the bones of this place, destined to repeat the words he had spoken years ago?

Is this one of my ancestors?

The house came into sight, but it had changed. Only a scattering of snow powdered its walls and the stone glowed through in shades of amber, here and there darkened with smoke. The yard too was only half covered, with patches of cobbles showing beneath the white. Leah still couldn't see Jack. He was hidden to her.

The boy tilted his head, lifting his chin as if to look at someone standing next to him. 'I know there is much to do, Jack, and only you left to do it, but it is even more important for us to thank the servants when you are reduced to two, and your burden so much the greater. We shall hope the yield improves next year, for all our sakes, but for now, Christmas is Christmas, is it not . . . ?'

His voice was beginning to fade. Leah's foot slid on the ice concealed beneath a patch of snow and as she fell, the doll slipped from her grasp. She put a hand out to catch herself, expecting to land on unforgiving cobbles, but instead, her arm sank into snow up to the elbow. Her fingers closed on the freezing whiteness as if she could cling to it and pull herself back to – to *what*, exactly?

When she stood back up, there was the snow-covered yard as it had been, churned by footprints and tyre tracks, filled once more with silence. Cath and Charlie might have just left; it felt like only a moment had passed, but the day was failing, with long shadows purpling the snow. And Leah was cold.

It might have been the winter chill or a reaction to what she thought she had seen, but she started to shiver. She knew she hadn't imagined what had just happened: she had actually *seen* where the doll had come from. She'd heard the words spoken by the boy who received it, been close to glimpsing the man who had fashioned it – and she'd lost all trace of them when the doll slipped from her fingers.

Is that what you wanted to show me?

She turned the doll so that she could look into its face, suddenly anxious that it mustn't be broken – because it wasn't just a doll, was it? It was a Christmas present.

The doll wasn't any more damaged than it had been before. The snow had saved it as it fell from her fingers. Gingerly, Leah touched the back of its head. She'd assumed the flattened shape to have been a mistake, or perhaps to have been a result of its age, but now she realised it had been made that way deliberately, designed to be lying down, like the effigy of a child sleeping – or something else? The boy's words came back to her: 'I hope it is not meant for my burial doll.'

A profound sense of disquiet crept over her as she continued to stare at the doll, but it showed her nothing else. Leaving it outside felt like abandoning its owner to the bitterly cold darkness, surrounded by sharp, glistening things – but what else could she do? And after all, the boy was *gone*.

She came to a decision and made her way carefully back through the barn. The heap of rotting and broken implements was reduced to dull gleams of metal, the details lost to the fast-thickening shadows. She could no longer make out the hole in the wall, so she placed the doll on the slaughtering bench, its head striking the surface with a dull sound as she laid it down. She turned away, leaving it there, and hurried back to the house.

Breathing a sigh of relief, she closed the front door against the onrushing night and all that she had seen. She didn't want to think about what it meant; she certainly didn't want to consider the word *ghost*. It had only been a kind of picture, she told herself, a waking dream that had overwhelmed her senses for a time. It would never happen again and soon enough she would forget all about it, for she was moving on – that was what this place was meant to be about. *Moving on*.

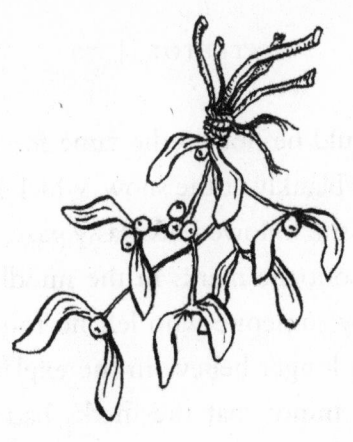

Chapter Five

If spirits played in the field during the night, if she received any further visitations, Leah knew nothing of it. She hadn't even lain awake wondering about the events of the day, although she had fully expected to. Instead, she awoke from a deep, dreamless sleep to find the sun already high in the sky, but she cowered under the duvet a little longer, unwilling to step into the cold air.

In the end, she made herself throw off the covers all at once and rushed to wash and dress.

When she looked outside it was a relief to see the snow was still there and everything as it had been before. Yesterday's vision felt more than ever like a dream, though she could not shake off the sense of strangeness hanging over everything.

Leah rested her hand briefly on Bear's furry head. If the doll could call to its master, making it possible for her to see him, why could he not do the same for Finn? The little teddy bear gazed blankly at the snow, which lay everywhere, silent, and when she followed his glassy gaze, she realised she could still make out the marks in the middle of the field – the ones made by someone who left no footprints.

Leah could no longer believe in the explanations she had tried out in her mind: that the marks had been made by local children playing tricks, brushing away the tracks they'd left, or that she'd inadvertently trampled over their footprints without noticing them; even that the traces had been left by birds. Nothing could have spoiled that pristine surface and made it so perfect again. Even fresh snowfall would have settled into every hollow left behind.

Could they have been made by the boy in the yellow waist-coat? Perhaps he'd made the snow angel too. He wouldn't have been thinking of her when he'd done it, though. He couldn't have imagined that she would one day be living in his house, looking out of his windows. She wondered what he might have made of that idea.

Her moment of introspection was broken when her mobile let out a cheerful beep, calling her back to reality. When she picked it up, she saw a text from Trish:

U bored yet? Just checked – *1* spare seat on the flight! Come to Lapland!!! Decide SOON, not long left . . .

Leah considered the possibility of downing tools and running away – for that's what it would be, wouldn't it? To her surprise she felt a tug somewhere deep inside her, as if, despite everything, she was somehow connected to this place, as if she was actually home.

She texted back:

Go, woman! Enjoy yourself! I'm busy!

She found a Santa hat and a winking emoji and appended a couple of Xs. Then she added:

PS. Pretty sure this place is haunted!!

After a moment's hesitation she added another wink and her finger hovered over the Send button. The message turned blue as it went off into the aether. She tried to picture Trish's face. Would she be staring at her phone in just the same way Leah was staring at hers?

Beep.

Awesome! Adds value!! Don't go scaring them away!

Leah laughed, and it felt good. She sent another message, a more heartfelt one this time, telling Trish to have a splendid time, to say hi to Rudolph for her, to pass on all her love to Curt, to give Becca a huge hug.

Then she went to find her sledgehammer and headed for the kitchen.

First she donned a face-mask and knocked out the shelves in the pantry, battering them to the floor. Then she started on the wall that separated it from the kitchen, demolishing it in clouds of plaster dust and shattered laths. She'd checked the wall hadn't been supporting anything before she'd started and quickly discovered it was a flimsy partition; it didn't take long to reduce the whole thing to piles of debris at her feet. The room immediately felt more open and welcoming, but even more importantly, it felt *different*.

She swept the detritus into a corner and left the dust settling. That was good enough for the moment; she had other things to do.

After Leah had washed off the grime and changed, she put on her warmest jumper and thickest socks, donned her coat and boots, pulled on hat, scarf and gloves and slung an empty rucksack over her shoulders before stepping outside into a beautiful day. It was crisp, cold and quiet, the sky pale, the sun blazing white. With a bounce in her step, she set off down the track towards the road. She was going to visit Cath, but first, she would do the neighbourly thing and buy a Christmas card and mince pies. On her previous visit to the village she'd noticed a little shop attached to someone's house about a mile down the road. She'd drop in there before heading over to Ingleby Nook (*like a fireplace*) and hopefully Cath would be at home rather than somewhere about the farm fixing fences or rounding up livestock or whatever they did at this time of year.

As she walked, she looked out across the empty fields. Before she'd moved here, she'd pictured herself wandering over them, chatting to families enjoying Sunday outings, or ramblers, or local dog-walkers, but there was no one enjoying the outdoors at all. Was it simply too cold, or did everyone tend to head off in some other direction? Perhaps it was only these particular fields that were shunned – perhaps no one wanted to go near her farm . . . or maybe something had driven them away.

Probably estate agents and prospecting property developers, she thought, *and who could blame them? They'd have a tight community here, wouldn't they?* Leah pictured a bunch of happy, smiling people chatting in the pub, everyone knowing everyone else's business. They'd be a bit suspicious of her as an outsider, but they'd surely soften when they realised she wasn't just going to use the farm as a weekend place or holiday let. And they could all come round, when she was ready, when the house was done up properly, maybe at some future Christmas. They would gather in the living room, drink mulled wine, sing carols, all laughing together and clinking their glasses with good cheer.

She blinked. That wasn't the plan, though, was it? By then, the place would have had its makeover: it would be fresh and modern and desirable and up for sale, ready for its new family. *Wouldn't it?*

The end of the track was a welcome sight as Leah's feet were already beginning to feel numb, but her relief was short-lived as the road at the bottom turned out to be hardly any better, with drifts burying the pavements. She sent a quiet 'thank-you' to the few hardy vehicles, Land Rovers or other 4x4s, probably, who had been out and about, for they had left a twin trail of compressed snow behind them. No one was in sight, so she slid her way to the middle of the road, hefted the rucksack straps higher onto her shoulders and trudged on towards the next turning. It was marked by a wooden sign saying simply Ingleby, which had recently been swept clean of snow. *Bet that's Charlie's job*, she thought with a smile; she could almost see his grudging face as he sped off to do his mother's bidding.

For now, she walked past, towards the little shop she had reached so quickly and easily on her last visit. As she went, fine specks began to drift into her face like grains of dust. The creak of her steps, the rattle of the zip on her coat, the buffet of her hood in the breeze were the only sounds she could hear. There was no traffic, no sign of any other living soul. The sky had turned as white as paper.

As she crested the next slope, a small grey building came into sight. A single bulb shining in the window illuminated a haphazard pile of tins and packets: baked beans sat next to bags of pasta; tinned green beans were perched on top of boxes of dog biscuits. Prices were handwritten on bright orange stars which were almost obscuring the seasonal display behind them: a cardboard manger, sagging as badly as her barn door, peopled with little pop-up cardboard figures, no doubt drawn by local children. A wistful smile touched her lips as she pictured the heads bent over their task, scribbling in the blue of Mary's cloak, the yellow of the haloes.

A jangling bell over her head made her jump as she pushed open the door and ducked under a strand of spindly tinsel. The smell of dried goods enveloped her as she brushed off her coat in the doorway before turning to pick up a battered wire basket from the unswept floor.

A woman she thought must be the owner was standing a

little to one side of the counter, watching her with folded arms. The apron wrapped around her thin waist had once been white; it wasn't just faded but dirty. She called out a greeting, but the woman didn't reply.

'Snowing again,' Leah tried again, and this time the woman did at least nod in return.

Not deaf then. Trying to hide her dismay – the shop-keeper had been chatty enough on her first visit – she turned and started filling her basket with bread, butter, milk and some other basic supplies. She spotted a half-crushed box of Christmas cards, the kind with dull but worthy pictures of robins and village scenes and skaters on a lake, half-hidden in a corner of a shelf. It was a pity she'd only be using one of the twenty, but she added it anyway.

At least there was a welcome sight by the counter: beneath the hazed glass of an elderly display case were some mince pies, sitting on a tray lined with greaseproof paper. The crooked shapes, thick pastry and icing sugar dusted haphaz-ardly over the top proclaimed them home-made, just what she'd been hoping for.

'I'll take six, please,' she told the woman, who was now hovering uncomfortably close. That felt like a good number, and it must surely please the dour shopkeeper, given how con-spicuously empty the place was, even if it was nearly Christmas.

The woman pushed herself away from her end of the counter as if it were a great effort, scooped the mince pies roughly into a paper bag, spun it carelessly to twist the cor-ners and slapped it down in front of Leah as if it contained potatoes, not pastries.

'Um . . . I just moved into Maitland Farm,' Leah started. 'I called in a few months ago – when I was looking around?' At least she was warming up at last; her fingertips were starting to ache from the heat of the fire.

The shopkeeper said nothing but she inclined her head in what might have been a nod of acknowledgement.

'I'm going to call on Cath at Ingleby. I thought I'd take her something.'

'Oh, aye. You're 'er, then.'

'Her?' Leah frowned.

'The one what scared 'er lad.'

Leah's cheeks flushed and she started thrusting her purchases into her rucksack. Was that the reason for her cold reception? She couldn't believe Cath had told this woman such a thing. Why act so friendly if all she was going to do was blacken Leah's name?

She shoved the bag of mince pies on top of everything else, no longer caring if they crumbled, and paid. She couldn't think of anything else to say as she left, but she forced a smile, not wanting to make an enemy. The shopkeeper's lip curled with amusement – or was it contempt?

Leah stomped back along the road, the tingle fading from her hands as numbness returned. How many people had Cath told? What if they all looked at her that way? It was so unfair – she hadn't asked Charlie to come and play in her barn, had she? In fact, she hadn't even known he was there. But perhaps they thought of it as more his place than hers. She was a newcomer, after all. An outsider.

She paused and looked around, across the empty fields

blanketed in layers of white. She had a sudden sense of connections hidden in time, old ties accrued by people who had known each other for generations, who had bonds she could barely understand, let alone sever: bonds formed by shared labours, marriages, friendships and secrets going back down through the decades, the centuries, even.

Damn them all, she thought, stomping down harder as she quickened her pace. The snow was blowing horizontally now, melting on her eyelashes, touching her cheeks with ice, so wet it was almost sleet. She was suddenly overwhelmed with the desire to stop in her tracks and cry. She had had such plans . . .

Should she even go to Ingleby Nook? The turning was close by, but wouldn't it be easier to retreat to her new home, shut herself inside where all was still and quiet, with no one to look at her, no one to judge her?

Leah blinked the thought away. She'd faced worse things in her life – and she hadn't even liked the woman at the shop, so why should she care what she thought? Cath had probably only mentioned what had happened in passing. Leah pictured the bluff, forthright woman. Would she spread a nasty tale about her on purpose? No, surely not – if she had anything to say, she'd tell her to her face. And perhaps it hadn't even been Cath. It might have been Charlie, buying sweets, chatting to a friend, and the nasty thin-faced woman had been eavesdropping.

The sign for Ingleby appeared in front of her and when she peered along the lane, she thought she could make out its chimney-tops, as Cath had said she might if she looked over the fields.

Leah bit her lip. It would only be a brief visit, after all. And she'd been invited: it was the neighbourly thing to do.

Built of similar stone to Maitland Farm, Ingleby nestled into the lee of a rising hill. Its roof was clear of snow, no doubt melted by the warmth rising from within, and the windows glowed with the red, blue and yellow of flickering Christmas garlands. Leah could already smell the place: cinnamon and nutmeg and baking pastry, as tempting as if it were a gingerbread house to lure little children. And she *was* lured, even enchanted. She stopped for a moment in the chill lane, feeling more than ever an outsider. What must Cath have thought of her own bone-cold, uninviting house?

As if sensing Leah's presence, the front door suddenly swung open and Cath appeared in the gap, her hair wilder than ever, waving her arm in a wide arc.

Leah couldn't help grinning as she waved back.

Leah's nose had not deceived her: Cath had been baking. Jam tarts gleamed like rubies as they cooled next to ginger biscuits shaped into bells and stars and stockings; a Yule log awaited its coating of chocolate. There were mince pies too, their tops deliciously flaking and golden-brown.

'You're just in time.' Cath grabbed a pair of oven gloves on the way to the Aga, a huge affair of dark-green enamel bursting with heat, and she pulled open one of the little square doors to remove a loaf tin. The smell of sweetened bread overwhelmed the rest for a moment, making Leah's mouth water. When had she last seen bounty like this?

Through a half-open door, she glimpsed a comfortable

sitting room, sofa cushions still sagging in the shape of their occupants. A Christmas tree stood tall in the corner, glittering with baubles and lights. The fireplace was laid in preparation for the evening, with a big basket of logs at hand; no one would be going cold in this house any time soon.

Leah swung her rucksack to the floor, realising that she might have bought cards, but she had neglected to write one before she came in – she hadn't even brought a pen with her. She felt even worse when she pulled the unpleasantly grease-spotted paper bag from the top of the pile.

'Everything smells amazing, Cath. Erm – I brought you these.' She handed them over. 'I'm afraid they're nowhere near as good as yours.'

Cath thanked her and set them out onto a plate before pursing her lips. 'I see you've met Mrs Jepson at the shop. She's a one, isn't she? Still, it's the thought that counts.'

'It might have to be,' Leah said, an unexpected giggle rising to her throat. 'She's no baker, that's for sure.'

'Oh, she doesn't make them herself, not that one. Still, they never are as good as your own, are they?'

Leah nodded, though she'd never made a mince pie in her life. Then she laughed and confessed, 'I have to admit, I'm no baker myself. I'd probably just drink the brandy.'

Cath laughed in turn and patted her arm. 'That's for the pudding, love – mind, I always keep a nip of the good stuff back. I've been at it since before Charlie broke up from school. It never ends, does it? I'd have brought you some of mine when I came, but—'

She didn't finish the sentence, but Leah could guess the

reason. *You're t' one what scared 'er lad.* Still, that was in the past, wasn't it?

Leah smiled as Cath placed two of her own mince pies on mismatched, flower-patterned plates, still steaming from the oven and redolent of fruit and spice and butter. Almost as if on cue, Charlie stuck his head around the door and called, 'Mu–um—? Are they ready yet? I've been waiting *ages!*'

With a wordless sigh – *a mother's work is never done* – Cath grabbed another and held it out to him.

He took it and shouting, 'Hello!' left the room – then paused to shout, 'Thanks, Mum!' just as Cath was about to go after him.

Cath tossed her head in mock despair and gestured towards the pine table dominating the room. 'Hope you don't mind if we sit in here. It's much cosier when the fire's out in't good room.'

'Happy to. It's lovely.' The comfort of the warm kitchen was already seeping into Leah's bones and when, after a moment, Cath set steaming mugs of tea in front of them both, Leah closed her eyes and sighed in contentment. Being here felt like civilisation, like home, like childhood. She hadn't realised how much she had been missing it.

'Sugar?' Cath asked, and as Leah shook her head, urged her, 'Drink up, get some warmth in you.' She took a mouthful herself, then asked, 'So, how are you getting on with that old place?'

Leah grimaced. 'Slowly, to be honest. I'm clearing the house – and making more mess than anything, at least to begin with. I'm trying to make plans about what I'll do with it as I go. I'll be starting in earnest in the New Year.'

'New Year, new start? Well, that's what the place needs, right enough. It's well gone time to forget the past.'

Leah sipped at her tea. 'Forget the past,' she echoed, remembering her earlier determination to do just that. She wrinkled her nose. 'Why did no one take to the farm, do you think, Cath?' She'd asked the question almost before she'd known she was going to. 'It's a shame that no one's ever really settled there. It seems – well, stuck in time somehow.' She didn't say, *haunted*. She wouldn't say *ghost*.

Even so, Cath looked uncomfortable before she shrugged. 'I don't rightly know, love. Folk did take it on from time to time, but no one lasted in it. There's some as tried to farm it again, but it never took. Maybe they didn't know what they were doing – posh new wellies and a bright red tractor might make you look the part, but farming's no job for amateurs, is it? But the old 'uns round here, they say the soil's poor, no heart in it any more. Well, that's what they reckon, any road.' She brightened. 'But that's not what you're after, is it, love?'

Leah sat a bit straighter, no longer sure if Cath saw that as a good or bad thing, then jumped as the door banged open. A man's face appeared in the gap, his dark hair mussed and damp. He sniffed dramatically and said, 'Spare a hungry man a tart, can you?'

Cath chuckled and gestured at the cooling racks. 'Help yourself – but you might want to say hello to our guest first.'

He straightened, looking horrified at the sight of Leah

sitting at the table. 'Sorry – so sorry! I didn't realise we had company.'

He rubbed at his chin and stepped into the room, revealing a hand-knitted jumper with the sleeves, like Charlie's, fraying at the wrist. His eyes were the same clear hazel as Charlie's, though his hair was several shades darker and his face was more defined than Cath's, his cheekbones prominent. He rounded his shoulders as if conscious of his height.

'Sorry to intrude,' Leah said. 'And for eating your mince pies, too.'

'This is my brother,' Cath announced. 'Leah, meet Drew Slater.'

He pulled a face at that before striding towards Leah, his hand out to shake. '*And*rew,' he said, a little pointedly. 'Pleased to meet you, Leah.'

'He doesn't like being called Drew,' Cath said, forgetting she'd told Leah this before, and went on, 'But we have some Scottish blood in us, from way back when, and that's the Scottish way, isn't it. So it's tradition, that's what I think.'

Andrew rolled his eyes and Leah smiled at their banter as Cath added, 'This is the one who's taken on Maitland Farm.'

'Oh, aye?' His smile faded, to be replaced by a look of concern. He snatched a jam tart from the rack and began nibbling around its hot centre.

'I'm really sorry I disturbed Charlie,' Leah said. 'I didn't mean to scare him.' As she looked at Andrew's puzzled expression, she decided that if Cath had been talking about her, she hadn't done so with her own brother; his concern was about something else. She wondered what that might be, but Drew was speaking again and she turned her attention back to him.

'What's that, then? Well, if you did, he was probably messing about. At yours, was he? He shouldn't have been, not at *that* place. I've told that boy often enough. I can't think what the attraction is – well, other than it's forbidden, of course. Boys, eh? Nothing but trouble, all of 'em.'

Leah fell quiet for a moment before saying, 'I hope you don't mind me asking, but . . . well, is there something about the farm that makes you say that? Is there anything about the place that I should know?'

Andrew shot his sister a worried glance before saying quickly, 'Oh, it's nothing. Nothing to worry – I didn't mean—' He looked down at his hands, then repeated, 'Honestly, it's nothing for you to worry about.'

Leah didn't want to be rude, but it was *her* place, not theirs, and they clearly knew more about it than she did. She remembered the estate agent's bright words, the patter that never let up, not for a second. Had he been chattering on like that so she wouldn't ask questions? And questions kept niggling at her: about that horrible doll, the marks in the snow, the boy she'd heard talking to another unseen person in her yard – she knew there must be more to tell about Maitland Farm. Suddenly she wasn't so much daunted as annoyed. That sense of *connections* she'd felt earlier, the buried layers going down, not through the snow but through the years, returned.

'It's a funny old place,' she said. 'I know that, believe me. You're not going to put me off or upset me or anything, but I'd really appreciate it if you told me what you know of it. Are there any stories about the farm or its owners?' She looked into Andrew's eyes, but he glanced away. 'I've got this really strong feeling there's something,' she went on, 'and – well, I live there now. So I feel like I should know.'

Andrew stirred, as if about to speak, but Cath sent him another sharp look and he settled. It was she who said, 'I will tell you about it, love,' she said, 'but you mustn't mind it, right? You must remember it's something that happened way back when, understand? I don't even know why it's still got such a name for itself, really. It's history, after all: long ago in the past.'

'History?' Leah wasn't sure what she'd been expecting, but it wasn't *history*.

'Aye – it's nothing for you to be concerned about, like I said. And anyway, it wasn't even in the house.'

'*What* wasn't?' Leah couldn't help but feel alarmed, despite Cath's attempts to downplay whatever it was had happened.

'It's just that – well, it was like this: a boy died there, a long time back, as I said. He didn't just die, in fact, he was killed. There was a labourer on the farm, some comer-inner, most likely . . . anyway, he'd heard all these old tales about winter and sacrifices to the land or some such thing. So apparently he thought it would fix whatever was wrong with the place. He . . .' Her voice trailed off, then she added, 'It was a long time ago, like I said.'

Maybe not so long ago as all that, thought Leah, wondering if the boy she had seen in her yard, talking so happily of presents and parties and Christmas, was the one who'd been murdered.

I hope it is not meant for my burial doll.

She shuddered. Was that why he lingered there?

No one spoke; no one looked at each other.

'So what happened?' Leah asked after an awkward moment. 'Do you know who this man was?' Then she had a thought and, blushing, added, 'Did he have some relation to Ingleby?'

'Oh – no, nothing like that,' Cath said quickly. 'It was the Maitlands he was tied to, not us.'

Us. Just as if they'd been there. Perhaps the past wasn't so very long ago to Cath either. And the way she'd said '*the Maitlands*' . . . Leah bit her lip, suddenly relieved she'd never mentioned her maiden name to anyone here.

'It was always the Slaters who held Ingleby Farm, for years and years back,' Cath went on. 'Centuries, really. Anyway, people around here – we protect our own, see? They couldn't have such a thing happen and just stand by, could they? It had to be dealt with. So some of the folk from round about, they all got together and took matters into their own hands, if you see what I mean.'

Leah really didn't. 'Took what matters into their own hands?'

'Rough justice, I suppose they'd call it now. Nothing to be proud of, mind—'

Leah thought that perhaps she did sound proud, just a little.

'—but you see, it wasn't in the house. And like I said, we protect our own, always have.'

Yes, I suppose they did. She pictured the look in Cath's eye when she'd said, '*Scared him off good and proper.*' And the way the woman in the shop had rebuffed her.

The kitchen no longer felt so cosy; the mince pie had turned bitter on her tongue. Leah tried to adopt a neutral expression to hide the anger she was feeling: at the estate agent for his careless sales spiel, intent only on selling the place, no matter what was wrong with it – and with Josh, for spotting the farm in the first place, for his unbounded enthusiasm, and then dying and leaving her with all this. And most of all, she was angry at herself.

She felt Cath's hand on her arm and started, jolted back to the present. This was nothing but a yarn to them, long consigned to the past. They hadn't looked into the face of the boy who'd died, hadn't seen his shape imprinted in the snow—

She forced a smile.

'There, now,' Cath said, 'I knew we shouldn't have told you. But these are old houses round here, love, and they've all got their stories. For hundreds of years people have lived and died and been born in them, and it weren't always easy, let's face it. They weren't all shipped off to homes or hospitals, not back then. Not here.'

'Of course,' Leah murmured, but it was hardly the same thing, not compared with murder – maybe even two murders, considering what Cath had been saying. But she wanted to show them that of course she understood, she wasn't just a city girl, an outsider – what was it Cath had called the man? *An inner-comer?* No, a *comer-inner*, that was it: a *Johnny-come-lately*. She suddenly wished she was back at home, away from their warm, welcoming, sweet-smelling kitchen. She would climb under her duvet and hold Finn's bear close until outside, the indifferent stars made the snow gleam as bright as day.

She smiled politely again and said, 'I really should be going. Thank you, Cath.'

'Oh, now, you don't have to – why don't you stay for a bit?' Then, almost without a pause, she added, 'Drew will drive you, won't you, Drew? Save you that trudge back.'

Leah started protesting that no, she was fine walking, although she could see through the window that the light was already fading from the sky and it would soon be altogether dark. She must have been here longer than she'd thought.

She glanced at her coat on its hook behind the door where Cath had stowed it. It hadn't really dried out much and she flinched at the thought of pulling those sodden sleeves over her arms. She didn't want to risk trying to find the shorter route over the field in the waning light so she'd have to walk back the long way round. But she didn't want to put them to any trouble, nor, if she was honest, did she really want to be confined so closely in the Land Rover with Andrew's quiet awkwardness while they jolted their way along. She was still shaking her head, even as Andrew was reaching for his own coat.

'Of course,' he said. 'We wouldn't think of letting a neighbour walk home in this. It won't take two shakes. Besides, it'll get me out of doing the washing up. Hey, Charlie!' he suddenly hollered, throwing open the hall door. 'Your mum's got a job for you!'

Leah laughed when she heard the boy's answering groan and when Andrew winked at her, somehow, in spite of herself, she found herself smiling back.

★

When they stepped outside, the air was so bitingly cold that Leah couldn't help feeling relieved she didn't have to walk. She shivered in her damp coat as she climbed up into the Land Rover and settled herself as Andrew ground it into gear. The fields were spread with shadows; their boundaries were marked by trees like silently watchful figures.

We protect our own.

Leah wondered exactly what they'd done, Cath and Andrew's predecessors and the 'folk from round about'. Was that one of the things that had brought the community together – had they bonded over some shared terrible act? In the half-dark, the idea of everyone knowing what everyone else did was almost sinister.

She snatched a quick look at Andrew, but his smile was guileless as he started down the lane, the Land Rover rocking into the ruts beneath the snow and bumping its way out again. In the headlights, tiny particles of snow still flickered in the air.

'What did she mean?' Leah asked suddenly.

Andrew didn't turn. His cheek was turned a sickly colour in the glow of the dashboard. He pressed his lips closed.

'Cath said it was rough justice, but what did they do, exactly? Sorry if you think it's not my business, but it *is* my farm, and – well, I need to know.'

He fell back on his sister's excuse. 'It's years back.'

'Still.'

He rubbed his face and looked surprised, as if he hadn't expected to find his hand encased in a bulky glove. 'They protected their children,' he murmured.

'I understand that, but how?' Somehow it was easier to press Andrew than his sister. Enclosed in the front like this, they might be the only people in the universe. She could almost feel the silence lying thick and heavy in the fields, waiting to flow back after they had passed.

'They hanged him. It was no more than he deserved. And, like I said, it's history.'

But it wasn't Andrew who'd said that, it had been Cath. Were the two of them so connected?

They didn't speak again until they pulled up in Leah's yard and before she could tell him not to, Andrew had jumped out and come round to help her down from the vehicle. He didn't meet her gaze but instead tilted back his head to look into the darkening sky as he asked, 'You've got a child?'

Leah whirled around, thinking her young visitor had returned, then realised Andrew wasn't looking at the out-side of the house. He'd seen her bedroom window, where a single light shone and a little teddy bear watched. The rest of the house was dark. She didn't recall leaving the light on up there, but that didn't mean she hadn't; it didn't mean anything.

'I had a boy. He died,' she said, turning back to meet his gaze, not blinking. She didn't know where it had come from, this sudden directness, let alone the need to tell him. It had been months ago and yet it felt like yesterday, as if the intervening time had been swallowed by a void: numb; cold. She looked at the snow all around her.

'I'm sorry.'

That was what everyone said, and it didn't help. She opened

her mouth to say goodnight, but instead found herself adding, 'Finn went on a school trip, on a bus. There was an accident – he wasn't standing in the road, not that; he was just sitting on the bus with his best friend – they were on the back seat. Apparently the teacher told them not to mess about, to put their seatbelts on, but . . . well, you know kids. Someone stepped into the road without looking. An old lady, they said. The man at the wheel was a good driver, everyone told me that, and somehow he managed to stop in time . . . but Finn didn't. He fell off his seat into the aisle – and he kept on going. He banged his head on one of the seat legs, so badly he got a blood clot on his brain. They brought him back home – well, to the local hospital, anyway. He was with us for a bit longer, but he wasn't *there*—'

She stopped, shocked by the way she had run on, and to a stranger. Only then did she realise, with a start of horror, that Andrew had put out his hands and was holding her shoulders. He was saying something – or nothing, probably, just the broken things that were all anyone could offer.

'I'm sorry.' It was her turn to apologise as she pulled away from him. 'I didn't mean to—'

She hurried to the door and started scrabbling at the lock with her key. Why had she told him all that? The words had spilled from her like she'd been punctured and everything she'd been holding so tightly inside had burst free.

She pushed open the door and only after she'd stepped into the dark hall did she turn to see that Andrew was already sitting behind the wheel again. He was nothing but a shadow among shadows, but she saw when he raised a hand to wave. She waved back, then shoved the door closed against the night and leaned her forehead against the cold, hard wood.

When Leah could move again, she retreated to the bedroom. The light was too bright, too modern for this house, so she snapped it off, grabbed Finn's bear and crept under the duvet, emerging briefly to recover her mobile phone from where she'd placed it by the bed. She looked for a text from Trish, but there wasn't anything new, so she started, *You won't believe what I've done* – then deleted the words and started again: *I'm such an idiot—*

She deleted that too and hit the off button. The screen went dark. Why upset her friend? If she carried on that way, Trish would be showing up on her doorstep with plane tickets and that wouldn't be fair. She wanted Trish to enjoy her holiday, not be worrying about her all the time.

She stared at the dead screen, thinking about what Cath had said, about all the ways and all the places the boy could have died. The barn, perhaps, filled as it was with all those rusted, broken-down implements, though of course they wouldn't have been rusty then. They'd have been bright and polished . . . and *sharp*. And there was the chopping block, too, and the slaughtering bench, with its waiting axe.

Looking back at her mobile, a reminder of civilisation, of *before*, Leah wondered if she should complain to the estate agent – if a place had a bad history, didn't they have an obligation to tell the buyer? But she recalled what Cath had said about all the births and deaths in all the old houses for miles around, going back for centuries. She was quite right, of course there would have been plenty of deaths, and they were long in the past. Perhaps one little boy hadn't seemed worth mentioning among all the rest.

She awoke her phone once more and opened the web browser.

Maitland Farm, she tapped into the search box. *Murderer. Hanged.*

There was nothing relevant in the thousands of results Google brought up, or none that included every search term, even when she scrolled down, pressing harder, as if that would help bring a long-hidden report to light.

There must be something, she thought. But Cath had called it rough justice, so maybe nobody outside the village had ever known what had happened, nobody who didn't belong in this place, at least until she'd come along.

But I do belong here.

She cleared the search box and started again, tapping in *Maitland Farm*, then adding the words *murder* and *child*.

This time, when she leaned over the screen and saw the name *Samuel Maitland*, she felt an odd prickle. Was that the boy's name? There was scant information, and nothing she hadn't heard already from Cath. The boy had been the heir to the farm, but he was killed by a labourer. It didn't say how it happened and it didn't give the labourer's name. But she knew that already, didn't she?

It is even more important that we thank the servants when you are reduced to two.

Only one labourer had remained on the farm and that was Jack. The other person the boy had spoken of was a woman:

Martha. Had Samuel Maitland invited his own killer to a Christmas party?

Leah held Bear against her neck, feeling the soft tickle of the fur, but she couldn't help picturing another toy, one given to a little boy at Christmas. *I hope it is not meant for my burial doll.*

Words leaped into her mind, Cath's words: *He'd heard all these old ideas about winter and sacrifices to the land or some such thing. He thought it would fix whatever was wrong with the place.*

She grabbed her phone and searched again, this time typing in *sacrifice* and *child* and *doll*. After a moment's consideration, she added the word *winter*.

This time useful results bloomed under her fingers and she began to read, following the flood of information about midwinter sacrifices meant to rejuvenate the land. She was surprised to discover just how widespread the practice had been, right around the world and in wildly differing cultures. During the darkest time of the year, Celts and other pagan peoples across northern Europe made Yuletide sacrifices to ask for the gods' blessings on their forthcoming crops. And then, mainly because she spotted the word *Christmas* among the results, she found herself reading about Saturnalia, an ancient Roman festival held in December which was said to be the root of modern Christmas celebrations. Back then, it had honoured Saturn, the God of Agriculture. The Romans would light candles, decorate their homes with evergreens and indulge in feasting and drinking in a spirit of togetherness. Masters would wait upon their servants in a reversal of the normal social order, and they gave gifts—

Leah gasped and sat up, ignoring the duvet slipping from her shoulders. The traditional gifts for the time of year were *sigillaria*, wax figurines or dolls, and at least one well-respected historian claimed they represented sacrifices made in primitive religious rituals to ensure a good harvest.

Now, of course, December's various pagan celebrations had been completely subsumed by Christianity, the early Christians wishing to displace such ungodly rituals with their own rites. Leah thought of the little manger in the shop, the image she'd had of children's heads bowed over their work as they coloured in the Holy family. The twenty-fifth was chosen to celebrate Christ's Mass, even though there was nothing in the Bible about His date of birth and nor had Saturnalia even been held on that specific day; that was supposed to be the birth of Sol Invictus, the unconquered sun. It was, she read, a natural choice, because in the calendar of Julius Caesar, the twenty-fifth was the shortest day: the Romans' Winter Solstice.

She frowned, bending over the screen. As the days grew shorter and night held sway, they had believed the sun to be dying, but after the solstice, the sun returned and the dying god was born again in a cycle of death and renewal. And the earth would also be renewed, as one season gave way to the next.

It seemed that winter had always been associated with death, before life returned once more to the land in spring.

Leah turned off the phone. She'd always thought the religious solemnity of Christmas had declined rapidly in modern times into nothing more than shopping and parties

and binge-drinking, not to mention a massive burst of con-
sumerism, but it turned out the opposite was true: this had
always been a time of feasting and partying, in defiance of
the hardship that winter brought. That, and perhaps it was
also an attempt to drive back fear – fear of the perils and
privations the depths of midwinter might bring.

Despite all the ideas circling in her mind, Leah's eyes at
last began to close. She must eventually have slept, because
she dreamed she was walking through the orchard, ducking
beneath the lowest boughs, raising her hands to pluck apples
from the trees and instead finding small white berries that
burst between her fingers. She brushed the juice from her
damp, sticky hands and looked up to see the living plant
wrapped around the dead. The moon shone down on it all,
a much larger milky-white berry, ripe and full: perhaps the
goddess of them all.

Then, somehow, she was standing at the entrance to the
barn. She could no longer see the moon, but it still gave
her light, gleaming from the snow, limning the edges of the
forms within.

The figure lying on the slaughtering bench was not a
boy; it was too small for that. And the bench itself was no
longer merely damp for rivulets of moisture had pooled on
its surface, drenching the doll, running along every crack in
the wood and dripping to darken the floor beneath.

A giggle rang out behind Leah and she whirled to see a
shadow moving in the doorway. Was it a boy? She couldn't
see his face, but she called out his name and hurried after him.

In the yard, she had to shield her eyes from the moon's

vivid light. There was nothing there but snow churned by tyre tracks and footprints. Silence had grown out of the land and was spreading across the snow, filling the world.

Leah awoke, realising she was no longer in bed but standing in the hall, and it was dark. She peered around. The flags at her feet were speckled with darkness too – were they damp? She bent and put her fingers to the stone, but she couldn't tell if it was moisture under her fingers or only the dead cold. She rubbed her fingertips, thinking of the sticky juice of the berries, and shook away the vision. It had been a dream, that was all: she hadn't been outside, she hadn't been in the barn. She had gone to sleep with the idea of sacrifices and murder running around her head, a murder in her own home, and of course it had given her strange dreams.

Leah went upstairs and got back into bed, relieved to find Finn's bear waiting for her where she must have left him, tucked securely under the duvet. An odd light penetrated the windows: the moon must be at its height, but not wanting to see its face, she turned her gaze away. She wrapped her arms around the soft little form, allowing herself to imagine that it was Finn curled against her, all warm and close, but there was only the little toy that had once been his.

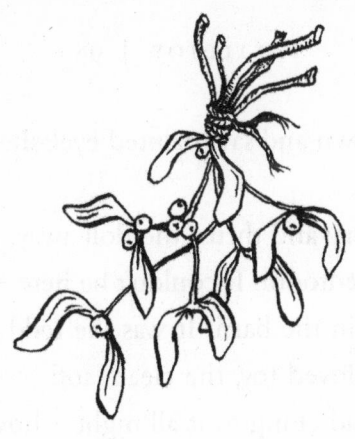

Chapter Six

This time when Leah awoke, for a moment she didn't know where she was. She listened for the sounds of Josh making breakfast in the kitchen below, for Finn slopping water over the side of the bathroom sink, but there was nothing, although she thought she could smell something – frying meat, perhaps? She blinked at the window, not recognising its shape. Then it started to come back to her, her new life, but she kept it at a distance, looking instead at something on the windowsill that should not be there: a teddy bear, his back turned towards her as he watched the snow.

And that smell wasn't frying bacon after all. It was a musky scent, rank and unpleasant, and it wasn't drifting through the air from the kitchen below but closer still – and Leah realised her arms were wrapped around something that she was clutching against her like a child.

She looked down and saw painted eyelashes, cracked skin, ragged sackcloth.

She let out a cry and thrust the doll away, pushing herself back across the bedroom. It couldn't be here – it *couldn't*. She had left the doll in the barn. It was the teddy she had taken to bed, Finn's beloved toy, the clean, soft bear that he'd had all his life. She had clung to it all night – how could it have been taken from her?

The dream returned: the slaughtering bench receiving its gift of blood, a child who vanished into the moonlight. She spread her hands in front of her face and stared at her fingers. Was that the trace of mistletoe juice on her skin, or was it just grime from the horrible doll?

Sacrifice, she thought. She had been reading of sacrifices and the dolls that represented them, and now this horrible thing was here.

And other words came back to her: *Falling yields. Exhausted soil. It makes for a poor living . . .*

Was that the reason this doll had come to her now, not as a relic of the past, but a demand for the future? She pushed it to the floor, not caring if it smashed into pieces, and made a decision: if the land was thirsty, if it demanded sacrifice, that's exactly what she would give it.

Leah set out towards the field, awkwardly lugging one of the packing boxes. She heaved its unwieldy weight over the top rung of the gate and let it drop into the snow on the other side before climbing after it herself. For only the second time since she'd taken possession of the keys she was standing on her own land: once her ancestors' farm, now hers.

She picked up the box again and adjusted her grip. The doll was almost covered by the other things she'd thrown in on top of it and she was glad of that, because she really didn't want to look into its face. In the barn she'd found some stuff to use as kindling – a few sticks, some dry straw – and added a bundle of papers she'd finished with and some torn-up cardboard boxes. Sitting on top of those was a tin of lighter fluid and a box of matches. There were some hand-tools too, also discovered among the discarded things. They might be rusty, but she thought they'd do the job.

I'd burn it if I were you.

Cath had been right, but she wasn't going to do that in the house. The vision of Samuel Maitland had faded the moment the doll slipped from her hands; she thought if the boy and the doll were connected, this would surely be the end of them both, and so she would banish them at the very border of her land.

She paused. She'd been thinking so much about the doll that she hadn't considered its master. What might have happened to his remains – where would he have been buried? Burial dolls were supposed to be effigies of the deceased; hadn't they sometimes been displayed right at the graveside? But the people hereabouts had avenged the crime, so they must have found the boy and surely they would have taken his body to the churchyard for a proper Christian burial. Exactly where he had been killed, she had no way of knowing. She glanced at the white expanse around her. If it held some darker secret, she had no way of reading it.

Leah waded through the snow until she reached the wall at the top of the field. It had resolved from a black line into the mottled grey of lichen-clad stone against the deep green of the firs. She dusted off the snow and pulled some coping stones from the top, then laid them on the ground next to each other to create a flat surface, leaving gaps between so any moisture could run off.

An intermittent breeze tried to snatch the papers from her hands as she screwed them up and placed them on top, so she pinned them in place with the cardboard and the sticks. Then, setting aside the lighter fluid and tools, she tore the box she'd used to carry everything into pieces and added those, then stuck the straw into the gaps.

Her fire was pitifully small and the air dreadfully cold, but she was not about to let such things beat her. She took the lighter fluid and drenched the lot, then reached for the doll.

The thing looked more ancient than ever, especially in contrast with the brightness all around. A pang of guilt chimed inside her: this was a part of history, after all – but it didn't belong here and she wanted none of it.

It went on top of the heap, reminding her of a body on a funeral pyre. *But that's exactly what it is, in a way*, she thought: her own little sacrifice, to quiet the land and the restless spirits that walked upon it.

She covered the doll in lighter fluid which ran down the cracks in its skin and pooled around the painted lashes in the eye sockets. Then she stepped back and walked around the fire until she was upwind. Even so, the first match she struck was immediately taken by the breeze and the next broke in her fingers. Leaning closer, but carefully – it wouldn't do to get caught in the flare – she struck another, and this time it caught. She tossed it towards the pile – but nothing happened; it was already extinguished.

She removed a piece of cardboard from the fire and holding it between her knees, she struck another match and set the little flame to its edge.

I'd burn it if I were you.

She threw it down and this time, with a dull rushing sound, flames shot upwards, their edges gleaming in different colours, tasted the things she'd given them, then shrank away. She thought the fire had died, but no, the paper was continuing to curl and blacken and at last a thread of flame began to explore the doll, deepening in hue as it devoured the dry sackcloth. There was a sudden hiss – not fire, but sand, bursting from the doll's body, and Leah realised she would now never know if something had been concealed within: blood, hair or bone.

The wax was beginning to melt, softening and smoothing out until it became almost lucent. At last it appeared like new skin, then the fire grew hungry and the eye sockets distorted, parting from the structure beneath and sliding away. The doll no longer had a face. It couldn't watch her any more. There was only age-darkened wood resisting the flame.

Leah jumped when it cracked with a dull sound.

After a time, nothing remained but ash and debris. The doll was unrecognisable.

She picked up the other things she'd found in the barn: hammer, trowel, an iron crowbar. A short distance away, by the wall, stood a small fir tree, its symmetrical branches shifting and whispering in the breeze. It struck her that if Josh was still here, it might have been their first Christmas tree in their new house together.

While the fire cooled, Leah scraped snow from the base of the tree with her boot, then set to clearing the rest with the trowel. She could have left the fire's remnants to be dispersed by the wind, but she knew she'd feel better knowing they'd been buried. The ground beneath the snow was bare of grass or anything living and as she'd expected, it was hard as stone. She'd hoped to find some kind of spike, but the crowbar was the best she could manage, so it would have to do. Using it like a chisel, she dug it into the ground and hit it repeatedly with the hammer, ignoring the rust crumbling from it, until she'd loosened the surface of the earth enough. It took some time, raising blisters on her palms and distorting the iron crowbar, but at last she had a shallow hole.

Thanks to the bitter air, the fire had already gone cold. Leah carefully picked up the stones that had formed its base and tipped the ashes into the hole before piling on the broken clumps of earth. She placed the coping stones on top to press it down. It almost looked like a grave, though small; too small.

It has to be enough, she thought. Looking around the field, she almost expected it to be different, but it was just the same: white and blank and silent. The sun had risen to its highest point, but it had no heat to offer.

Leah retraced her steps towards the farm, wondering at herself. Had she really presented the land with a sacrifice? And if the boy *was* connected to the doll in some way, didn't that make it rather sad, even cruel, to banish him by burning it?

All the same, the first thing she did when she went inside was to unearth a paintbrush and a tin of white emulsion and carry them up to her bedroom. She moved the pile of boxes to one side to get to the odd discolouration on the wall, telling herself the face that had so disturbed her really was nothing but a stain in the plaster; that it had no features she could see, no eyes to look at her as she obliterated it with a few deft strokes.

The boy wasn't *her* ghost – and in any case, he'd already had justice of a kind, hadn't he? Samuel's killer had been hanged: the people who lived here had done what they could for him. She was one of them now, and so had she. What unfinished business could he possibly have with her?

Now he was gone and she needn't see that echo of his shape again, only a pale glow in the middle of the wall that would remind her how bright and clean this place was eventually going to be.

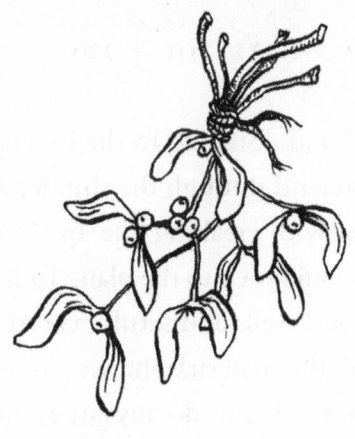

Chapter Seven

Leah stood in the master bedroom, seeing a vision of the future: a double bed dressed with bright new linen; matching bedside tables on each side; a capacious wardrobe with gleaming doors; a dressing table and mirror set by the window where the light would fall on the face of whoever was seated there.

For now, the near-empty room was undeniably drab. The chimney forming a crooked ridge down one wall opened onto a hearth that was littered with a tangle of twigs, probably dropped by jackdaws or some other birds trying to nest in the chimneys. Bits of decaying carpet failed to entirely conceal the scuffed floorboards. Other than the old wardrobe where she'd first hidden the doll, there was nothing else in the room. The walls were bare save for remnants of wallpaper showing twining flowers, which might once have been white and pink but were now badly yellowed. *Were they apple blossom?* she wondered, listening to the breeze playing in the branches of the orchard through the thin leaded glazing, dry rattles interspersed with creaking like an over-strained rope.

This time, she would stick to the plan. Today she was going to strip the floor and walls and scrub everything clean, then draw up a list of all the materials she would need in the New Year. She hadn't intended to do anything drastic this side of January, but her attack on the kitchen wall had felt good – as if she had not just been making the house anew, but striking a blow; a warning, perhaps, for it to behave.

She started with the carpet, not realising how sour it smelled until she began to pull it up, filling the air with loose fibres. It should have been a simple task, but the disintegrated, spongy residue of the underlay turned to noxious dust that stuck to the floor; she ended up having to scrape it all away and soon it was coating every surface, settling in her hair, on her clothes. When she wiped her face with her sleeve, it came away black, as if she were covered in soot. But at least she was getting rid of it. The room would be so much better when it was done.

As if in answer to her thought, she again heard the hollow rattle of the trees, a little like throaty laughter, but she ignored it and took up a Stanley knife, changed the blade and started to slice the carpet into smaller sections so she could bag it up. Once she'd taken all the detritus outside, a process that took hours, or so it felt, she swept up as much of the dust as she could, then stood back to examine her handiwork. She was sweaty and exhausted and covered in grime and her skin itched, but the room already looked much improved.

Now to clean the wardrobe, she decided. It was empty save for the rows of shelves and pegs for hanging clothes, or perhaps, originally, bonnets and hats.

The right-hand door rattled against the frame as she pulled it open. She tried to pretend it didn't come as a relief to see that the doll wasn't there, staring out at her, but of course it wasn't. She had burned it.

She dusted down the shelves, having to stretch up to reach the back of the topmost, then kneeling to do the one on the bottom, which turned out to be the grimiest, as if no one had touched it in years. When she peered into the very back, she spotted a clump of something lying in the dust: a curled, organic shape that made her think of dead spiders. She gritted her teeth and swept the thing towards her.

She stared down at it before picking it up, not quite sure what she was looking at. It was withered and browned, brittle as a pressed flower. She turned it in the light, tilting her head. *Is that a hint of green?* she wondered as she realised she was holding two leaves with desiccated berries clinging to each stem.

Mistletoe.

Perhaps it had been brought inside from the orchard one Christmas past to decorate the house, although how it had come to be in the wardrobe, she couldn't imagine; she'd never heard of it being used as a ward against moths or other insects. She twisted the leaves, so closely entwined, and they separated.

The trees outside the window shifted uneasily.

Leah started to throw them into a rubbish bag, then stopped and examined them more closely, suddenly certain she'd seen something odd, even through the patina of grime. The leaves were so dry and discoloured they might be years and years old, and speckled with darker patches, but for a moment she thought she discerned some pattern within their markings. Each little stain bore the trace of an indentation at its heart, as if the marks had been made on purpose with a needle or a pin. She turned one of the leaves again and stared at it, and finally she could make out letters: a J and an H.

Leah stared in wonder. Someone had pricked letters into these leaves and saved them – but why? Had they received such a special kiss under the mistletoe they had wished to preserve the moment?

J.H. Could that be for Jack – a murderer?

She examined the other leaf and saw that too had initials marked into it, this time an E and an M.

M – for Maitland?

Whatever the answer to the riddle, Leah did not wish to so lightly discard this remnant of a memory that had been kept so long. She cast about for somewhere to put the leaves, then, so she didn't accidentally sweep them away with her duster, she laid them against each other and slipped them into the breast pocket of her flannel shirt.

Behind her, she heard the crackle of fire.

She whirled around. The fireplace was empty, even the fallen twigs cleared away. She told herself it was only the trees she'd heard, the knocking of their dead limbs, but in the next moment she saw the sinuous flash of flame.

She blinked. She knew she was tired – was fatigue causing her to hallucinate now?

Leah felt the heat from across the room as the hearth burst into life. The flames leaped higher, sending a bright glow emanating from the stone fireplace, and she started at the sharp crack as a log split. She half-expected to see the doll's face in the fire, come back again – why had she thought she could ever be rid of it? But there was only wood, fissured to the heart with a red glare.

She must have been working too long. She was dehydrated. She needed to rest, to get out of this room, the one she knew she would have shared with Josh. She had to stop imagining these strange, impossible, *crazy* things.

Leah shut her eyes, suddenly unable to breathe as she felt a presence in the room, filling the space around her, but this wasn't the doll; it was something else entirely. If she could bring herself to turn and see, would it be Samuel Maitland standing there? Had he come looking for his toy, only to find it burned, so now he'd come in search of the person who'd destroyed it?

But it wasn't a boy's voice she heard. It was a woman's.

'Samuel is already so excited.'

Leah twisted around and opened her eyes to see there were two women by the window. One was seated at a dressing table, in much the same place Leah had imagined placing hers, while the other stood at her side.

The seated woman was richly dressed, her hair swept upwards and teased into tight curls, all held in place by an arrangement of combs and pins. Her posture was very straight, as if supported by a corset, her dress black and high at the neck, with long sleeves trimmed at the wrist with lace. The

skirts were full, embellished with ruches and drapes and pan-
elled with figured satin, and she perched on the edge of her
chair, at an angle to the table, to accommodate an elaborate
bustle. Her companion, who looked like a maid, was similarly
old-fashioned in her dress, with a plain white cap and an
apron with feathered straps worn over a faded print frock.

The dressing table itself was not what Leah had envisioned
but a solid, heavy thing of gleaming mahogany. Her gaze went
to the mirror set over it and there she saw the reflection of
the seated woman's eyes. Neither of them reacted; the woman
was clearly unaware that she was there.

Still, Leah turned her head away – and saw the transforma-
tion that had been wrought on the room. It was no longer
empty. A four-poster bed dominated, its barley-sugar pillars
holding aloft swathes of crimson drapery, the once plush
cloth so moth-eaten that in places the light shone through
it. There were numerous chairs: arranged about the fire, on
either side of a small round table, or pushed against the wall
as if at any moment their mistress might grow tired and need
to sit. The remaining floor space was busy with rugs in a
miscellany of colours. An open door revealed the wardrobe
to be stuffed with clothes, white linens folded on the shelves,
and gowns in blacks and browns and deep blues and greens,
with a variety of caps and bonnets hanging from the pegs.
An antique washstand stood by, its marble top crowded with
a basin, china dishes, glass bottles and a ewer for water, with
a chamber pot set into the frame beneath – but it wasn't an
antique, was it? It wouldn't be for another hundred years.
The crystal bottles gleamed. One hadn't yet had its stopper

replaced and Leah could smell some sort of musky scent, cut with the chemical sharpness of carbolic soap.

The fireplace had changed too. An embroidered screen now shielded anyone sitting there from the fierce heat. The mantelpiece was adorned with a tasselled velvet cover which in turn was covered with what Leah thought of as car boot sale bric-a-brac: a flat-backed china shepherdess; a bouquet of feathers and dried white blossoms covered by a glass dome; a picture of Queen Victoria and her children.

Leah stood lost before it all, her heart racing. She focused on the floor at her feet, hoping to find something in the room that remained the same, part of her world, but even the boards had changed, now scrupulously clean and gleaming with polish.

'He so wants to dress the tree, to make everything cheerful,' the mistress said, her incised, confident intonation proclaiming her class, 'just as it has always been, and so we must. We shall cut the tallest, I think, and defy everything! He does not quite grasp our present difficulties, Martha, and that might be for the best, after all.'

Leah once again stared at the woman's reflection. The word that came to her was *handsome*. Her features were symmetrical, her face a neat oval, although her expression was sombre and her cheeks pale. Her dark eyes were so serious they were almost severe. She also looked tired, bone-weary.

'Perhaps the garnet collar, Martha, for the party? I do not think I shall need the opals again. I may dispose of them . . . it would be of no matter.'

This last was said in such an airy fashion that Leah knew

she did care, very much – and she caught the look of contempt the maid cast her before the girl lowered her eyes. It was the look of someone who knew what it was to have little, towards one who had perhaps still to learn.

'Shall I brush that gown with the crimson bodice to go with them, Ma'am? Though the blue's so pretty.'

The maid half turned towards the wardrobe and although she was certain they couldn't see her, Leah still flinched. Martha was younger than she'd first thought, perhaps in her early twenties, and pretty, though her face was scrubbed bare, her blonde hair drawn back tightly under her cap. She had long, pale eyelashes, a snub nose and sweetly curled lips – which now curled a little more, taking on an almost snide expression.

'Do so.' Her mistress sighed, then, changing her mind, said, 'Ah no – perhaps the blue with the opals after all, just this last time, Martha. We shall not be so very many, but we will have the Slaters and the Jepsons from the village, and the parson and his wife, and our tenants. Their children shall be coming too, and you will be there, and Jack, of course.' The woman leaned forward, gazing deeply into the mirror, into her own eyes. 'It was a nice idea of my husband's, was it not? He said it was an old tradition, for masters and their men to mingle together at Christmas – although I know it means you are very busy beforehand.' Without waiting for a response, she added, 'It is a custom that I am glad to continue, of course, now he is gone.'

'And the late master's cousin, Ma'am – will he be attending?'

'Ah – Ellis.' She looked troubled. 'I imagine he will grace

us with his presence, yes, since he has stated his intention to take a house in the village. He insists that he must help to pull the farm around somehow and I suppose – well, I suppose I must allow him to do so.'

'It seems a good offer, Ma'am. Very generous.'

The maid spoke carefully and yet the older woman looked surprised, as if the girl had overstepped her bounds, or maybe her words meant more than she had expected.

She replied stiffly, 'Indeed. Though I imagine he would have preferred to spend his days travelling the Continent, had his means allowed it.'

The maid bowed her head, concealing her expression, as she straightened the silver-backed brush and mirror set upon the dressing table. She selected an ivory comb from a decorated box and held it out in the palm of her hand. The mistress scarcely glanced at it before shaking her head; she was clearly thinking of other things.

'I do wish Ellis were a steadier man, Martha, though I suppose I should not say it, and in any case – well, to whom may I speak? There has been no one, for so long. I heard such tales of Ellis from my husband – but they were not close and he did allow the reports may have been a little . . . well, perhaps exaggerated. Debts and dissolution—' Her voice tailed away, as if she had forgotten her maid was listening. 'Indeed, he hoped they were overstated. It is his place to offer and mine, as you say, to be grateful.' She did not sound grateful; she looked distinctly unhappy. She stirred and said, 'If only the harvest had not been so very dismal! And there is no one who remains on this earth in whom I can confide, no one who calls me Isobel and not Mrs Maitland, the widow. I may have cast off my mourning, but he is still in my heart.' She placed the palm of her hand against her cheek as if the heat of the fire was troubling her.

'I suppose it must be very trying, Ma'am,' said the maid.

Leah didn't think she appeared to believe it very trying at all, but of course Mrs Maitland couldn't see the girl's face.

'Shall I have Jack cut the holly, Ma'am, for the party? There's some growing down the lane, with red berries too. And there's mistletoe – should we have that?'

'Mistletoe?' Isobel sounded startled, although Leah couldn't work out what was so unusual about the request. 'Why Martha, do you mean to be caught under it, you little cat? It is bad luck to bring greenery indoors before Christmas Eve, or so my husband always said, and my little gathering comes before that. He would have been most decided on the matter.'

But Martha wasn't looking at her mistress any longer. She had taken something from the pocket of her apron and was staring down at it in consternation. 'Bad luck, Ma'am?'

'What is it you have there? Show me.'

Martha bit her lip, then opened her hand.

Leah felt a shiver when she caught sight of what the maid was holding: a cluster of fresh green leaves, complete with white berries.

'Martha, you *didn't* – why, has someone imposed upon you already? Jack Hirst, I suppose!'

The girl's lip twitched.

'Have you indeed a follower, Martha? You must tell me

at once if you do. You should have a care, you know – I suppose you admire the man's looks, but you must think of your position here.'

'Of course, Ma'am.' Martha spoke demurely, her eyes downcast, then she raised them. 'But anyone can be kissed under the mistletoe, Ma'am – it's only tradition, like all the rest, in't it? It's *expected*. It don't mean – well, it means – it's supposed to mean things'll blossom, don't it? And love – it can make it strong and make it grow.'

'Whatever do you mean?'

'My mam, she told us all about it. This, it's summat the maids hereabouts used to do, when there was more than one of us, at least. It's just a game, that's all, though they do say it brings down a blessing on a couple, and maybe even on places too.'

Isobel looked dubious. 'Please, explain yourself, Martha. What was it the maids used to do?'

Suddenly eager, the maid held up the sprig of mistletoe and spread its leaves. 'You pick a leaf and you take a pin,' she explained, 'and you mark out the young man's initials – *your* young man's initials, I should say – right there, on the leaf. Then you wear it next to your heart. It means true love – that he'll be true to you and good to you, and that love will grow, even in the winter. Me mam said the leaves are meant for the man, see? Look at their shape? They're like a woman's shape, aren't they, all ready for him, and the berries – well, they're meant for the woman, of course.'

'Martha!' Isobel Maitland sounded scandalised. 'You let your tongue run on quite enough. Perhaps it is just as well we no longer have a houseful of servants, if this is how they talk.'

'It's only how it works, Ma'am. I din't decide on it. It's tradition.'

Leah put her hand to her shirt pocket and felt the shape of the leaves nestled within.

'Tradition.' This time it was Isobel's lip that twitched. 'Well, I do not like the sound of it, though I doubt not that my husband would have been very interested in your tales. He told me of such things: how maids were used to peel apples on All Hallows' Eve to foretell whom they would marry. I believe they were to throw the peel over their shoulder, hoping it would land in the shape of the letter standing for their true love's name. There are many games of the sort, apparently, though he never spoke to me of this one. All he told me of mistletoe was that it was believed that the plant could be used to contact the dead – at least, they do believe that in France.'

She sighed and looked around the room. 'I will admit that I used to imagine,' Isobel continued, 'when I was a good deal younger than I am now, of course, what it might be like if such things really worked. Surely it would make you afraid, if it truly did? But it has been a long time indeed since I believed in magic, and longer still since I left the nursery. But very well: tradition wins out, even if it is not quite its time. See how you carry your point, Martha! You shall tell Jack that we shall have the holly, and the ivy too, as well as our tree, of course – and yes, even the mistletoe. Why not?' Her voice turned melancholy. 'For we must not forget that this may be the last such gathering my son will ever see at Maitland Farm.'

The girl was still fingering her mistletoe sprig, but she looked up at this, as if surprised. 'Really, Ma'am? Are things truly so bad?'

Isobel twisted towards her maid. 'Oh, do not worry yourself, Martha. The harvest shall be better next year, of that I am certain. I am only a little despondent today, that is all. And I will always make sure you are taken care of, no matter what may come.'

'And the letters, Ma'am?'

'The letters?'

'On the leaves.' Martha waved the mistletoe in the air.

'Good Heavens, Martha, you cannot mean it! You forget yourself.'

Martha looked crestfallen. 'Sorry, Ma'am. It's just – we're so very alone here now.'

Isobel stared at her.

'And it might help make everything grow, Ma'am, not just – I mean . . . I thought it might help, that's all.'

Isobel smiled indulgently at the maid. 'I know you mean it kindly, Martha, but you must know this is all nonsense. And you cannot expect—'

You cannot expect me to do it, is what she was going to say.

Leah could almost hear the words hanging in the air, even as Martha echoed, 'So *very* alone.'

Isobel stared at the leaves as if she did not know what they were, and then said, 'I know that things have been difficult for you too, Martha—' She fell silent, then, her voice brighter, cried, 'Oh, it cannot hurt, I suppose – very well, let us try our luck with the power of the mistletoe.'

'You really mean it, Ma'am?' But Martha did not wait for an answer. She set down the leaves on the table and rummaged in the decorated box once more, pulling out a long hatpin with a pearl at one end. 'This shall serve.'

She picked up the mistletoe, divided the sprig and handed Isobel a stem with a single leaf and a clinging berry; she kept the other for herself.

'So this one's mine,' she said, and paused. Giving her mistress a sidelong glance, she murmured, 'Well, after all, let it be—'

She started to prick at the leaf, bending low over the table, focused on her task. When she straightened, Isobel caught hold of the leaf and read what she had written there. 'J— H—'

She laughed softly. 'Hmm. So . . .'

'Now you, Ma'am. Two leaves, two names.' Martha giggled.

Isobel looked at her sharply for a moment, then shook off her obvious reluctance. 'Very well – but you must tell no one of this, Martha. Though I do not suppose they would believe it of me if you did.'

Martha's eyes opened wide. 'No, Ma'am! Of course not – for then the charm would not work.'

Isobel tossed her head. 'I do not expect the charm to work at all, Martha, but I imagine that at least it can do no harm. Still, if Fate or whatever magic there is in the world could ever make me love such a fellow, I shall be forced to believe in it after all, and you shall have your victory.'

She took the hatpin, spread the leaf on the dressing table and quickly pricked out the letters. 'There, you see: here is an E, and here the M.'

She picked up the leaf – and dropped it with a sudden exclamation. To Leah, it looked as if she'd been stung.

'What is it?' Martha asked, reaching for her mistress' hand. 'Oh, Ma'am, look at your fingers!'

Isobel examined her fingertips. 'It itches,' she said, 'really quite intensely. Do you feel it, Martha?'

'No, Ma'am, not at all – but look, it has given you quite a rash. It must be working. Perhaps that's the charm in it!'

'Nonsense, girl. It is nothing of the kind. I must be sensitive to the plant, for that is where the sap has touched my skin. I must have some aversion that you do not – well, that has paid me back nicely for my indulgence! How odd that I never before knew.'

She took the fine lace handkerchief Martha handed her and wiped at her hand. 'There. I suppose I have never actually touched the horrid stuff before. It has always been cut by others. See that you take it away, would you?'

'But I can't, Ma'am,' Martha protested. 'We've only done the first part. Now we have to wear the leaves next to our hearts.'

'Well, that is something I certainly cannot do, that is clear enough. So much for your customs – see what they have done? Even now I feel my breath is shortening. I must not touch the mistletoe again; indeed, Martha, I will not.'

Martha bowed her head and gathered up the leaves as Isobel reached for a pot of some sort of ointment and smothered her fingers with it, still exclaiming at the discomfort.

Leah could see the flesh was angry, with what looked like little raised welts spreading across her fingers.

Martha said sulkily, 'Shall I bring anything else, Ma'am? Some water, perhaps?'

Isobel gasped in a breath and when she spoke again, her voice was wheezy. 'I think you have done quite enough—' Then she stopped and as if regretting her outburst, said more calmly, 'Oh no, Martha, it is all right. I begin to feel a little better.' She put a hand to her throat.

'I shall take them away,' Martha said, picking up the leaves and slipping them into her apron pocket. Then she clapped her hands and cried, 'Oh, Ma'am, I know! I shall sew two little bags with material from the scrap-box. I can have them done in a trice. We'll put the leaves in there and that way we can keep them close to our hearts all we like – and never feel anything at all.'

She whirled about, excitement shining in her eyes, and walked directly towards Leah, who stared at her, then stumbled to one side when she realised the girl wasn't going to stop. As she did, she saw that the floorboards in front of her were no longer polished and gleaming but old and greyed and cracked with dust and the passing of time.

She turned back, wondering if Martha had seen her after all, but the girl had vanished – everything had. The bedroom was as she had first viewed it, empty, sad. It seemed even more so after her vision of it so full of furniture; the silence lay deeper now the women's voices had faded. The grate was cold, the winter chill already creeping back in.

Leah slipped her hand into her pocket and withdrew the old, faded, brittle leaves of mistletoe. She stared at them. There was no doubt these were the same leaves, for that was the reason for what she had just seen, wasn't it? The doll had shown her the child; the leaves had shown her the women who had pinned their dreams and hopes into their surfaces, however disbelieving one of them might have been. Now, wearing them next to her own heart, they had yielded their secrets.

All he told me of mistletoe was that they believed . . . it could be used to contact the dead.

Leah shivered. She didn't know if she was afraid. Was there something wrong with her – was she losing her mind? But they had spoken of Samuel and he had been real. She closed her eyes. She hadn't *wanted* to see them – she hadn't wanted any of this. If she really was having some kind of breakdown, couldn't she at least see her own ghosts, ones she'd welcome, instead of these people?

Then she thought, *Perhaps they are my own ghosts. They could be my ancestors.*

She looked around the silent, empty room. It had felt so warm in her vision, so lived in. Now it was bereft. The change from their world to hers was so very marked that for a brief moment she could almost wish them back again.

Chapter Eight

For the rest of the day, Leah avoided the bedroom and busied herself downstairs, removing some rotten wood around a window frame and repairing the gap, although the whole time she couldn't stop herself wondering what might be happening in the room above her, whether long-vanished lives were still going on behind its closed door.

Some time during the morning, it began snowing again. She watched the snowflakes drifting across the sky from the window and after a while, pulled on her boots and stepped outside. The sky was a uniform white, flakes floating out of it like scraps of ash. The sun might almost have vanished from the world.

From where she stood, Leah could hear the sound of ice cracking, and then that of wood striking wood. Something was out there, out of sight – was it another vision? She pushed down a swell of fear. This was her home: it had to belong to the living, not the dead.

She thought of Trish's text – *Don't go scaring them away!* – and she tried to laugh, but the sound was thin, fading too quickly in the cold air. She swallowed. Shouldn't it be a comfort to believe that ghosts were real, that there was some possibility of seeing the people she loved again?

She walked towards the orchard, wondering if the sound her footsteps made was quite right; if there wasn't some echo of other steps, just a little out of time with her own.

The snow was falling thicker now, like icing sugar shaken from a sieve. Flakes clung to her coat and she blinked them from her eyelashes. It deadened sound, deadened everything. Leah put out her hand as a child might, trying to catch hold of it, but by the time she felt the cold on her skin the flakes had already vanished.

'Indeed, yes. He must have made it for the boy himself.'

Leah started, trying to peer through the snow, but she could barely make out the yard ahead of her.

'Oh yes, it is part of a quite ancient tradition. My cousin had an interest in such things. He wrote a monograph once, did you know of it? I dare say they must have discussed it between them.'

The voice was a man's, clear, well-modulated and educated, but not one Leah had ever heard before. If anyone replied, she didn't hear them.

'It was indeed most kind, particularly from a labourer.' The same voice. 'One does not expect Christmas gifts to be given upward, does one? Not from servant to master. Ah, Jack, there you are! Yes, we are speaking of you, you see.'

Leah struck out at the falling snow. It fled her touch before swarming back again, more thickly than before. For an instant she thought she could see the outline of a figure amid the wild dance, but it dissolved and was gone.

She lifted her face to the sky. The world was insubstantial, nothing lasting for more than a moment. It buffeted and caressed her and she almost felt it wasn't hiding everything but making it visible: revealing a design that lay beyond the surface of the world.

She heard a new voice, lower than the first. It was perfectly distinct and close to her ear.

'You paint me a cleverer man than I am, sir.'

She spun around, only to see more snow, more *nothing*. She could picture the speaker, though: broad shoulders, strong arms, black hair almost covering his beetling brows. His hands would be callused; perhaps his heart, too.

Jack?

She didn't call his name. She didn't know what would happen if she did. Instead, she ran, her hands held out, as much in fear that Jack Hirst might suddenly appear as that she would fall.

She couldn't even see the farmhouse – she might have been anywhere – then she stumbled into the patch of trodden-down slush in front of the door and pushed her way inside, wondering if she was, after all, any safer in here, if there was any point in slamming the door.

She paused there, panting for breath, listening for any

other sound, but there was nothing. She was just beginning
to think it was over when she heard something heavy being
thrown to the ground. Then she recognised the sound of an
axe striking wood.

She pressed her fingers to her eyes and pictured the bench
in the barn, damp and hungry, awaiting – what?

They would have used it for slaughtering.

Is that what she was hearing? And what would come next?
The shriek of a pig, the panicked cries of cattle, or something worse? But there was nothing, only the axe's steady fall.
Still, she couldn't help but picture Samuel Maitland, staring
upwards, his eyes wide and blank, like a doll's.

No. The boy had gone. She'd banished him.

And the doll was burned – but the mistletoe remained.
Had the men whose initials were pricked into the leaves
been summoned too? Isobel had thought mistletoe could
contact the dead.

And what had Martha said?

The leaves are meant for the man.

But the sound didn't appear to be coming any closer, and
when Leah drew a deep breath she realised the blows had
ceased. What if the axe's wielder was coming for her? She
steeled herself to feel the door shaking at her back, but as
time passed there was nothing, only the dusty, quiet hall.

She went up the stairs and pausing on the landing, stared
at the door she had closed so firmly, not expecting to have
to enter the master bedroom again so soon. She turned the
handle and opened it.

Everything was just as it had been: empty. The women had

gone and only dust stirred, the floorboards answering her steps with a hollow sound. She walked towards the window where the dressing table with its bottles of scent and silver-backed brush and mirror, the little decorated box, had stood. She half expected it to appear again. Would Martha's mistletoe be there, all fresh and green? But the maid had taken the leaves away, hadn't she. She was going to sew them into little bags to protect Isobel Maitland's skin, so they could keep them next to their hearts.

She raised a hand to the pocket of her shirt. The mistletoe leaves hadn't been in little bags when she found them. They had been abandoned. And she was still wearing them – they had been with her the whole time she was outside, listening to voices in the snow. Even when she'd run away, the leaves had remained next to her heart.

Ellis and Jack – could they have been drawn to her by such brittle things? She reached into her pocket and drew out one of the leaves, staring at it as she had when she first found it. She wondered why she hadn't just thrown the things away. She turned it so the light caught the markings where Martha had set her pin.

J.H.

Jack Hirst. Murderer.

Her fingers closed into a fist and the leaf crumbled, its curve first bending before it snapped in two. The letters were quickly spoiled as she rubbed it between her palms. She let the fragments fall to the floor, then stepped on them and kicked them through a gap in the floorboards.

I'd burn it if I were you.

Disquiet ran through her. Fire would have been better. She'd burned the doll and she hadn't seen the boy again. She dropped to the floor and ran her hands frantically across it. Were those fragments beneath her fingers, or only black dust?

Her visitors were gone. *Gone.*

Leah left the room without looking back. There was nothing she could do here: the house belonged to the past and to the dead. She'd thought to change it, but it was she who was changing, hearing strange voices, seeing strange sights. Its emptiness surrounded her as she ran down the stairs. Who would ever want to live in this place? Even she hadn't – not when she'd first seen it. It had taken death to bring her here. But she had lived through that somehow and she would not allow herself to be broken now.

Leah pulled open the front door and stared out defiantly, as if daring the murderer to appear – but no one did. Everything was still.

But the sound she'd heard earlier must have come from the barn.

Leah stepped into the snow. If the farm wanted to show her something, let it show her.

She followed a trail of her own footprints, the patterned soles of her boots perfectly clear in the snow, and then she saw there were other prints written there: a different pattern, one made by larger boots and marked by studs, perhaps hobnails, around their edge.

Within moments, the barn was looming in front of her.

Nothing had changed. The harrow, spades and forks and billhooks, tools for working wood and stone, for land and fencing and hedging, were still there. There was the chopping block and the slaughtering bench, the shining, sharp-bladed axe leaning next to it as if it had never been touched. Then Leah blinked, because there was something different after all.

She smelled it first, a sweet, pleasant scent, one that reminded her of summer, before she saw the firewood that had been freshly chopped and stacked in the corner. Was that what she had heard? Not death, not slaughter, but the cutting of wood to provide warmth and comfort. Was it meant for her? But it was here, in the present, not in the past – or she thought it was. She approached it slowly, touched one of the raw edges, felt the dampness of sap.

Where had it come from? There was no reason she could think of for it to be here. Had one of the ghosts somehow reached into the present to provide it for her? She recalled her fear when she thought Jack Hirst was coming for her – but perhaps it hadn't been Jack. Ellis was a master, not a labourer, but he had come to the farm to help Isobel, so might he have been trying, in some strange way, to help her too? She and he were both outsiders, after all – *comer-inners* – and yet both of them were also Maitlands.

Leah shook her head. They didn't even know she was here – how could they? And yet their world had touched the present, had left footprints in the snow, had provided this wood for her.

Or she really was going mad. The footprints might have been her own, melted and distorted by the sun. The sounds she'd heard could have been the creaks and echoes of a place that was new to her. And all the strange things she'd seen, the voices she'd heard – well, her mind must have supplied the rest.

She reached out and touched the wood's fresh-hewn edges once more and a new thought came: not of a long-dead labourer, but of Andrew Slater, a sympathetic neighbour to whom she had revealed too much of her grief. He had pitied her; she knew that, and so he must have come here to do her a good turn, to make things a little more comfortable for her.

The anger and fear drained away as she saw again his silhouette behind the wheel after he had brought her home, how he had held her as she cried. His face had been in shadow, but Leah had noticed the little gesture he'd made.

She closed her eyes, trying to replay the sounds she'd heard earlier. Andrew must have called at the house first. It was he who'd walked here, leaving those footprints behind him, and knocked on the door. But she had been so confused she'd taken it for something else.

Would it have been in character for him to come here and help her, saying nothing about it? She didn't know him well enough, but she thought it probably was. He had that kind of quiet awkwardness about him and she could well imagine him considering carefully what she might need, what he could do that would be of use to her.

It was that, rather than anything else, that made her eyes sting. She should thank him, invite them all over, maybe. That would force her to pull herself together, to get on with everything she intended to do to this place.

And if she was wrong?

She could all too clearly picture what would happen if

she thanked him for cutting wood for her fire and he hadn't even thought of it. Would that story spread, too? How long before the village began to gossip about the delusional woman who'd moved into Maitland Farm, the one who thought she could live among them like a normal person? Outside the barn, the wind scoured the fields with a hollow moan. Snow whispered across snow; there came again the creak of a dying tree.

Leah hurried back to the house, going straight to the living room and the ancient fireplace. The mirror was as she'd left it, turned to the wall. She ran a finger over each of the urns she'd placed on the mantelpiece before picking up the smaller. The smooth marble was cold against her skin as she twisted the lid.

The ashes inside were soft and grey, heaped like snow. This had once been her son's bones, his body, his blood. Leah could not connect it with her grinning boy, always rushing about, intent on some task he'd dreamed up, who woke her by leaping onto her bed, who would bargain with her to let him stay awake just a little bit later. This could not be all that was left. These ashes were pale, faded as her memories would fade, leached of colour as the world outside had been.

Could objects really bring people back from wherever they went? Samuel had been drawn by his doll; the mistletoe had brought Martha and Isobel and the men they thought they might love.

How could Leah be closer to her son than this? She reached into the urn and stroked the ashes, which felt grainy and dry.

When she withdrew her fingers they were tipped with white and she raised them to her face, pressed them to her lips.

The room remained empty. She reached out with her senses, as if she could send them roaming into every room and then beyond, into the yard, the barn, the fields. She knew he was not there and she squeezed her eyes closed, although they were as dry as the ashes on her lips. Was it only that this had never been his home? Would he have come to her if she'd stayed in the city? What if he was searching for her there even now, wandering their old rooms, calling for her in a voice no one else could hear?

Leah replaced the lid and set the urn on the mantelpiece, her hands shaking.

Then she put her hand to her pocket.

The other mistletoe leaf was still in there, the one marked E.M. She should get rid of that too, banish all of it. But she remembered the wood stacked for her fire, that simple act of kindness, and instead she turned from the hearth and went up to her bedroom. She took off her shirt without looking in the pocket again and threw it over the boxes she still hadn't bothered to unpack.

She changed into her pyjamas, relishing the cold air that tightened her skin, climbed into bed and pulled the duvet up to her neck. As she lay there, she stared at the ceiling. Whatever she had seen, it felt unfinished – but she was wrung out, exhausted. If a ghost came to her now she wouldn't even care. She would stare into its eyes until it saw her too; maybe then it would be the one to be afraid.

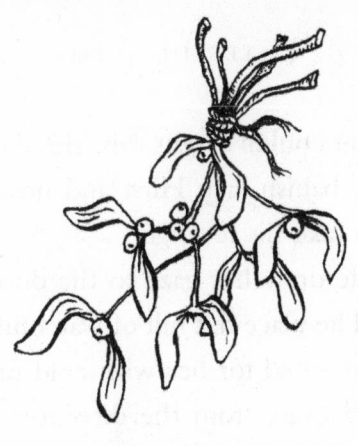

Chapter Nine

There was something in the room. Leah was certain of it the moment she jolted from sleep. Her vision was speckled as if it were snowing, billowing flakes obscuring the familiar objects around her. Breath misted from her lips. Why was it so very cold? It couldn't only be that it was midwinter. She could see nothing, but it didn't matter; that *nothing* had darkness in its heart.

All her bravado evaporated as Cath's words echoed in her ears. *I'd burn it if I were you.*

She hadn't burned the leaf. She'd been stupid and left the crumbled dust in the house, so short a distance away, beneath the floorboards of the bedroom across the landing. Was Jack in there now? Had he come seeking Samuel, his victim, only to find her instead?

She was chilled right through to her bones; her hands

were shaking. She couldn't fight this: she didn't know how. She had tried to banish Jack Hirst and now he was angry. He had come to take his revenge.

A creak outside drew her gaze to the door. Was that the house, settling? The place felt full of watchfulness, of hatred. Its malevolence reached for her with cold fingers.

Another sound came from the direction of the landing, and the bedroom beyond: fingernails scraping against wood. At once Leah pictured someone scrabbling across the floor to reach the fragments of leaf that had fallen between the boards. Or was he trapped beneath the floor and was now clawing at the wood, trying to find a way out?

She closed her eyes and curled in on herself, wondering where she might hide – but there was nowhere. There was only the old wardrobe, in the room where *he* was – and anyway, she didn't think she could hide; it wouldn't make any difference. He would know where she was: he would feel her presence just as she had felt his, and he would come to her.

She couldn't breathe. She was a child again, caught in a nightmare, unable to wake, unable to move, unable to escape—

The room darkened.

Leah flinched. She wanted to draw the covers right over her head, but how would that help? She strained her eyes, peering into the dark, trying to make out the door, telling herself clouds had covered the moon outside the window; that there wasn't anything wrong, that all was just as it should be.

She tried to make out the faint line at the bottom of the door. She could see it at either side, but in the centre – was someone standing there, blocking out the light? The scraping had stopped. The presence was no longer trapped. It was *out*.

Hinges creaked.

Leah did move then, rolling away so her back was to the door, pulling the bedclothes even more tightly around her.

She did not need to hear the footsteps to know he was walking across the room towards her. She did not need to look into his face to know who it was. She squeezed her eyes tight closed, even as she felt chill air against the nape of her neck – cold, yet humid too, a little like breath.

The duvet rustled next to her and she couldn't stop herself letting out a soft whimper. She clamped her teeth together and tried to hold onto the bedclothes, but still she heard the whisper of cotton against cotton as the duvet was lifted and someone slipped in, the mattress sinking as someone settled into place next to her.

Telling herself she was dreaming, she shifted towards the edge of the bed, trying to counter the effect of the weight of her unknown companion, but the duvet was pulled away from her again, allowing a freezing draught to find the space behind her, unfolding along her spine, prickling her tender skin. *He* was lying next to her. He had come to her like a husband to his wife, as if that was where he belonged, where *she* belonged.

A hand touched her skin.

She couldn't stop herself from crying out – and the sound made everything worse. It was like the noise a child might make, still lost in their nightmare, but Leah was certain she wasn't asleep; she felt certain she would never sleep again.

The hand reached for her once more, gently slipping under her pyjama top and resting for a moment at the hollow of her waist. Then it moved upwards, insinuating, tender, but so very cold—

—and she found she could move after all. In an instant, she was out of the bed and whirling to see that it was empty.

Was he still there, unseen to her? How could she know?

She careered from the room and onto the landing, swung around the top of the stairs, catching herself on the balustrade, then rushed down. Grasping for the newel post at the bottom, she snatched back her hand from the touch of something she did not recognise – was that a coat thrown across the carved acorn?

She hurtled into the living room, barely pausing to strike out at the light switch, half expecting it wouldn't work – then yellow light flooded her vision.

She slammed the door behind her and still panting for breath, she closed her eyes and leaned back against it.

When her heart had calmed a little, she opened them to see that the ceiling was hung with mistletoe.

It was heaped over the mantelpiece, its bright green stems heavy with berries, its fresh leaves curling around the ancient beam. It was piled in the hearth and upon the table, even draped along the back of the settle. She looked up: a handful hung over the doorway, just above her head, as if waiting for her. Had it been festooned around the newel post too – was that what she'd touched?

Had Jack obeyed Isobel's orders, harvesting this mistletoe

and bringing it into the house for the party – or was this for *her*, this plant meant for kissing under?

She reached up and snatched at the sprigs above her, hating the touch of the pliant leaves, the damp crush of berries against her skin.

Suddenly angry and relishing that anger, Leah dragged the door open. Jack was not there; she saw only the empty form of her own coat, hanging from a hook, but mistletoe was indeed twined around the newel post, creeping through the house as it had crept through her orchard. Leah grimaced, then strode to the front door and threw it wide.

Winter air swirled about her, stealing her breath away. The world was bathed in moonlight, setting all the whiteness agleam. It was unearthly and it was beautiful, absolutely pure and clean, and for a moment she just stood and stared.

Then she threw the mistletoe into it.

She went back inside and started pulling stems away from the carved acorn and the balustrade. They refused to break but she unwound them until her arms were full of the stuff. She threw that outside too, as far as she could, then hurried back for more, gathering it up from the living room, snatching it from the settle, dragging it down from the ceiling, feeling as if the plant was fighting back, clinging to her hands, wrapping itself around her arms. Returning from the hall, suddenly dizzy, she stumbled – and felt herself caught by the elbow.

Leah wrenched herself away and staggering, almost fell into the living room, where she found herself blinking against the warm glow. Shadows were flitting around her and she could almost hear snatches of some quick, merry music, the sharp notes of a fiddle answered by the energetic stamping of feet.

She shook her head and grasped at some mistletoe which had fallen from the mantelpiece, feeling as she did a blast of heat from the hearth, though it was as empty as the rest of the room. But she could sense people dancing around her as she crossed it once more. This time some unseen form grasped her arm, spinning her around to face – *what?* There was nothing.

She pulled free and went striding across the hall to dispose of her burden, throwing it onto the pile outside. She was glad of the cold air against her face. Still hearing the music, she had to force herself to go back into the living room, but it remained empty, for all she could sense movement all around her, feeling the steps of the dance in her toes and fingertips.

A skirt brushed against her ankles and was gone. Then came the touch of a hand at her waist, and another, fingers grasping for her hands; the press of a body close to hers.

Leah pushed them all away, instead turning to sweep an arm along the mantelpiece, pulling the last of the mistletoe into her arms. She could almost picture the fiddler's face, his eyes closed over his flashing bow, the notes lower but quicker still—

She threw the remaining mistletoe into the snow.

All at once, everything stopped: the whirling movement, the wild dance, the strains of the fiddle, the touch of hands she could not see. Leah stood at the door of her empty house, looking out into a beautiful night. The world was at peace. There was no one but her, staring at a heap of mistletoe already dying at her feet. There was nothing else but silence; nothing but the snow.

Chapter Ten

The night was filled with thoughts of mistletoe, dreams of mistletoe, the touch of it on her skin, the grasping tendrils entangling her limbs. Leah awoke scratching at her arms and her first thought was of the heap she had left outside her door. Would it really be there? But her fear and revulsion were already fading like a dream, banished by the daylight – and perhaps that was all it had been.

At least the house felt empty. It was quiet. The space beside her was bare. She reached out and stroked the sheet, thinking of Josh. His touch was never so cold. If her family had been here she'd have been busy wrapping presents now, Finn all chatter and excitement, joining in with the Christmas carols spilling from the radio—

She leaned over and picked up her mobile, something that

belonged to a world that had always been so present, so safe. The first thing she saw was a text from Trish.

☺🌲🎅🌲☺ LAPLAAAAND!! ☺🌲🎅🌲☺

She smiled at the thought of her friends all wrapped up in their Christmas adventure. She tried out different responses in her mind. *So jealous* would make Trish think she was unhappy to be left behind after all. *Happy Christmas* was too vague; Trish would know she was hiding something. She settled on *Have fun! Hug Santa for me*, added kisses and a glass of wine emoji, then opened her web browser. After a moment's hesitation, she typed *"meaning of mistletoe"* into the search box.

All the things she had expected flowered in front of her: the tradition of kissing under it in the festive season; placing evergreens in the house to retain a little life amid the barrenness of winter; a belief in the powers it must hold over the season's dark magic; the association of evergreens with everlasting life. Still, she hadn't expected there to be so many links, so many stories.

Everyone knew the Druids revered it, believing it to have magical properties, although she couldn't find anyone claiming to understand why, just that they gave it to their people to hang in their homes to protect them and ensure fertility. She hadn't known about the ancient Greeks, though; there was quite a lot about that, how they also revered it, considering it sacred – when Aeneas went in search of his dead father, it was only by plucking the golden bough of mistletoe that he could visit him in the land of the dead.

She read the Norse legend, how treacherous Loki killed the god Baldr using a weapon made of mistletoe, and how, when he was restored to life, Baldr's mother turned the plant into a symbol of love, her tears becoming its berries. That was probably why the Vikings also believed it had power to resurrect the dead. 'I wonder if Trish knows there's even mistletoe up there,' she said out loud to the empty room.

She quite liked the idea that mistletoe was believed to provide a home for the host tree's life through the winter; some people even believed it carried the soul of the tree.

And here was an echo of Isobel's words: the French had once named it spectre's wand, believing anyone holding it would be able to see ghosts – and that they could make them speak.

Leah stared at that, then sighed and turned off the mobile, not sure what good any of this was. The mistletoe that might or might not be waiting outside her door had begun to feel truly mythical. She was reluctant to see any sign that everything really had happened; it might be better to have imagined it all – or to find out she'd placed the mistletoe around the house herself, then pushed it so far from her mind she'd forgotten its existence, just like she had brought Finn's toys along on this venture.

'Time to get up,' she told herself forcefully, but she couldn't quite stop the sigh, or the confusion whirling around her head. She found some clean clothes, threw a jumper over the top and went downstairs. There was no point in putting it off – it would change nothing.

And there it was.

The mistletoe was outside her door, but not as she remembered leaving it. Ice shone from each stem, each curving leaf, each translucent berry, turning it into a sculpture, something miraculous.

I did once imagine . . . what it would be like if such things really worked. Wouldn't it make you afraid, if it truly did?

Leah imagined plucking a pair of leaves ripe with berries and inscribing Finn and Josh's initials onto them. She could wear them next to her heart; she could wait for them to come to her.

She shook her head, as if to deny the very idea. Her husband and son were *gone*. It was hopeless; she might as well whisper their names to the snow.

She gathered up an armful, the mistletoe crackling and snapping in her hands, shedding crystals of ice as she walked carefully through the rutted snow. There was no way she could burn it; fire might melt the ice but it wouldn't consume these green stems. Instead she stacked it in the furthest corner of the yard where it would at least be out of sight.

By the time she'd finished moving everything, Leah was glowing and feeling much more herself. And so she went to see where it must have come from, following the path from the barn to the orchard. She could no longer feel the frozen ruts beneath her feet, only the soft give and settle of deeper snow. She could still hear the trees, though, the now-familiar clacking and creaking that made her think of dead men's bones.

But the trees no longer looked dead. Everywhere was the brightness of fresh green. The mistletoe was thriving, creeping along every branch and twig, gathering here and there into clusters that hung low and heavy like the nests of some unearthly creature. It had claimed the orchard for its own.

Leah took a deep breath, telling herself to be glad of this sign of life. After all, it was a festive plant for a festive season, wasn't it, as much a part of the time of year as holly or Christmas trees.

Still, the sight filled her with foreboding.

Some even believed it carried the soul of the tree.

The idea no longer seemed altogether pleasant. And this is what had found its way into her house . . .

Leah searched the snow for footprints or some other sign of the person who had picked the mistletoe, but the ground was smooth and undisturbed.

Trying not to feel as though she was retreating, Leah crunched her way back to the barn. The scent of cut wood wafted from inside, prompting her to pick up one of the old galvanised buckets and fill it with logs for the fire. Wherever it had come from, she decided she didn't care; she would take from it what comfort she could.

It didn't take long to set a fire in the living room grate, then stack the rest of the logs on one side of the hearth, ready for when the flames caught. The sight reminded her of Cath's homely living room with its lights and its Christmas tree. Tonight her room would be just as cosy. She'd sit close to the flames, watching them dance, keeping the night and everything it held at bay.

She pushed the thought of the coming evening away and went through to the kitchen to gather her cleaning things, ready to continue where she'd left off. There was no fear left in her, only a strange calm. 'It's time to concentrate on practical matters,' she muttered, as if that would force her mind away from ghostly visitors who chopped wood and draped her rooms with mistletoe. She would get another of the bedrooms ready for decorating and then do some of the fun stuff, like choosing colour schemes, deciding on wall-papers and paints to make the house cheerful.

As the day wore into the afternoon, Leah cleared win-dowsills of cobwebs and curled-up flies and dust, and many more bags of mangy old carpets joined the damp heap in the yard. She'd polished some of the greying wood, to see if, with a little love and attention, she could get it to gleam as it had in Isobel Maitland's day. It wouldn't be a quick job, that was quickly obvious, but it wasn't beyond her either, and that made her smile.

Maybe she would have approved, she thought, running her hand over the acorn newel post.

The sky had turned a livid deep gold and in no time at all the sun was sinking out of sight, bleeding against the fur-thest fields. As Leah made what she promised herself would be her final trip outside today, she realised it was snowing again, though barely this time, the flakes so fine she could only make them out where they danced in front of her eyes, as if they existed only for her.

She brushed their moisture from her hair as she returned to the living room, eager to light her first fire in the new house, putting from her mind the memory of the one she'd set in the field. She scraped a match into life and set it to the crumpled newspaper and kindling and once it took hold, she fetched a warm cardigan and a book, ready to bury herself for a time in other people's lives.

A loud knock rang out into the night.

Leah sat bolt upright in the old velour-covered chair, her heart thudding. She should never have touched the wood – she was such a fool. Of course Andrew hadn't chopped it – he barely knew her, and she'd terrified his nephew. So no, it hadn't been him, which meant it must have been Jack. After all, he was the labourer: the barn was his territory, the axe was his. He belonged out there with the slaughtering bench and its memories. He'd made the doll she'd so ruthlessly committed to the flame—

She tried to still her wild thoughts as she waited for another knock, or any other sound. She wasn't even sure whether it had come from outside or from somewhere in the house. She remembered the unseen body in her bed, the hand resting on her flesh before moving up her back, and shivered. The fingers had felt so cold – cold as the grave. Now she had lit a fire, one *he* had prepared, and he wanted to warm himself by its glow.

Three sharp raps sounded, and this time she was sure they had come from the hall. They echoed around the stairway and were gone.

Leah leaped to her feet. The living room door was open, just a crack, but hadn't she closed it? She could almost hear her mother's voice in her head: *Don't leave the door open and let the heat out, Leah – were you dragged up in a barn?* She took a step just as the rapping came again, this time followed by a muffled voice calling, 'Hello? Anyone at home?'

With a rush of relief she realised who it was. Cursing herself for a fool, she hurried into the hall, shouting, '*Co-ming!*'

When she yanked back the bolt and opened the front door, two figures stood there: Cath, with a large woolly scarf wrapped over her hair and covering much of her face, and Andrew, shifting awkwardly. The dainty plate covered with cling film looked tiny in his callused hands.

'Are you busy?' Cath asked, pulling down her scarf and softening her words with a smile. 'I forgot to send you off with some of these the other day. Charlie's at his friend's tonight, so we thought we'd give you a knock, since we were passing. Hope it's not a bad time.'

Andrew held out the plate with a smile.

'Oh – of course not,' Leah said. 'It's lovely to see you both. And thank you – your baking's delicious, Cath. You shouldn't have, but it's lucky for me you did! Come on in—' She ushered them into the hall, her heart still rattling.

'At least I've actually got a fire going this time,' she said, gesturing through the open door into the living room, pleased to see it was already lending the place a little life. 'Tea?' she went on, and then on impulse, 'or perhaps something a little stronger? After all, I dare say the moon's over the yardarm by now, let alone the sun. I've got some wine in one of these boxes somewhere.' She'd bought a couple of bottles for just such an occasion: a visit from new friends or neighbours, popping in to share a little Christmas cheer.

At first Cath didn't say anything, which made Leah wonder

what time it actually was. The sun set so early at this time of year and she hadn't checked her watch, had simply stopped work when she was tired. Would they think she was a complete lush?

Then Cath grinned and said, 'Well, I wouldn't say no, love.'

'Just a small one for me,' Andrew said. 'Got the Landy outside.'

Leah wondered how she had missed the sound of the Land Rover pulling into the yard – it would have saved her from the panic only now subsiding in her veins. She must have been too engrossed in the fire's crackle and hiss. But she realised she was staring at him, although he wouldn't meet her look. Perhaps, after their last conversation, she shouldn't be surprised. After all, he hadn't asked for her confidences, had he?

Or was it that he had chopped all that wood and he was waiting for her thanks? Leah opened her mouth, not yet knowing what she was going to say, but Andrew looked up and gave her a tentative smile. 'We wanted to see if you were all right.'

'Oh – I am, really. But thanks – I appreciate the thought. Why don't you make yourselves comfortable? I'll be back in a sec.' She kept her tone bright and as they nodded their understanding, she hurried to fetch the wine. She came back with the bottle clutched in one hand, glasses in the other and the bottle opener stuffed into her pocket. At least Andrew didn't offer to open it for her.

As Leah pulled the cork and poured, she glanced at him, watching the way he gazed into the fire and then away, passing over the neatly stacked logs without pause or change of expression. If it was a pretence of nonchalance, it was a good one.

She hadn't been paying attention and had over-filled the glass, but with a murmured apology she handed it carefully to Cath, then passed the next glass to Andrew before raising hers in a silent toast. As they sipped, all of them making appreciative faces, Cath scanned the room as Andrew had, as if trying to make out what Leah had been working on – but she'd not touched this room yet, other than to clear out the mistletoe, and there was still no sign that Christmas was approaching. A brief thought came that perhaps she should have left it there, to lend some festive cheer, and she pushed it away.

'Got a funny feel to it, this place,' Andrew muttered, almost spilling his drink, and Leah realised Cath must have stretched out from the armchair where she was ensconced and kicked his ankle.

'Of course it has,' his sister said. 'That's exactly what you're sorting out, isn't it, love?'

Leah nodded, though she knew that wasn't what he'd meant. He wasn't talking about the unswept flagstones or the peeling walls or the cobwebs swathing the corners. He didn't mean the lack of tinsel or furnishings or family pictures. He knew there was something wrong at Maitland Farm.

If Andrew could see it so easily, why hadn't she been able to when she'd first been shown around? Surely she should have sensed it at once? But after what had happened to Finn and Josh, she'd felt nothing at all.

She adopted a neutral tone, hoping that this time he'd explain a bit more. 'Has it? What is it about this place, do you think?'

Andrew shifted on the settle, although Leah didn't think the hard wooden seat was the reason for his discomfort. 'Things happen, I s'pose, like we said. Best to let 'em be, eh?' He fell silent again and started turning his glass so that the light shone through it. 'Nice, this.'

'It is. Lovely, love,' Cath added.

Leah picked up the plate, took off the wrapping and offered it around, admiring Cath's industry, for as well as the mince pies, she'd included a selection of tarts and slices of Christmas cake. 'I'm surprised Charlie hasn't polished it all off,' she said with a grin. 'This looks amazing.'

Cath let out an abrupt laugh. 'Had to sneak these out, I did, once his back was turned. P'raps I'll give him the ones you brought me instead.' She went bright red and shot a startled glance at the glass she was holding. 'Oh, sorry, love – I didn't mean that.'

Her apology was drowned by Leah's spurt of laughter. It felt good to share a joke, and she had to force herself to stop. After all, she didn't want them thinking a crazy woman had moved in next door.

'Quite right,' she said, 'that'd show him. And all the more of the good stuff for us.'

She imagined the expression on the face of the sour woman at the shop if she'd heard them, and that set her off again in another peal. After a moment, Cath joined in, while Andrew looked from one to the other as if they'd gone quite mad, though in an *ordinary* way, a pleasant way. He ate half a jam tart in one bite, only trying belatedly to catch the crumbs.

Leah dismissed his concern with a wave. 'Don't worry about the floor. You can't do any harm, trust me.' And then, faced with his unguarded smile, she asked, 'Where did he go, do you think?'

'Who?'

'I mean – what do you think they did with him, the man they hanged here? Would they have taken him away? They buried outcasts at crossroads didn't they, or on unhallowed ground? Near a churchyard maybe, but not inside it.' Her voice faltered. The wine must have gone to her head. She'd scarcely known the question had been lurking in the back of her mind, let alone meant to run on like that.

'Goodness!' Cath replied. 'What on earth brought that on? Well, I suppose that's what they would have done, and quite right too. Now, love, what are you doing for Christmas?'

'Sorry?' It was Leah's turn to be stopped in her tracks.

Cath bent over to set her glass on the floor. 'Don't worry, it's not the wine talking. We were saying earlier, Drew and me, she'll be on her own, and it's no place to be alone – not here. We're just doing the usual, nothing special. It'll be me, Drew and Charlie, dinner – mind, we go all out; we like our food, as you'll have seen' – she patted her belly – 'and board games and the speech on telly, all that. Don't bring anything, we've plenty and more. It might not be what you're used to, but you'd be very welcome. We'd like to have you join us.'

Leah couldn't speak. She hadn't expected this kindness. That they'd been thinking of her at all made her want to cry. She thought of the friends she'd left behind, of Trish in Lapland with Curt and Becca, the three of them riding on a sleigh, laughing in the snow.

'That's so sweet of you,' she said. 'If you're really sure I wouldn't be intruding. I mean, I'd hate to get in the way.' She saw their expressions dispelling such concerns and finished, 'I'd love to.'

'That's settled, then!' Cath looked genuinely pleased. She caught up her glass, swirled the liquid and took a mouthful. 'We'll enjoy having the company. Cheers, love!'

They chinked glasses again. They'd ignored Leah's question about the farm's history again, but she brushed that thought away. Why had she even asked at all? *Let the past be the past.*

They laughed and joked and made plans until Cath sighed, looked at her empty glass and announced, 'Well, love, we'd best be off.'

They stood and made to leave the room then Cath stopped dead. 'Well, look at that! Isn't that nice. You're getting in the spirit after all, lass.'

Leah followed Cath's gaze. There, hanging above their heads in the doorframe, was a sprig of mistletoe. Its leaves twitched in the air stirred by the fire, its berries catching the light.

Leah blinked, almost ready to believe she was seeing things again. How on earth could she have missed this stem last night? She was almost certain she had torn it down from that very spot, but she wasn't imagining it now. She reached for the sprig, at once eager to snatch it away and unwilling to feel its touch, but Cath stopped her.

'Nay, don't spoil it, love. Bad luck, that. You don't want to bring down bad luck, not on *this* house.'

There was something about the emphasis in her words. Leah froze, her fingers not quite touching the leaves, then let her hand fall. She would rip the wretched stuff down once they'd gone.

'See, p'raps there'll be love in the place again one day.' Now Cath's tone was coloured with amusement. She looked meaningfully at her brother, standing next to Leah. 'Best not throw it away before it can start.'

Leah didn't know if Cath was talking about her throwing away love or the mistletoe or both together, and she didn't care. Josh's urn was right there on the mantelpiece, with her son's next to it, here in this very room. She had no wish to kiss anyone.

But Andrew, taking her by surprise, said, 'God's sake – we'll never get any peace if she doesn't have her way!' and he pressed his dry lips to the very edge of hers.

Leah pulled away from him. Her vision blurred: for a moment everything was dark and when the illusion cleared she found herself staring at her own form – but from a distance. She was still standing close to Andrew under the mistletoe. She blinked, not quite taking it in, until she realised she wasn't looking at herself at all: it was another woman standing there. She was dressed entirely differently this time, in a shining dress of light blue silk, severely pinched in at the waist and cut low to reveal a stunning opal necklace at her throat.

And the man was not Andrew. Instead of broad shoulders

and an awkward stance, the person in front of her was slighter, with a very upright posture. He wore a straight-cut black jacket over a starched wing-collared shirt, with a waistcoat adorned with a racing print. His hair was a rich brown, the colour of chestnuts – like her own, Leah realised, though his was darkened by some kind of oil. His face was pale and slender, made striking by the intensity in his deep brown eyes. Looking upon those eyes, Leah could easily feel that were he to turn, he would see her too; he would see everything.

But he wasn't focused on her. He was gazing at the woman in front of him, at the widow, Isobel Maitland. When he spoke, his voice was low and musical, yet his words were pleading.

'What can I do, Isobel? I have offered to help you, to be everything to you – and I have promised most devoutly that you will be everything to me.'

'Ellis, please! We are not alone. My guests – we must not be too much together.'

For a moment Leah's eyes widened: then she realised that of course Isobel did not mean her. Indeed, Isobel was glancing about the room as if to check who might be watching from the corners. She touched the opals about her neck as if to take comfort from the stones, which gleamed from within, lent fire by the light from the hearth. *She was right to choose to wear them*, Leah thought, realising this must be the Christmas gathering. The Slaters and the Jepsons, the parson, Martha, even Jack himself might be here at this moment, but she could see none of them.

Ellis smiled wryly, revealing a dimple in his cheek. He was

a handsome man, although Leah thought he knew that as well as anyone. 'Oh, but why mustn't we? We are close in relation, Isobel, if nothing else . . . *yet*. We may surely speak to one another with perfect propriety. There is no harm in that – and in any case, no one is watching us. They are intent upon the dancing, you see?' He lowered his voice and, his tone more intimate, added, 'Will you not at least give me hope, the chance to change your opinion of me?'

'I have no opinion.' Briefly, Isobel's hand went to her heart and Leah remembered the little bags Martha had intended to sew. Was she even now wearing a mistletoe leaf marked with this man's initials? Had the charm begun to work its magic upon her?

'I have tried so hard to be worthy of your esteem, Isobel,' he murmured. 'You see, you make of me a better man.'

Her voice was gentle, kind, but when Isobel raised her eyes to his, Leah could see they were cold. 'I do thank you for your kind attentions, Ellis.'

'Is that to be all? You will not have me, then?' His tone was still soft. 'Not even for the family name? For the farm, for the good of all those who rely upon you – who could perhaps rely upon us both?'

'Do you think me selfish, Ellis? Is that what you would wish for us, a marriage of mere convenience?'

He drew a breath, as if to steady himself, and said, 'I know nothing of "convenience", Isobel. I wish only for you.' He reached for her hand and grasped her fingers. 'When I said you would be everything to me, I meant it – indeed, I mean it still – and most truly.'

'I am grateful.'

'Are you?' Now he sounded to Leah as if he had lost hope. 'Ah, Isobel, I would not have your *gratitude*. And yet I see only disdain – disdain for a man who would uproot his whole life, who would change everything, only to be near you – a man who has already helped you all he can. A man who asks – no, who begs – to be allowed the right to help, to support, to protect you with all his heart.'

Her cheeks flushed crimson and she lowered her gaze to their intertwined fingers, but Leah noticed that she did not immediately pull her hand away.

Ellis looked down at them too. 'One kiss, then?'

'Oh! I told you that I was grateful, but that—'

'No! You misunderstand me, Isobel—' He let go of her hand and gestured above them and Leah saw there, hanging over the lintel – just where it was in another world and time, and looking in every way identical – a sprig of mistletoe, the translucent berries glistening in the firelight, just as they had been moments before.

'We have to exchange a kiss now, you see, even if the first is to be the last. It is tradition, is it not? And one must surely follow tradition, for we would not wish to bring bad luck upon the house, would we? Or each other.'

He smiled, a nice smile, Leah decided, demanding nothing, and leaning forward, he raised his hand to Isobel's cheek. He rested it there so tenderly that Leah lifted her fingers to her own face, recalling the last time she had been touched that way; her own last kiss. Then she remembered that her last was not the one she had immediately thought of – it had been Andrew who had kissed her, not Josh, and it had been nothing like this.

Ellis never lifted his eyes from Isobel's, and her expression was hidden as he pressed his lips to hers.

He straightened, whispering, 'There. You see, Isobel? No one has noticed – and no one sees anything peculiar in our closeness. And no matter your choice, you shall remain my cousin, if you so wish – for I shall always be yours.'

She did not answer; perhaps she could not. She stirred, but he had not removed his hand from her cheek. He continued to gaze into her eyes, as if he could not bring himself to let her go, and he stretched his other hand up to seize a berry from the sprig of mistletoe, which jolted and spun as he plucked it from the stem.

'There is another tradition hereabouts,' he said, and now his voice was so low that Leah could barely hear him. If there was anyone else in the room, she guessed they too would not be able to make out a word of their conversation.

'Upon receiving a kiss, the man must pluck a berry, which he must keep close about him' – he slipped the berry into a pocket – 'like this.'

Isobel's eyes widened and Leah wondered if Ellis had somehow heard of the women's little game. Did it mean anything if he had? Isobel had made her choice. The charm had failed; it hadn't made her love him.

Did Martha fare better with her charm? Leah wondered if Jack had come searching for Isobel's maid in the night. *Is she here?* – but if she was, Leah couldn't see her.

Ellis was speaking again, drawing Leah's attention back as

he said, 'And whenever he presents her with the berry, the lady must kiss him again.'

Isobel's concerned gaze raked the room, though she did not move away. Was she being persuaded after all?

But Ellis had not finished. 'And the woman must also take a berry,' he said, lifting his hand to pluck another, 'if she wishes her love to prosper – and perhaps our love shall yet prosper, for I must hope your reluctance is no more than a brief scruple, or concern for the memory of my poor cousin. He will not be returning, Isobel, and I know he would be happy for us, do you not see? He would be glad to know you are cherished, and by one who will always put your concerns and needs before his own. We shall be together, Isobel, for I know – I feel, here in my heart, that we are meant for each other.'

Isobel was silently shaking her head, but Ellis gave a wry smile and stepping forward, pressed the berry to her lips. 'My cousin loved his traditions, did he not, Isobel? I feel he would have enjoyed this one too. The man keeps one berry about his person. The woman, however— Come, let us complete the act.'

Leah saw Isobel's face pale, as if she had only just realised his intent, and she shook her head more firmly, trying to stop him, but the moment she opened her mouth to protest, he thrust the berry between her lips. When he stepped away, he said, 'Would you really refuse me, then, Isobel? Will you not reconsider? Or at least promise to think on what I have to offer you? Give me some reason to hope, at least.'

When Isobel opened her lips again, no sound emerged. A single tear trickled down her cheek.

Ellis gently wiped it away. 'Come Isobel,' he said, his tone brighter, 'it is only for tradition, is it not? For Christmas . . .'

As his voice tailed away, Leah heard the ragged quality of Isobel's breath.

'My dear, whatever is the matter? It is only a little festive game – only a kiss between cousins—'

Isobel's hands were at her throat, her mouth working as she struggled to draw in air. A choking sound emerged; she fell to her knees and Ellis bent over her, trying to pull her hands away from her neck. Her face was ash-white and her eyes were bulging.

'Isobel, please!' His voice was fading. 'Isobel—'

For a moment, the woman's staring, frightened eyes were all Leah could see, and in the next instant there was only an empty doorway adorned with a sprig of mistletoe.

Leah swayed, putting out a hand to catch herself, and cried out when another hand caught her arm.

'Crikey, love, did he have that effect?'

Cath's cackle of laughter brought Leah back to the present, but did nothing to dissipate the vision. Still half immersed in Isobel's world, she couldn't breathe; she reached for her own throat, trying to pull sweet air into her lungs. She could still see Isobel in her mind's eye, lying dead at her feet, killed by the single mistletoe berry pushed between her lips. Then she was gone.

Someone pulled at Leah's arm and she snatched it back, turning to see Andrew's bewildered expression.

'I'm sorry. I didn't mean – I should've thought.'

Cath's exclamations joined his and Leah tried to push

away everything she had witnessed. 'I'm so sorry,' she began, straightening, 'but it wasn't you – I don't know what happened. I just suddenly felt woozy.'

'The wine, maybe,' Cath said, putting a warm hand on her shoulder. 'Are you okay now? P'raps you've been overdoing it, trying to get this old place sorted?'

'Happens to us all.' Andrew patted her arm as if reassuring a horse and Leah had to bite back a sudden urge to laugh. If that laughter escaped her lips, she wasn't sure it would sound entirely sane.

'You sure you're all right, lass?' Cath added. 'We'll not go, not if you're feeling a bit giddy still.'

Leah stepped away from the wall – *Look! I'm fine! I don't need support!* – and pronounced herself better. 'I'm absolutely fine, honestly – I've just been working really hard, that's all. I must have been a lot more tired than I'd realised. Maybe the wine on top was a bit much, that's all.' Leah found herself echoing their reasoning, as if to prove she was as well as they were.

At last they accepted her words and bustled into the hall and the strange scene she had witnessed was subsumed by the practical matters of finding coats and scarves and gloves, exchanging farewells and sending greetings to Charlie and promising to 'not be a stranger' until at last she was standing in the doorway and watching them go. She was still waving as the Land Rover's red tail-lights spilled across the snow and its headlights forced a path into the dark, until they were nothing but a pale glow rising from the lane.

She took one last look around the yard, which was innocent

of visions or presences or any movement at all. The snow
was the same deep blue as the night sky; the glitter it threw
back from the doorway's light echoed its stars. She wondered
what secrets were hidden beneath that shining surface. She
almost felt she could see everything, if she could only learn
the right way of looking.

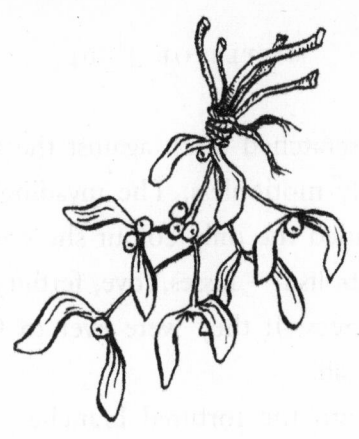

Chapter Eleven

The snow was constantly changing: now rose-tinted or grey, now golden or lavender, made new with every dawn or noon or evening and yet just as cold, just as still. Leah looked up into a blank white sky. The air was raw and sharp as a blade, but she realised that she wasn't feeling the cold – had she grown used to it, or was this another sign that she was becoming a part of this place? Was winter creeping its way inside her, along each vein and sinew, like ice making its way around a tangled skein of mistletoe, or mistletoe winding itself around a tree?

She looked at the sprig she was holding, wondering, *Did this let me see the dead?* But of course it couldn't answer her, and there was no one to ask. With a shudder, she threw it onto the top of the heap, glad to relinquish the touch of its springy, pliable stem, and made her way to the orchard.

The trees were scratched black against the white, all their branches perfectly motionless. The invading plant hanging from them provided the only colour she could see. For all its romantic symbolism – kisses, love, fertility – the parasite was killing her trees. If they were ever to fruit again, she must be rid of it all.

Leah peered into the tortured branches, then stretched up and grabbed a handful of stems, leaves and berries, but when she tried to drag them away from the tree, a deluge of powdery snow engulfed her. She shook it off. Of course it hadn't been real, but for a moment it had almost felt as if the wiry stems had tightened about the branch, not just determined to keep hold of its host but squeezing her fingers like a threat. She pulled harder – and leaped aside with a shriek as the whole branch suddenly broke off, crashing to the ground to the sounds of crackling wood and shattering ice.

She drew in a deep breath, trying to compose herself, before examining the fallen branch. It looked like only the mistletoe had kept it attached to the tree, for it was black inside, rotten right through. When she took off a glove and poked the spongy mass, it left dark smears on her fingers and gave off a musky, mushroomy scent. She had to fight to stop tears rising in her eyes. She had suspected the trees were damaged, but it was quite another thing to see how deeply the decay was seated. Her visions of apple blossom and the autumn's bounty to come dissipated on the air.

Suddenly angry, Leah grasped another handful of mistletoe, this time trying to snap the stems, but they were too wiry to break and too tightly enmeshed in the branches to tear away.

She knew, even as she tried for a third time, that it was no use; this wasn't something she could do by herself. She would have to unravel every knot and stem, bring ladders and, step by step, cut each individual piece away from every branch.

Would it be better to raze the whole orchard to the ground and start again? she asked herself, visualising flames leaping from tree to tree, devouring everything – but maybe they'd burn so fiercely that sparks would spread to the barn roof, maybe even engulf the house, too.

Would that be such a bad thing, burning the old to make way for the new?

She could claim on the insurance and write this whole thing off as a brief, surreal interlude. She could go back to town, return to the world of cars and buses stinking of diesel, of towering buildings and grey streets, of all-night supermarkets and corner-shops, of anonymous crowds rushing everywhere, heads down, faces hidden beneath hoodies, hats and umbrellas – and noise, everywhere: car engines, sirens blaring, phones ringing, the never-ending chatter of the city.

But this place was her future, wasn't it? And anyway, it was only mistletoe.

When Leah returned to the yard, something else had changed. A new shape had been cut into the snow, one she was certain hadn't been there before: a smooth channel, as if some heavy object had been dragged along. She raised her head – and froze. A man was standing a short distance away, bent over an odd shape lying crumpled on the ground – *a body?* But then she saw there was a boy there, too – and with relief she realised it was Andrew and Charlie, and the form wasn't a crumpled figure; it was nothing but snow.

She mentally shook herself. They were building a snowman, that was all, just like normal people did. The trail had been made by the lower part of its body being rolled through the snow, and now they were patting it into shape. Charlie's merry voice echoed across the yard; Leah didn't catch the words but Charlie had spotted her and was waving wildly at her, crisscrossing both arms over his head.

She grinned, returned the wave and started towards them.

'There you are,' Andrew called, his breath billowing from his lips. 'We just popped by to say thank you, for the wine and stuff. And, you know . . .'

He didn't need to say it. She knew what he meant: *To see if you were all right.*

Then another memory popped into her head: *Crikey, love, did he have that effect?*

Mortification reddened her cheeks and she reached up to rub them, hoping Andrew would think it was just the cold. 'Everything's absolutely fine,' she said, hoping for a breezy tone. 'Thanks for dropping by last night. It was really nice to see you both – and good of Cath to bring treats round, too.'

'I was at Adam's,' Charlie interrupted, 'and we made a *much* bigger snowman than this!'

Andrew laughed. 'Well, we're not done yet, are we? And there's plenty of snow, isn't there? Go on, then, lad, let's get another ball going. Roll it nice and tight, that's it. Come on, I'll race you.'

He made as if to run, then stopped and watched as the

boy darted across the yard and scooped up another big armful of snow.

Andrew left him to his task and turned to Leah. 'Hope you don't mind, but he really wanted to come along, and then when you weren't here, he thought we could surprise you.'

'Of course I don't,' Leah said. 'It's nice to see him. And all this snow's just lying around going to waste. Tell you what, why don't I help you? That way we can beat Adam's snowman hands-down.'

She soon forgot her dismal, dying orchard as they sought out fresh heaps of snow, rolling it into ever-larger balls for the snowman's body and head, until at last it was time to start assembling their creation. Charlie picked out a spot near the front door – 'Like he's coming to visit, see!' – and Andrew pushed the first, biggest ball into place, then heaved a second onto the body and started to pat it down.

'You've done this before,' she said and went to help, grabbing handfuls of fresh snow to press into the gaps. It felt clean, simple fun, creating echoes in her mind, but good ones: of building a snowman with Josh and Finn, miles and years away. She'd never imagined that in another life she would be here, doing something like this with another man and another boy.

Andrew stretched to position the snowman's head on top of its body, then lifted Charlie up so the boy could draw a face onto the snow: a wavering line for its mouth and two gouged holes for its eyes.

Once he was happy, he wriggled until Andrew set him back on his feet and they all stood back to examine their masterpiece. The snowman's face was rough-hewn, its mouth a grimace, the hollow, misshapen eye sockets staring blindly at Leah's front door. She laughed at it; after a moment, they all did.

Then Charlie said, 'It's a pity your boy isn't here. He could have helped.' Andrew's head swivelled towards him and he opened his mouth as if to stop him, but Charlie was off again. 'He wouldn't have had to go on a bus – he could have come to school with me, in the Landy. Couldn't he, Drew? He'd have liked that, wouldn't he?'

Leah couldn't answer; she couldn't even speak. It wasn't the fact of her son's absence or even surprise that Andrew must have told the boy about Finn's accident; it was the idea that was in his words. Would Finn be with her now, running around the yard, *alive*, if she had only gone along with Josh's dream from the start? If she hadn't resisted this place?

She looked at the drab walls, the blank windows, the snow encasing the roof, but the house had no answer to give. And she tried to pull herself together – Charlie was just a child, voicing everything that popped into his head – but she couldn't seem to stop staring at him. She'd had plenty of regrets. She thought she'd covered all the 'what-ifs' she could imagine, but she hadn't considered this. If she'd answered the call of Maitland Farm at once, they could all have been building this snowman together – more than one snowman, even, a whole snow-family . . .

Dimly, she heard Andrew telling Charlie off, and when she turned, she saw that the boy's face was creased into a frown. She'd done it again: she'd had another funny turn, gone missing from the world, shown the cracks that lay beneath the surface, and she'd upset a young boy who hadn't meant any harm.

'Andrew, it's all right,' she said, 'really. Charlie, how about we put my scarf round its neck? And we can find some stones for its eyes.'

The boy pulled a face, still upset, then a moment later, cheerful again, he said, 'I'm off to get some twigs for its arms—' and he ran towards the orchard.

'Oh – Charlie, no!'

He whirled, flapping his coat sleeves against his sides, pulling another face as if to say, *What now?*

Leah didn't know why she didn't want him near the place, only that the idea of him coming back with his arms full of that blackened, spongy wood still wrapped in mistletoe filled her with dismay.

'Come back, Charlie,' Andrew said firmly. 'You don't go running about someone else's place like that, not without asking.'

'I didn't mean that,' Leah said quickly, thinking of the way Cath had looked at her when they'd first met, and how she herself had invited Charlie to play there whenever he liked. 'I don't mind him around the place, I really don't. It's just – well, the orchard, you know? I've found some of the trees are rotten right through and I'd hate for him to try to reach for something and have a branch come down on his head.'

'Hold up, there, Charlie, I'm coming with you. Don't you go near them trees, d'you hear?' Once he'd stopped the boy rushing off, Andrew nodded at her in understanding.

Charlie pulled another face. 'I'm *not*! I'm only going to the bushes.'

He pointed towards the path and with relief Leah remembered the hawthorns poking their long black twigs from the other side of the wall. She grinned and gave him a thumbs-up, trying to lighten the mood, but this time his expression didn't change; he turned and started running again.

She watched him go, then Andrew spoke at her ear. 'I didn't tell him.'

Leah turned, startled.

'About the bus, I mean. About what happened to your lad. I never would have. I don't know how he got that in his head, I really don't.'

'Ah – thank you, Andrew,' she murmured, then feeling the need to stay more, she started, 'I—'

But there wasn't anything more she could say, not without her emotion spilling from her.

She'd faltered, but Andrew went on, his tone low and urgent, full of a meaning she wasn't sure she could unravel, at least not just yet. 'I wanted to make sure you were all right. And to see if you needed help with owt.'

'Really, I'm fine. It was kind of you to come.'

'There's nothing I can do for you, then? Some of the heavy stuff, maybe. You got enough wood for the fire an' that?'

She stared. Was this a hint that he'd helped her already? But he met her look with nothing but kind concern and the moment passed.

'Honestly, I'm fine,' she repeated. 'I'm really only making plans at the moment, trying to work out what needs to be done, how I want the place to look. So there's no heavy work to do, not yet. January, that's when I'll really get going.'

'New Year, new start.'

Cath had used those same words. Leah nodded and met his smile and the silence stretched between them, becoming something not entirely comfortable, until Andrew half turned away and stared at the path. 'Now, where's that boy got to?' he muttered, raising a hand to shield his eyes from the glare of the sun on the snow.

Leah peered towards the path too, but there was no sign of Charlie. Had he gone into the orchard after all? Perhaps he'd been entranced by the mistletoe and tried to reach it. Maybe he hadn't been able to resist trying to climb a tree, not realising how dangerous it would be to trust his weight, no matter how slight, to that rotten wood.

As if at that moment a branch really had broken under him, a shriek rang out. It was high-pitched and inarticulate; it didn't sound entirely as if it had been made by a child, but Leah instinctively knew it was Charlie and as she started to run, she felt she'd already known what was going to happen.

As they approached the barn Andrew tried to catch her by her coat sleeve, but he missed and she slipped past him. There was another pained cry as she swung around the corner – but the path was empty.

She replayed the sound she'd heard. It had been so clear. Could it really have come from the orchard? Was that why Andrew had tried to stop her? Now she could hear his voice, although his words were spilling out in such a rush she couldn't make out what he was saying.

She hurried back to the barn and for a moment wasn't certain of exactly what she was seeing. Two figures were struggling together, with a shadow playing across their forms: the outline of a man's feet hanging in the air, twisting first one way and then the other in the breeze.

But the figures she saw weren't from the past: they were Andrew and Charlie, and the man was kneeling, trying to lift the boy from the ground. As she got closer she could see Charlie's face was white and shocked.

'It was a man,' he cried out to her. 'I saw a man.'

The shadow across his back swung again, the dangling feet in endless motion, a clock that wouldn't stop ticking.

Andrew shushed him. 'There's no one else here, Charlie,' he said, and then he added quickly, 'I don't think it's that bad, lad. Your mum'll patch that right up.' He shot a glance at Leah and she could see that despite his bluff words, his expression was tight, full of concern. To her he blurted out, 'A thing and a half to be lying around, that. It's just waiting to happen.'

An accident, that was what he meant. *An accident waiting to happen.* Leah moved towards him, but Andrew held out a hand to stop her.

'It's all right. I've got him.'

He got to his feet, the boy in his arms. Charlie's skin was clammy, his eyes half closed like an infant ready for sleep. Without opening them he wrapped his arms around Andrew's neck and Leah's gaze moved downwards. The boy's jeans, torn through above his calf, were sodden with blood. She caught a glimpse of a shocking bright red through the rip, the darker edges of an ugly wound.

'What happened?'

Andrew gestured with his chin as he strode past her and she saw the bench meant for slaughtering. The axe was no longer propped against it but lying on the ground. The blade was dark.

'Best to put that thing away somewhere, eh?' Now he was recovering from the shock, he spoke more softly. 'Not that he should've been poking about in there, mind.'

'Oh God, I'm so sorry. Charlie, are you all right? I didn't even know he'd come in here.' She still couldn't imagine what had happened. Had Charlie been pretending he was going to fetch twigs for the snowman and instead sneaked in here to play? Or perhaps he'd tried to pick the hawthorn and found the stems wouldn't break, or they'd fought him off with their thorns. Maybe he'd come into the barn to find something to cut it with . . .

The image that came to her, however, was that of a dour-faced labourer, his brows drawn down, his expression glowering, reaching for the boy with one hand, his axe in the other, full of some wild belief that sacrifice was necessary for the land, for the farm—

And the past was *close*. Leah knew that: she had heard it in the voice of a child inviting his murderer to a Christmas feast. She had seen it in the stare of a dead woman's eyes and felt it in the touch of a cold hand in the night. Here, the past didn't fade to nothing but instead, bled through to touch the present at any time it chose.

And Jack was a murderer: a *child* murderer.

I saw a man, Charlie had said. Why had she ever allowed

him to play anywhere near here? And yet she found herself saying, 'You could bring him inside. I'll have something to clean it, I think, and to wrap his leg—'

'His mum'll do it. She'll want him home.'

Leah was silenced. *Of course she will.* Cath would have everything he needed, that and the comfort that could only be offered by his mother. And Charlie would want her too, though his eyes were still half closed, as if he wasn't even listening. His head tilted towards her, loose and heavy on his neck, like a doll's.

'It just moved,' he said suddenly, fuzzily. 'I think the man did it.'

Leah's eyes widened. Had Charlie seen Jack Hirst? Might he be able to see the other ghosts too, or sense them all around him? But that was all he had to say. He closed his eyes and buried his face in Andrew's coat.

His uncle spoke soothingly to him as he carried him to the Land Rover and settled him inside.

'Are you sure?' Leah began, but she let the words die unsaid as she realised how little help she could offer. She wasn't prepared for this, or anything else, if it came to that. Even her car was buried so deeply in the snow that it was useless.

Andrew shook his head, although she was relieved to see that his expression had warmed again. 'It'll be all right,' he said. 'Don't you worry, lass. It wasn't your fault. I should have been watching him, not—'

Talking to you, Leah mentally added. But Andrew didn't know this place; he had no idea of the secrets it held.

All she could do was watch as the Land Rover lurched

its way towards the lane. She winced at the thought of how much the jolting must be hurting Charlie's poor leg. Her heart hadn't quieted. How could he tell her not to worry? That cut had looked really nasty – and what if it got infected? After all, who knew what germs that blade might be carrying, let alone what curse, what ill will?

Of course Charlie shouldn't have been playing in the barn, but hadn't she known, like a premonition deep in her bones, that something would happen? She should have got rid of that damned axe as soon as she'd found it, maybe even blocked off the barn altogether, although quite how she'd have managed it, she hadn't a clue. After all, if Finn had been here, she never would have left such a thing lying about, would she? Had it really been so long since she'd needed to think of anyone else's safety?

Andrew's distraction was her fault too. He wouldn't have been speaking to her quite so earnestly if she hadn't been acting so oddly the evening before. And even in the midst of the accident, she had been distracted by shadows and dreams: she had seen a hanged man swinging over Charlie. Andrew said they'd hanged the man who'd killed Samuel Maitland, and now she knew where they'd done it. They hadn't dragged him into the village as she'd first thought, but had dealt out their rough justice right here, in her barn.

Of course, deep down she had known that, just as she'd known, that day she'd got home and found the house empty and had seen the note from Josh left on the kitchen counter.

Don't go into the garage. Call the police. I just miss him so much.

Then, as if it made everything all right:

I love you.

She tried to shake the image away, but it doubled in her mind: the shadow of a hanged man, not a labourer long dead, but the man she loved – though she could not bring herself to look into his face. For of course she had gone into the garage, and straight away, and the first thing she'd seen had been his feet hanging in the air, turning a little one way, then swinging back the other. Josh had not been suspended from a beam in an ancient barn but from a hook set into the ceiling of an ordinary garage.

She found herself brushing away tears. A hanged man – would that image haunt her always? And a dead child. Those were the things that had brought her to Maitland Farm. Had its influence been reaching out to her even then?

A picture came to her: sitting with Andrew, Cath and Charlie on Christmas Day, everyone at the table wearing paper hats and wide smiles, pulling crackers and reading out the bad jokes to a chorus of groans and grins, cutting into a fat, glistening turkey.

So, Charlie, did you see a ghost in my barn?

And each of them falling silent, turning to stare at her with masked expressions and guarded eyes. But of course that wouldn't happen. She couldn't ask him, so she would never know what he had seen.

Another picture formed in her mind, this time of the cut on Charlie's leg. She saw the dull black point at the centre of the wound; the decay starting somewhere deep inside him, the same rot that had taken her trees. The branching design of it would be like mistletoe as it spread through his veins, purpling his thigh, wrapping itself about the limb.

No. Charlie would be fine. Cath would clean the wound and dress it – she was probably always patching him up after one scrape or another – and they would have their Christmas and the rest of their lives.

She walked back across the yard. She was going to take a look at her barn. She supposed she should be afraid, but after what had happened to Charlie she felt nothing at all. If a murderer was waiting for her there, she wouldn't care: she'd take that axe and swing for him herself.

But there was nothing there, no odd shadows, no sensation of anyone watching her. She stooped to pick up the axe from the slaughtering bench – the first time she had touched it herself – expecting to be jolted out of her world and into another, but nothing happened. She just stood there stroking the smooth wooden handle, worn to the touch of another's hand.

She could see a trace of blood on the blade, but it was already drying. Leah grimaced but despite her resolutions, she couldn't bring herself to throw the axe away. It was a part of the story this place had to tell her and it wasn't finished, not yet. And Charlie would never come here again; they must all see to that.

She leaned the axe back against the slaughtering bench,

blade pointing downwards, so that if it fell it wouldn't cut anything else.

It was only then that she noticed what was waiting for her there, lying on the bench. A wax doll. Had Charlie not seen it? Even though he'd been shocked and in pain, wouldn't he have said something? The thing was face upwards, staring into the shadows of the roof beams. But she had burned it, hadn't she – or had she dreamed that too? Could she no longer trust her memory at all?

But when she looked more carefully, she could see this doll was different to the one she'd seen before. Its face wasn't cracked and desiccated but fresh and smooth, like a child's skin, and its hair wasn't wiry black; it was red.

Leah started to reach out towards it, then at the last moment she snatched her hand away. Was she seeing into the past again, when the doll had been new? Perhaps she had been wrong about the colour of its hair.

Then she focused on what it was wearing. The garment wasn't a waistcoat, or even yellow, but dark blue and quilted, just like the coat Charlie had been wearing when he came to visit her. Fraying wool from a hand-knitted jumper poked from its cuffs.

And its eye sockets were not empty, like the first doll; these had been set with two rough black stones, like those they'd intended to use for the snowman's eyes.

Horror crept over her. *This was meant for Charlie.*

Her gaze went to the wall behind the bench, the part where it had crumbled away. Was the hole wider now? Leah peered into the dark hollow, wondering if that was where this new doll had come from – but it couldn't have; surely she'd have seen it when she tried to put the older one back. And in any case, if it had been walled in with the first, why did it look so clean and fresh?

The axe had been blooded, but it wasn't yet sated. It wanted more. It wanted sacrifice. It had tasted the boy and now it hungered for him – or its true owner did.

He'd heard all these old ideas about winter and sacrifices to the land or some such thing. He thought it would fix whatever was wrong with the place.

This doll wasn't a gift for her or for Charlie. It was a sign, a symbol: it was his burial doll.

Leah snatched it up and stuffed it into the hole in the wall. She tried to block it in with some of the stones and plaster that had fallen to the floor, but it wouldn't be covered. Just as before, the debris fell away, revealing its dead black eyes.

Her breath coming short, Leah stumbled from the barn, pulling off her gloves and rubbing at her face. Her fingers were coarsened with cold, the skin across her knuckles cracking as if it too were made of wax.

She bowed her head and as she hurried towards the house, the snowman loomed into view, a sentinel standing guard, for all it had no twigs for its arms, no scarf about its neck, no stones for eyes. And tomorrow she would step outside, having forgotten it, and it would shock her all over again. She wanted to knock it down, kick the snow away until not even a trace remained to remind her of this day or Charlie or Andrew or any of it. She wanted it all to be gone. *A new start*, she thought. The words felt like mockery now.

Leah stopped in front of the snowman, remembering Charlie's excited chatter and the way Andrew had leaned in towards her, his solicitousness, his caring. She set her hands to the snowman's chest, meaning to push it over, then stopped herself. What if they came back and saw what she'd done? Charlie would be upset all over again.

She turned her back on it, trying to put the hollows of its eyes from her mind, and closed the door behind her. Her fingers no longer felt like a part of her. She forced herself to flex them, trying to warm the blood; to make it flow again.

Leah did not light the fire that night, or even enter the living room. She made herself a sandwich and took it upstairs with the last of the wine left over from her neighbours' visit. The aroma of it reminded her of sitting by the fire, feeling its warmth, driving back the empty spaces with laughter and talk of Christmas, but now the wine was cold, the taste flat, the house so very quiet.

She sat up in bed, trying to warm the glass between her palms, though they too were cold. Finn's teddy bear kept watch from his place on the windowsill, staring out just as the snowman, at this moment, was looking in.

'What are you looking at, Bear?' she murmured. Nothing but clouds crossing the moon, sending their bewildering shadows dancing across the fields. Perhaps Bear could see the black line of trees where she'd burned Samuel Maitland's effigy. And, of course, the endless snow. Leah couldn't imagine the fields ever being green again. The snow would always be there, keeping her and the house and the barn and all of Maitland Farm in its grip.

But perhaps spring must be summoned, rather than waited for.

She gulped the wine down.

She couldn't stop thinking about Charlie – the image of his fists, grinding out a snowman's eyes; his cry, *I saw a man.* His body, limp in Andrew's arms. And Finn was constantly in her thoughts too, out of reach behind the falling snow, but always there, the echo of his laughter emerging through its veil.

She closed her eyes and saw his face smiling up at her, laughing. He was clutching something in his hands. Was it a Christmas present? Some kind of action figure, perhaps; he'd liked those. He moved his lips but she couldn't make out the words or remember what they might have been, and that, with the darkness pressing in around her, was worse than anything else.

Leah shuffled off the bed and went to the wall where she had painted over the image of a boy. Had it really been Samuel Maitland who had appeared there, or had it always been Finn, come to show her she was never alone? And she had banished him with a few strokes of her brush. She ran her fingers over it. Was the plaster slightly raised where he had been?

She sank down and sat with her back to the wall. She could not bear to see the boy's outline again; she could not bear to know that it was altogether gone.

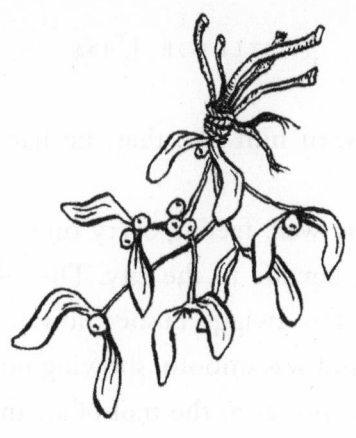

Chapter Twelve

Leah set out early the next morning into another clear day, full of quiet resolve. The sky was pale above Maitland Farm, the sun bright and comfortless. Behind her, the buildings were cocooned in snow. There was no trace of her presence there; even her fire had done nothing to melt the whiteness from the roof. The barn resembled just another slope in the field. The sight made the scale of the task of transforming the place feel impossible, but she couldn't allow herself to think that way; it was far too late for that.

She turned her back on the sight and indeed on the lane. This time she headed for the shorter route towards Ingleby Nook, the way Charlie used, the way Cath had pointed out across the fields. As she approached the wall he was running ahead of her in her mind's eye, red hair hidden under his hood, frayed sleeves flapping. Of course, when she'd last seen him like that, he had been running away from her.

She climbed the wall, feeling every one of the miles that divided her from her life in the city. The edge of the path was marked by a few twiggy bushes now reduced to black filigree. The ground was smooth, showing no trace of where the boy had gone, not even the trail of an animal or bird to mar its surface.

It was harder walking across the field than going by the lane. The snow was deeper here, but absolutely clean, the cold air fresh in her lungs. She stopped for a break when she reached a post-and-rail fence at the top of the hill, her calves aching, but feeling exhilarated – and caught her breath when she saw what had been positioned by a little wooden stile.

It was another kind of doll, but this one was a modern toy, an action figure in soldier's uniform. It leaned against a post, its camouflage clothing standing out clearly against the white. A plastic machine gun pointed towards Maitland Farm, as if ready for whatever might come from there.

It must be Charlie's. He had been playing a game up here and forgotten it, or maybe he'd grown too old for it and abandoned it here. Or perhaps he hadn't forgotten it at all – could he have left it here deliberately, to protect his home from whatever lived in hers?

I saw a man.

Perhaps that was why, in part, he kept making his way to Maitland Farm: not to explore the barn or play in its fields, but because he felt some instinctive need to keep an eye on the place. Leah looked in the direction of Ingleby Nook, still holding the soldier doll in her hands. Should she take it with her, present it to him with a cheery, 'Look who's home—'? But he might not feel safe if his guardian were to shirk its duty, and in any case, he'd have to explain to his mother why he'd left his toy in a cold, wet field.

Instead, she set it back where she'd found it, giving its head a little pat – for luck, maybe. At least this talisman wasn't anything like the doll in her barn – though was it so very different?

Leah supposed worse things had been given to this land in its time.

She thought of that ugly cut on Charlie's leg and grimaced, but she pressed on, keeping to the edge of the field. The deep snow made it hard going and her exhilaration turned to tiredness as her movements became mechanical. Her legs were sinking in above the knees and she had to drag her feet free, lifting them high for the next step then setting them down carefully so as not to fall into some unseen rut. At least the exertion was keeping her warm.

When she looked back, she could no longer see the farm, which felt like something of a relief. She couldn't see Ingleby ahead either, only another slope rising away before her. For a moment, she imagined what would happen if she never found it, only another hill, and another, and another, going on for ever. She might turn back only to find she'd lost her way, or the land had changed into something she didn't recognise. Charlie's talisman might have done its work and wiped Maitland Farm from the face of the earth.

But when she crested the next rise, there was Ingleby

Nook, although there was no sign of life, no smoke rising from the chimney, no child outside building a snowman. It looked cold and desolate and worry gnawed at her. What if Charlie had been badly hurt and Cath hadn't been able to patch him up? They might be at the hospital right now, a doctor in a white coat leaning over him to probe at that ugly cut with dark rot spreading from its centre along the veins – *tendrils* – under his skin.

She shook the thought away. Charlie had probably gone to see his friends to show off his war wound – like all boys, once the pain had gone, Finn had loved to show off his scabs and scrapes. Or the family could be visiting relatives; it was the festive season, after all. But Leah hadn't brought any paper on which to write them a note, and yet again, she'd forgotten their Christmas card. What could she do? Write a message for them in the snow itself, a huge 'Hi from Leah!' outside their door? She imagined their faces when they found it – they would think she was mad and that they'd better build a better fence, get a real soldier to guard it. She let out a spurt of laughter that hung before her face in a cloud of vapour.

I'm here now: I might as well check to see if they're home. Leah headed down the slope. It seemed to take both an age and no time at all before she stood in front of the door, her hand raised to knock.

After a pause, she did.

At first she thought they weren't going to answer, though rustling sounds spoke of someone moving about within. Then the door opened suddenly and without warning, making Leah jump.

Andrew stood in the gap. For a moment he looked as startled as she did, then he stepped back and invited her inside. Leah took off her boots and when she straightened he'd put out his hands for her coat, awkwardly formal, although once he'd hung it with the family coats behind the door, he smiled.

'Thanks for coming,' he said. There was genuine warmth in his voice, and another message too, one Leah wasn't certain she could read.

'I wanted to see how Charlie was doing,' she said. And then in a lower tone, 'You were right, Andrew, and I'm so sorry. That farm's no place—'

'Oh, he's fine. Don't you worry. He shouldn't have gone wandering off where he wasn't wanted – it's not as if he'd not been told, is it? He's just a bit shook up and embarrassed an' all. Quite right too. Come on in.'

He led the way into the kitchen. Cath waved from over by the sink, her bright yellow gloves covered in suds.

'He's in here,' she said, cheerily. 'Say hello to the walking wounded.'

Charlie was sitting at the pine table, his leg stretched out to rest on another chair positioned in front of him. He was playing with an electronic toy of some sort, which suddenly gave out a descending series of beeps. He grimaced at it before looking sheepishly up at Leah.

Leah grinned at him and his expression lightened.

'How are you doing, Charlie?' she asked. 'I was worried about you. I brought you something for when you're better, although it's not much, I'm afraid.' She went over, pulling her small gift from the pocket in her sweatshirt: a leather cricket ball, only a little scratched.

'Great, thanks!'

She watched him run his hands over it, at once wistful and pleased that Finn's ball would be played with again.

'I'm going to have a scar,' he announced suddenly, pride evident in his voice. 'Just wait till they see it at school.'

She laughed. 'Will they be jealous, do you think? Does it hurt, Charlie?'

He nodded and put on a brave face, although the breadth of his grin suggested it couldn't be all that bad, and sure enough, Cath said, 'He's making the most of it. He's had more ice cream than you can shake a stick at.'

'I should think so too,' Leah said. 'I wish I could have brought some more for you, Charlie.' She smiled again, secretly wishing she could see the wound and check for the black rot she feared must be creeping through him.

'There's no harm done.' Cath had divested herself of her washing-up gloves and come to stand at Leah's shoulder.

'Really? It's all healing nicely?'

'Course! Healthy lot, us Slaters. At least he'll know not to touch owt like that again. I've towd him.'

Leah turned and Cath must have seen the relief in her face, for her kindly gaze warmed, as if Leah was more in need of comfort than her son.

And maybe she was. Leah blinked back the tears suddenly springing to her eyes. 'Ah, Cath – that's just it,' she said, and found she couldn't go on. She glanced around the kitchen, taking it all in. She had felt so at home here. It was just what she would like her own house to be. They'd received even more Christmas cards, she noticed. They were brimming from the shelves, pushed in among the china teapots and tureens and the miscellany of mugs.

'What is it, love? He's sorry he went in your barn and talked a lot of nonsense, an' all. He didn't mean to mess with your things. He should have known better, and he does, really. I can't think what he was doing.'

Leah took a deep breath. It would be better to say it all at once, but still she faltered over the words. 'The thing is, I don't know the half of what's in that barn. Andrew was quite right, I should have got rid of it all straight away, but it's a big job. And the thing is – I thought—'

But it looked like Cath didn't want to know what she thought, because she was already spinning away, reaching for the kettle as if to deflect Leah's words. 'Cuppa tea, love? Andrew, pass us another mug, would you? Pot just needs refreshing. There's nothing like a brew to warm you up, is there?'

Andrew had been hovering by the door but he leaped at Cath's words and grabbed a mug – then put it back and chose another, this one finely shaped, with scraps of gold clinging to the rim.

'Cath, I think it's best if Charlie doesn't come to the farm any more.'

Now that she'd said it, Leah couldn't look at Cath or Andrew but instead, focused on Charlie. She was certain she saw a flash of relief, quickly smothered when he saw her watching him. Instead he adopted a sulky expression and buried himself in his game, fingers flying over the buttons.

'Well, that's fair enough, love. He can stick to coming along with us when we're over there. Me and Drew can keep an eye on him. We'll all be more careful in future – we know what boys are, don't we!'

Leah took another deep breath, thinking of the way they'd laughed over a glass of wine, just as she'd imagined for her new home. But it wasn't any good, she knew that now. Charlie hadn't been alone when he was injured – she and Andrew had both been there, a short distance away, but the accident had still happened.

I saw a man.

And Leah had failed to banish him: she had failed to make her farm safe. She couldn't protect Charlie. She had to admit the truth: Maitland Farm was haunted. Before she came here, she'd never believed in such things, but now she knew it was true. The ghosts here were real, and they didn't just linger like shadows on stairways or make noises behind the walls. They *moved* things, *touched* things. One of them was a murderer. He had seen Charlie and made a burial doll for him, and Leah was terribly afraid of what he might do if the boy went near him again.

She met Cath's gaze with a direct look of her own. 'I think it would be best if you don't.'

Cath looked puzzled, then she looked hurt as Leah's words sank in. *She doesn't understand, not yet,* Leah thought, *but how could she?* But she couldn't afford to be tactful, or let them think she didn't really mean it, not when Charlie's life might depend on it.

'The thing is,' she went on, 'it's all too soon for me. I

came here to be alone and that's what I want – it's what I need, just now. So I'd appreciate it if you didn't bring Charlie again. I think it best if no one comes at all. Then you won't— I mean, then there's no risk of anyone being hurt, not on my land. I don't want that. I don't want to be sued, either.' She forced hardness into her voice, as if that was her main concern, as if she were that selfish, so little worth knowing. That way, they wouldn't even *want* to see her again.

And she had come here to be alone, hadn't she? She had come here to do a job. She hadn't even made a decision to stay. It was still harder than she'd expected to watch the disappointment dawning on Cath's face. She couldn't bear to look at Andrew at all, although she could feel his gaze on her from where he stood, motionless, by the wall.

'It's best if I just get on with things as planned,' she went on, determined to drive them away. 'I'm going to be so busy. I probably won't even be staying myself – you'll most likely have new neighbours soon, and—'

But she didn't know what came after that 'and—'. Could she simply abandon Maitland Farm? She would be the last of the family, escaping its clutches . . .

Even as she spoke she envisioned a new family moving into the farm, one who would welcome Charlie with open arms, who would let him roam wherever he liked. Everything would be new and neat and safe, and perhaps Charlie would wander into the barn one day and find – what? – a man with murderous thoughts in his eyes and an axe behind his back? Could she ever risk that happening? And if she did hand the farm over to a family, what if they had children of their own? What might happen to them?

Time stretched out before her suddenly, years and years of her being trapped here, never able to leave or let go, tied to Maitland Farm and its ghosts for always. Maybe one day she'd be one of them herself; she was a Maitland, after all. But it only need happen to *her*, she could at least stop it touching Charlie or anyone else. She suddenly realised that if she took on this charge, she would have to keep her dearest friends away, too. She certainly couldn't allow any risk to Trish's Becca. If she was going to protect them, she would have to steel herself to losing them all.

Cath still hadn't spoken, and Leah, barely knowing what to say, ran on, desperate to fill the silence. 'I'm going to be so busy,' she repeated, 'so I really think it's best if we don't see each other.'

When Cath replied, the hurt in her voice was worse than if she'd been angry, although Leah could sense that there was anger there too, layered underneath. But all she said was, 'I'd be careful if I was you.'

It was Leah's turn to be puzzled, but Cath went on, 'It's being in that place. I can see it working on you – have done from the start, if I'm honest. I can see it in your face, hear it in your voice.'

Unconsciously, Leah put a hand to her cheek. She could not feel her own fingers; her skin was numb, though from cold or something else she couldn't have said.

'It's no good to take yoursen out of everything,' Cath went on. 'Cutting yoursen off from anyone who'll help drag you out on it. You shouldn't be there on your own, I always said it. Didn't I always say it, Drew?' Sharp edges had crept into her tone, a reaction, perhaps, to the blow Leah had dealt to their blossoming friendship.

Leah still couldn't look Andrew in the face, but she saw his head dip in acknowledgement of Cath's words. She remembered the way he'd leaned towards her in the car, the low, meaningful tone he'd used when he spoke to her. The dry kiss he'd placed at the edge of her lips. She jerked her head away as if to avoid that kiss all over again. Was some part of her decision really about that? She wanted to keep them all safe, but would it also be easier for her – for whatever other reasons she didn't want to think about – to keep him away?

'You want to listen to them as knows,' Cath said. 'Them as knows that place better than you do. Do it up, you reckon? Sell it on, make some brass? Don't you reckon there's better folk than you who've tried it all afore?'

'That's enough, Cath.' Andrew stepped towards Leah. 'I know it might sound daft to outsiders, love, but she just means that Maitland's been the way it is for as long as we can remember, and you'll not change it into some new-fangled flats or whatever with nowt but a bit of fresh paint and polish. It's got history. It's a part of this place.'

Leah wondered what he would say if he knew she was a Maitland herself. Perhaps they wouldn't have had anything to do with her if she'd been up front about that from the start; they would have stayed well away. But she couldn't drag this out any longer. She'd made up her mind. Besides, a thread of pride twisted somewhere deep inside her, one she hadn't felt before. She *was* a Maitland. If anyone knew what was best for the place, wasn't it her?

'Well, now it's mine,' she said firmly. 'I've taken it on and it's too late for all that – it's mine and I will live there if I choose, and I'll see whom I choose. It's not your concern. You don't have to worry about me. I'm grateful for your thoughts, and for – for everything, but I've made my choice.'

'That you have,' said Cath. 'You hear that, Charlie? You're not to go anywhere near. Can't say I'll be sorry not to think of you roamin' all over it. Never did like it, if I'm honest.'

The boy said nothing, only lowered his head.

'But it's Christmas,' Andrew said and Leah, taken by surprise, turned to face him at last. Clearly discomfited to find himself the focus of attention, he hesitated, then repeated, 'It's Christmas. It's about friends, isn't it? New friends as well as them we've always known. And you're coming to us, aren't you? You are still coming?'

Leah felt drained. She looked from Andrew's hurt expression to Cath's resolute one and then away from them both. She saw the thick ropes of tinsel strung from the cupboard doors, the child's drawing stuck to the fridge with a magnet shaped like a stocking; on it a man and a woman stood by as a boy ripped open a pile of presents. It looked like a family, not a father and mother, perhaps, but a complete unit, and it did not include her. The Christmas trimmings were alien to her now, too gaudy and too busy, artefacts from a realm she no longer understood. She had been right to try to escape it. She'd known, deep down, she had no place in any of it.

She wanted to explain, but she couldn't speak, so that

would have to be enough. Charlie would be safe and so would they and that was all that mattered. She shook her head again and turned to leave.

Andrew didn't speak any more either, but he led the way and when she stooped to put on her boots, she could feel his eyes on the back of her neck. He made no offer to drive her this time and she was glad of that. She wasn't sure she would have been able to refuse him, but she couldn't bear the thought of sitting next to him in their slow silence, of getting out of the Land Rover at the end of the journey and walking away, into the cold, empty, *haunted* house she had chosen for herself.

When she straightened, Andrew was holding out her coat and she twisted to put her arms into the sleeves, offering an apologetic smile. Andrew stared down into her face for a moment. He made to reach out for her, but Leah thrust her hand in front of her and found herself shaking his, like a stranger.

She glanced towards the kitchen and saw Cath watching with narrowed eyes. She could see what Cath had had in mind: Leah and Andrew, standing under the mistletoe; Leah being drawn into their big day, their *family* day, because she imagined that's what Leah might someday be.

And she had driven them away. She opened her mouth to apologise that she couldn't be what Cath wanted – but Cath pushed herself off the doorframe and disappeared into the kitchen before she could say another word.

As if to make up for his sister's behaviour, Andrew opened the front door and held it for her. While Leah had been destroying any chance of friendship with the Slaters, outside, the whole world had disappeared; mist had drifted across the fields, obscuring any boundaries. Leah could see the path that led from the door and, dimly, the gate at the end of it, but beyond that there was nothing.

As she stepped outside, Andrew said quietly, 'He made a present for you.'

She began to turn just as he closed the door behind her. Leah stared at it. She badly wanted to knock again, to walk back into that warm, welcoming home and tell them that she was sorry, she hadn't meant any of it – but how could she, when Charlie was at risk? And what else could she say?

She hadn't even said goodbye to Charlie.

She stepped onto the path. Her footprints, left in the snow so short a time ago, had already started to vanish. A bitter wind had risen and it was haunting the hills with a hollow sound, picking up handfuls of snow and throwing them down again like a child in a tantrum.

Cold air scoured her face, her lowered hood unable to keep it out. She cut across towards the field, seeing nothing but white ahead of her. She didn't know if Cath would appreciate her walking over their land, not now, but she wasn't about to go back and ask permission and anyway, Ingleby Nook was almost out of sight already. Only its turned cheek faced her, a single window set into it like an eye. If someone was standing there watching her leave, she could not make them out.

She began walking in earnest, pulling her hood closer about her face as the wind picked up, lifting the snow in swathes and hurling it at her, as if to hurry her along. When she looked askance into the field, there were shapes in it, spectres dancing amid the whirlwind, revellers in some ancient pageant.

I'll see whom I choose, she had said. Those words sounded so presumptuous now with Maitland Farm lying ahead of her. There, she would see whomever the farm chose to show her; whatever it decided she had to see.

She didn't notice the post-and-rail fence where she had found Charlie's soldier until she was almost upon it. At first she thought the toy had been snatched away by unseen hands, then discovered the doll was there after all, just drowned in white. She pulled him from the snow and dusted him off. It had been so easily buried, this child's toy which had once been loved and was now abandoned and would soon be buried again. There was no protection in it.

All the same, she placed the soldier back on guard before climbing the stile and starting down the hill. The wind gusted, heavy with freshly falling snow. The whirling shapes around her danced; strange shapes towered over her.

As she descended the slope, the wind's strength began to lessen and the snow fell more slowly. When the farm came into sight, it was the image of the perfect Christmas past, mocking her with its loveliness. The flakes were no longer thin and biting but fat and generous, so light they hung in the air, shifting and spinning on every breath. They fell like feathers and settled like down, looking as comfortable as pillows. Leah's whole body grew suddenly heavy. She had not expected the homeward journey to feel so much longer than the outbound — but perhaps it depended on whose home she was going to.

Brushing flakes from her face, trying to ignore the figures still dancing at the corners of her vision, she started on the last stretch. She would soon be home. By the time she reached it, the ice might have entered her veins. It would spread from her fingers and along each limb until it reached her heart, numbing her until nothing mattered any longer. It would teach her how to be a part of this place.

Later, as night drew in, Leah once again sat in her bedroom with a glass in her hand, but this time she was cross-legged on the floor in front of a crackling fire. The warmth in her fingers and toes and nose and cheeks had become a burn and she shifted uncomfortably. She could scarcely recall the events of the afternoon — she had no memory of the last few yards of the journey, or of lighting the fire, or indeed of carrying the wood upstairs, setting the tinder, finding the matches.

Charlie, Cath and Andrew were probably at this moment settled around a similar fire. She wondered what Charlie had thought of her words, if he'd even understood that she was banning them from visiting her for ever. She knew she'd caught that flicker of relief when she'd said he shouldn't go there any more, so he probably wouldn't be too disappointed. She wondered what he would do with the gift he'd made for her; had he already presented it to his mother? Or maybe he'd been so upset he'd fed whatever it was to the flames instead.

But he was all right now. He was *safe*. She had done the right thing; she had to focus on that. Even now, Charlie would be busy thinking of all the excitement of Christmas, the ordinary things: presents, hanging his stocking, a visit from Father Christmas, at least if he wasn't already too old to believe in such magic. Finn hadn't been and he never would be, now. If he'd been here there would be stockings hanging by every chimney, just in case *this* was the one Father Christmas chose to come down. And he would have been so excited when the actual night came, lying awake and listening for big boots scraping their way down the chimney, for every footstep creaking on the stairs or thumping on the landing.

Leah shifted, not liking to think of someone creeping through the house at night, even if it was Father Christmas. After all, he was a stranger too, wasn't he? Yet he had the right of tradition to enter her home, to eat her food, wander where he would, leave what gifts he chose behind. And he was supposed to be able to see everything, even into her heart, to judge whether she was bad or good; to decide which way the scales tipped, whether she should be rewarded or punished.

She wondered what decision he would make if he could see her now.

She shook the image away. It was such an impossibly long time ago when she had believed in Father Christmas herself and yet, since coming here, she had seen so many things – she had felt their touch, seen their effects – and she *knew* there was magic in the world. It just wasn't the kind she wished to believe in.

Leah gazed into the fire, though it brought no cheer. Flakes still fell thickly down outside the window and she imagined Father Christmas flitting across the moon in his costume red as blood, flying from house to house on the hunt for sleeping children, slipping down chimneys, squeezing through grates, passing across fires without singeing even a hair on his beard – and always by night, always in the winter dark, leaving only the echo of his laughter to remember him by.

Was that a rustle coming from the fireplace? Leah stared at the chimney, listening, before scolding herself.

She couldn't allow herself to become lost in stories. She had no excuse to spin tales of enchantment; her son had gone. Now there were bricks and mortar, all the things she must do, because what else was left?

She looked at Finn's toy, still on his vigil at the window, and murmured, 'What am I thinking, Bear?' Her words trailed away. Perhaps it was a natural part of winter, to imagine things out there in the dark – to tell strange tales while drawing a little closer to the fire. Hadn't people always told stories of ghosts, even while they lighted candles, feasted and made merry, kept friends and loved ones close, given them cheering gifts?

I don't want new gifts, she thought. *I want all the old ones.*

As if in answer, there was another sound: stomping followed by a scrape, as of someone walking about downstairs. Were they dragging something across the flagstones of the hall? Leah stared at the floor as if her gaze could pierce right through it. What would she see if it could? A rotund, jolly, white-haired fellow with a merry smile and a twinkle in his eyes? Or a glowering man with broad shoulders and rough, callused hands?

And was he too seeking children – or one particular child,

born to lord it over him and the farm, one whose mastery he resented? Or had he been driven by some deeper motive, one irrevocably bound up with the land he tended?

Another step, scrape, step; then came the sound of wood clacking against wood. Leah traced the direction with her gaze, then raised her eyes and looked at the door. The sounds faded. Had Jack paused at the bottom of the stairs? Was he staring upwards, listening for her in turn, for the sound of living breath?

If only she had burned Jack Hirst's leaf. Why had she only crumbled it in her hands, leaving the fragments to mingle with the dust beneath the floorboards? He could not have returned to her then. For she was certain it was Jack – she felt it in the chill that wrapped itself around her. Instead, she had left the leaf's remnants to mingle with the house, so now Jack was for ever a part of this place. All she had succeeded in doing was to make it impossible to be rid of him.

She jumped, her heart thudding wildly, at the pistol-crack of a splitting log, then wrapped her arms around herself, taking some comfort in the softness of her plaid shirt, for all it still had the musty smell of old carpets in its weave; despite the fact that she had no memory of slipping it on over her T-shirt when she got home.

When no more sounds came, Leah got up and went into the hallway. She paused at the top and listened, and when she was certain she couldn't hear anything, she descended into darkness until she felt the cold flagstones under her feet.

But it wasn't entirely dark. A wavering glow flickered in the gap under the living room door, brightening a little before fading away almost completely. Hearing the spit and hiss of a fire, Leah paused, not certain that when she opened the door, the house would actually be empty.

I still have to look . . .

At first, all she could see was the fire. She didn't know when it had been lit, but then, she didn't remember setting the one in her bedroom either. She could have done it herself.

The fire was not the only source of illumination, however. Snow was continuing to fall outside the window, each flake shining in the moonlight, an ethereal glow spilling across the floor like a chain of living fairy lights.

Leah stood motionless as her eyes adjusted and she began to make out a dark shape standing in the corner of the room. She had been wrong: the presence was still here, waiting in the shadows, watching her. She shot out a hand and scrabbled for the light switch and a second later a yellow glare flooded the room.

A Christmas tree was standing in the corner – a fir with no trimmings and no tinsel, no star and no baubles, but a tree nevertheless, its branches dripping as if a moment ago they had been covered in snow.

Who had chopped it down, brought it in and placed it here? Was this another gift from the past? Was she supposed to welcome it? Trim it with decorations? But even if she'd wanted to, she hadn't brought any with her; they had gone into storage with the rest of her life. She thought of the boxes stacked upstairs. She still hadn't opened them all, but she'd had no place for Christmas in her packing – though she'd brought Finn's toys here without realising it, hadn't she? How did she know her Christmas decorations weren't in there too?

Did she *want* to know?

But the simple green tree was fitting, Leah decided, without all the gaudy colours of modern decorations. Evergreens symbolised eternal life, even when all other life had faded; life intruding into her home after all, even if it had been given to her by a dead hand. She remembered being told stories of certain trees which, despite lacking a single leaf, would bloom at Christmas. That made her think of her orchard and its black wood, surely too rotten to ever blossom again. If she saw the apple trees covered in white flowers on Christmas Day, would she feel glad, or only more afraid?

She wondered which of the ghosts had given her the tree. Was it Jack, mocking her, showing that he could come in whenever he wanted? Or was it a gift from Ellis, to show her that this could be her home after all, that she needn't be scared?

Ellis: the man who'd pressed a deadly mistletoe berry between Isobel's lips.

Ellis had killed the woman he'd loved in this very room, which must have brought its own punishment, for he had been left with the burden of knowing what he had done. He would have had time enough for sorrow. Was he trying to make amends?

Leah shifted her focus to the flames licking the back of the hearth, realising the tree wasn't the only gift her ghost had brought.

The mantelpiece was drowning in holly and ivy, the glossy

leaves gleaming; and there was the paler green of mistletoe, twisting around them – and around the urns belonging to her husband and son.

She heard the echo of Isobel Maitland's words: *We shall have the holly, and the ivy too, as well as our tree, of course – and yes, even the mistletoe . . .*

She walked to the fireplace and lifted each urn down, setting them safely aside before sweeping her arm across the mantelpiece and sending the tangle of evergreens to the floor; then she did it again, to rid the surface of every last flake of bark and scrap of leaf and twig. Tomorrow, she would get rid of it all, and the tree too. She didn't want these gifts – she didn't want whatever Christmas could exist in this house.

Then she picked up the poker and used it to shatter the burning logs in the fireplace as much as she could. She couldn't put it out all at once, but she could leave it to die.

When Leah stood back and stared at the wreckage, another echo of Isobel's voice drifted through her mind. *It is bad luck to bring greenery indoors before Christmas Eve . . .*

Leah could not forget the sight of Isobel, gasping for breath through her swelling throat, staring up at Leah, almost as if she had seen her.

Had Isobel died because she had failed to heed her own warning?

Leah frowned. If these evergreens had been cut before their allotted time, it was not her fault. It wasn't as if she'd asked for them. If bad luck was to follow, it was nothing to do with her . . .

Was it? She closed her eyes. She'd been blanking out too

often these days. She'd brought Finn's possessions here without even realising she'd done so, wrapping them in boxes like gifts to her future self. Tonight she'd set a fire in her bedroom without being conscious of it. Had she lit this fire too, and brought this greenery inside without remembering? Should she be calling for a doctor?

No, I am sure I didn't. And I don't think anyone can help me, not with this.

She looked through the window at the moon's light gleaming from the thousands of snowflakes drifting by and realised it must already be long after midnight.

The evergreens had been cut true to their time after all. Today was Christmas Eve.

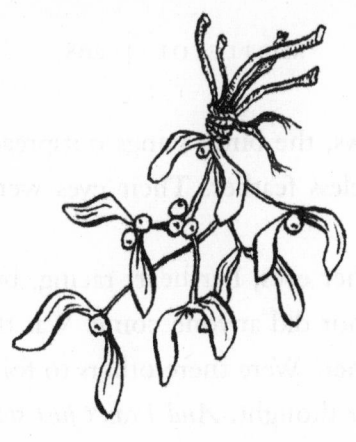

Chapter Thirteen

Leah awoke to a house full of sound and light. Somewhere, a woman was singing, her voice clear and pure, now fading away as if it were the remnant of a dream, then rising again stronger than before. Leah lay motionless, staring at the cracked ceiling until the sound ceased.

She threw back the bedclothes to find she was already partially dressed. She didn't remember going to bed, either. The fire had long since reduced itself to ash, but the vicious chill of recent days had lost its grip. Leah swung her legs out of bed and her toes touched unexpected softness: a rag rug, positioned for this very purpose. She didn't think she owned such a rug; she certainly had no recollection of putting it there.

Turning towards the door, she froze again at the sight of a glass case containing, on closer examination, a display of dead animals. A stuffed mouse and a sparrow ran from a weasel's wide jaws, the bird's wings outspread to show each tiny, perfect, useless feather. Their eyes were all the same: false, black glass.

Leah rubbed her eyes, her heart racing, but the spectacle did not vanish, nor did anyone come. Was this meant to be another gift for her? Were there others to follow? *There must be more to see*, she thought. *And I can't just stay here, caught in time, waiting – especially when I don't even know what it is I'm waiting for.*

She stepped out onto the landing, finding under her feet the softness of a crimson carpet which stretched down the middle, pinned at the edges by shining brass fitments. She caught the scents of beeswax and something else: turpentine? It smelled like something her mother might have used for polishing furniture; she always swore by her own weird mixtures.

She narrowed her eyes, staring at the brass handle on the door opposite, which was now bright and shining against wood not yet darkened by grease and dirt and time. Leah shivered as she walked towards it, though she still didn't feel cold. The door handle turned and the door opened smoothly, without a rattle or a creak.

The master bedroom was once again crammed with furniture: the bed she remembered, the multitude of chairs. The mirror over Isobel's dressing table reflected back the room, doubling everything, but her silver-backed hairbrush and comb were laid askew and her jewellery box had been left open, a necklace set with large, lustrous opals, the very one she'd been wearing the night she died, spilling out.

The crocheted circle it sat upon was crumpled and the little bottles were all awry.

The washstand gave off the sour odour of dirty water. The mantelpiece and its burden of china ornaments were dulled with dust.

There was no one in the room. Quietly, Leah closed the door again, then paused at the top of the stairs and looked around. The door across the landing also had a brass handle that was yet to tarnish and panelling that had yet to crack, as it had in her time. She felt she already knew what she would see as she pushed it inward.

But it wasn't there. Instead, the room was dark, the shutters closed across the casements allowing only narrow slats of light to peek through. The room was closed and private as grief and she knew that this was *his* room: Samuel Maitland, who had lost his mother to a single berry of mistletoe.

His bed, carved from richly gleaming wood, was positioned by the far wall. Leah imagined him lying there, curled away from the light, the blankets drawn over his head. He would not have been sleeping, she was certain of that. He would have been fixed upon something he could feel but not quite see, a presence that had passed out of reach.

Perhaps she would have been able to see him if she had not burned his doll. She had banished his ghost so now she wouldn't have to look at him, or have to witness his sorrow. She wouldn't have to see whatever Jack was going to do to him. Is that what she had wanted all along – to protect herself?

She tried to recall the boy as she had first seen him, but it was Finn's dear face that rose before her, his features present and clear in every detail – but it was only a picture; there was nothing she could hold. She thought of Josh, but it was different with him. She could almost feel the solidity of him, wearing his favourite sweater, his arms wrapped around her, but his face – that was a blank. She wondered now what expression he might wear, what face he would choose to show her if she could see him again.

She stared into the little room a moment longer. Everything felt wrong here, out of its time. It was as if the world had turned malleable and might at any moment fall away from under her feet. There was nothing here that belonged, and yet it all did, the strange things it had shown her: Isobel's death, Jack with his axe, the boy and his burial doll; they all went together with the farm and the land, and all of it fit except her. She had become a ghost in her own life.

She ducked from the room and pulled the door closed behind her. She hurried to the stairs and went down to the living room. When she opened the door, the Christmas tree had blossomed, bursting into splendid life, full of light and colour. It stood where she had left it the night before, but it could not be the same one, for she was no longer seeing glimpses of the past: this *was* the past. The tree was decked with all kinds of decorations: bright red apples, but also paper chains and paper roses; ornaments of sugar and gingerbread; gilded sweets, delicate blown-glass globes and painted pine cones; and lit candles were wired to the branches, which were sagging under the weight of so much bounty. The whole was topped by a golden star.

Leah stood in front of it, breathing in the scents of pine and cinnamon and ginger, the aromas of childhood, of Christmases past, and most lately, of Cath's kitchen, and she felt a sudden pang of loss. This was everything that Christmas should be . . .

And then she turned and saw the evergreens that must have been placed over the mantelpiece, all swept to the floor in a heap.

She frowned. *How could that be?* For surely that was what *she* had done in her own world, in her time, not in this. But now the two were so closely intertwined they were like mistletoe growing around a branch, rooted so deeply they never could be separated.

'Pardon the disarray. I was so overwrought, you know, at my sister-in-law's demise.'

Leah whirled to see Ellis Maitland standing in the corner, his expression grave. She stepped away, but his eyes slid past her and she realised he wasn't speaking to *her*.

Martha, the maid, must have entered the room while Leah had been standing with her back turned, gawping at the Christmas tree like an enchanted child. She curtseyed to Ellis before going to the fireplace and kneeling amid the tangle of greenery. She started to gather it into her arms.

'Forgive me,' Ellis said. 'I should have better controlled my feelings. Such a dreadful thing, though, was it not? Whoever could have imagined she should be so susceptible to such a tiny thing? A single berry – and all was ended in a moment.'

A stifled sound emerged from Martha, although she did not turn; she was intent on picking up every scrap of greenery. Finally, she straightened and began to replace it on the mantelpiece, straightening bent branches, twisting the ivy decoratively about the holly, thrusting the mistletoe into place.

Then she realised the girl's shoulders were shaking and as another sound escaped her, Leah's eyes widened. Was she *laughing*?

'Aye,' Martha said, turning towards Ellis. 'Who'd've thought?'

She lifted her arm until the sprig of mistletoe she was holding in her hand was suspended over her head. She stood there silently, waiting.

For a moment, Ellis stared – then he strode to her and grasped her shoulders, pulling her into a lingering kiss. When at last he released her she mock-gasped and thrust the greenery towards him.

'Best not take a single berry for that one,' she said. 'Best to take the whole bunch!'

He laughed. 'What, so that I can demand more kisses of you? It's a little late for that, I reckon, you pretty harlot. Far too late.' He slapped her bottom and she grinned more widely.

'Didn't I tell you it would work? She couldn't even stand its touch, let alone its taste. It's a dry time you would have had with that one and no mistake.'

He pulled a face. 'You think I don't know it? I'd had lectures enough to know her character by. And yours too, you minx. You know that she thought you lovelorn for the farm-boy?'

'He's no boy,' she said slyly, but she tossed her head, dismissing the notion. She reached into the bodice of her dress and withdrew a little pouch sewn from grey-and-white striped fabric. 'You goose, Ellis. Look! We worked the charm together, Isobel too, though it was my doing, of course.'

She teased open the neck of the pouch and carefully removed the mistletoe leaf concealed within. The pale green was speckled with darker marks and Leah leaned forward to make them out, although she had no need; she already knew what they said.

Ellis read them out himself. 'E – M. Why, those are my initials. Did you cast a spell on me, you little witch? Is that how you so enchanted me? I shall have to watch you more closely, shall I not?'

Leah stared at him, her pulse throbbing, remembering the scene she had witnessed between mistress and servant, when she had seen them mark the mistletoe leaves with the initials of their chosen lover-to-be: the man each cared for, or hoped to care for. But it hadn't been Martha who'd chosen the letters E and M – that was her mistress. Martha could never have done so; Isobel would surely not have countenanced it. Ellis had been paying court to *her*, no matter how unwelcome, not to a lowly maid in her household. And yet here was his leaf, worn close to the maid's heart, not the mistress.

Had she been lusting after Ellis the whole time?

Martha's face took on a look of triumph. 'It was her leaf,' she said, 'but it should have been mine – you saw to that, and more than once, too! It was more mine than hers, so when I made the little bags to keep them in, I swapped them. It's only how it should have been in the first place.'

'*Her* leaf? You mean Isobel took part in your pretty game too, by God? There was more to her than I guessed, then. And she chose *my* initials?'

Martha's expression creased into a sulk. 'Only since there

were no one else. And she didn't get to keep it, did she? It were *my* leaf. She didn't even get one. She had nothing but an empty bag next to her heart. And it came true, didn't it? She'll marry no one, now.'

'Ah, have I upset you? Well, God forbid I should do that.' Ellis grasped her around the waist and kissed her again. 'Though perhaps I should really have wooed her, and not just for show. I wonder what other bounds she might have crossed, our saintly Isobel?'

Martha raised her hand to slap him and he caught hold of her arm.

'Aye, wooed her and bedded her. I'll be forced to wear a mourning-band for the woman, after all – you do understand that, don't you?'

Martha adopted a sombre countenance. 'And I – I shall be so very sad.' She screwed up her lips as if to demonstrate.

'Ah, you're a heartless wench, Martha.'

'Me, heartless? She had me run ragged from sun-up to sun-down. "You shall come to our party," she says, "you shan't do a thing all night long!" – just as if I didn't have to work double getting everything ready in time – it was all, "Set the fires, Martha, bring a hot supper, Martha, clean the boots and the knives and the passage and the step, trim the lamps, rub the furniture, fill the scuttles, and don't forget the roasts, Martha, turkey and fowls, get them basted, get the puddings boiling, and always, her little bell ringing—"' Her face reddened as if she were still rushing about trying to do it all.

'Come, now. She wasn't such a tartar, was she? One

shouldn't think badly of the dead. Did you care nothing at all for her?'

'Oh – of course I did! How can you think otherwise? She was my own dear mistress. I shall cut off a lock of her hair and have it made into a *memento mori*. A brooch, so's I can wear it every day.' Martha looked sly. 'Or perhaps I'll have it blown into a Christmas bauble and put it on the tree every year to remember her by, her face all purple and her neck all swole.'

She laughed, but Ellis did not. His gaze went to the Christmas tree and he lifted his eyes upwards, to the star that shone from the very top. His expression became solemn.

'Now don't look like that, Ellis, like some whey-faced ninny. What would have happened to you, if you hadn't have done it? What would have happened to *me*?'

She threw herself against him and pressed her face into his shoulder, grasping his hands and pulling his arms around her. 'And it wasn't anything bad. It wasn't, Ellis. It was unny tradition – you had to do it. Anyhow, it was her that chose to kiss you. She shouldn't have kissed you, Ellis!'

'Tradition?' He looked down at her as if surprised to see her there and placed one hand on her head. 'Yes, I suppose so. I must pluck a berry, must I not? So that I may demand more kisses whenever I choose.'

'That's right, just like I told you.' Her voice went dreamy. 'Because you're the man. That's what the man does.'

Unseen by her, he lifted his hand away from her hair. 'That's what he does. But the woman—'

Martha's voice filled with bitterness. 'The woman has to

take the berry and eat it. She has to think on what she's done. It goes inside her and becomes a part of her and gives her pangs in her belly. After all, that's what kissing leads to in the end.'

'Do you think it was what she deserved?' He sounded like he was only half-listening to her.

'Deserved!' Martha put her hands on her hips and glared at her lover. 'Do you think this life is all *I* deserve, Ellis? Is it what you *deserved*, to be the poor relation, the one left with nothing, while she had all of this?'

'Your name stands true, Martha. Well, you have your wish. Who could stand in the way of it? You shall not be a Martha any more.'

'What?' She scowled.

'Do you not remember the sisters in the Bible? Martha and Mary were visited by Jesus. Mary diligently listened to his word while Martha was kept busy about the housework. She complained that Mary did not help her.' He paused. 'The name Martha means lady or mistress. And, likewise, you do not like to dirty your hands. Perhaps you will not have to, much longer.'

'What do you mean, perhaps? I'll not cook and clean now. Anyroad, I'll not be able to, not when it starts to show. And what do you think would have happened then? If she'd seen my belly start to swell I'd have been cast off quick-sharp. I've nowhere else, Ellis. And what would she have said if she knew who's it was, eh? We'd both have been finished. No – we had to do it. There wasn't any choice.'

Ellis went on in the same absent tone, as if he hadn't heard,

'The same women were sisters to Lazarus, did you know that? You're not one for church learning, are you, Martha? Our Lord raised him from the dead. Only think of that – of the dead coming back to look into the eyes of the living. What would they say, do you think? What might *Isobel* have to say?'

'Is your brain turning soft, Ellis? You must stop that talk. There's no one coming back from the dead here. She's gone. She can't speak to you or even look at you again the way she once did. You'll be the master now.'

'Hmm.' Ellis shifted uncomfortably. 'Well, come then, Martha. It seems I have paid your price already. Let us see how it tastes.'

'Stop talking like that. You know how it tastes and you've not complained afore. And anyhow, now you can always kiss me.'

But he did not move towards her and Leah saw that the sprig of mistletoe had fallen to the floor, to be trampled beneath their feet. The other, the leaf with his initials pricked into it, was clutched in the girl's hand. Martha pressed kisses on him, stopping his words, and Leah wondered if she was the only one who heard the echo of that *always* hanging in the air.

She looked up at the Christmas tree and saw the star shining atop it – and blinked. In another moment, the star was gone. The rest faded too, the candles and gingerbread, the paper flowers and baubles and apples, until only bare branches remained. Even the scent of cinnamon turned to that of dust, leaving the room forlorn.

She thought of Martha's jest about making Isobel's hair into a Christmas bauble, a *memento mori*.

'Remember that you will die,' she murmured aloud. That's what it meant – and yet nothing really died here, did it?

The twists of evergreen were still lying at the foot of her own hearth where she'd swept them to the floor – or had that been Ellis? She was no longer certain of anything. The mistletoe wound among it all, the agent of Isobel's death, which was not a tragic accident unwittingly caused by Ellis, but a deliberate act. He and the maid had arranged it all between them. Martha had killed her mistress as surely as if she'd placed the berry in her mouth herself.

Leah raised a hand to the pocket of her shirt, just over her heart. She didn't even recall choosing to wear it, but when she reached into the pocket she felt the dry curve of a leaf under her fingers. She drew it out and stared.

The leaf still bore the same initials. She held it up to the light, making out the tiny holes forming the letters E and M. The flesh around each hole bore the trace of a bruise, like black rot spreading from Martha's touch.

It had been there all along, close to her heart. She had worn it while she slept, kept it close when she awoke. Why? Had that been her choice, or had Martha – or Ellis himself – somehow made her do it?

She curled her fingers around the leaf, thinking to crush it to powder, but stopped herself. If she did that, it would remain here like Jack's had, mingling with the dust under her feet, the air she breathed. She would never be able to destroy it then. She should burn it or get rid of it some other way; or, she realised, she could keep it by her. She could face this.

This was her family history, wasn't it? She'd been so set

upon effacing the past from this place, erasing all that it had been, making it into something shiny and new. But if she destroyed this single fragile thing, her ghosts might vanish for ever – she might never see them again, and what would she be then? Someone who did not dare to face the past, who ran from everything. A part of her would be trapped in this moment always, instead of doing what she had resolved to do: start again.

After a moment, she replaced the leaf in her shirt pocket. She couldn't let go of her ghosts, not yet. Her own story might already be over, but theirs was not and she had to know the truth. She needed to see how the story would end for all of them.

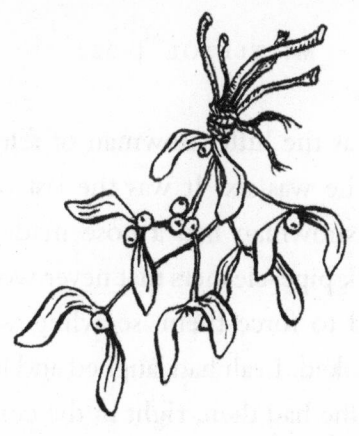

Chapter Fourteen

The Christmas decorations were in the first box Leah tried. She tore off the sealing tape and folded back the top to reveal crimson and gold, silver and green. Josh had laughed at them once, all these mismatched things they'd gathered through their lives, saying they should stick to a single colour and have everything neat, but he soon changed his mind when Finn began returning home from school with the things he'd made.

Cradling the box in her arms, Leah carried it downstairs, feeling a sense of inevitability as she placed it by the tree – the one that had appeared as if by magic, as if there really was some enchantment about these shortest days at the end of the year. It was the right thing to do, she decided. The season demanded its tribute.

She reached into the box without looking, knowing that everything would be there, and sure enough, the first thing she picked out was the little snowman of felt, the one Finn had made when he was six. It was the last decoration he'd ever made. The snowman had a nose made of glitter and arms of fuzzy black pipe-cleaners that never would go straight, though he'd tried to force them, scowling when they only became more crooked. Leah had laughed and loved it anyway.

She hung it as she had then, right in the centre of the tree. Reaching into the box again, she retrieved a wooden rocking horse that had come from a Christmas market in Germany the year before Finn was born. A man with a white beard, ruddy cheeks and a pipe had sold it to them and they'd joked for years afterwards that it had come from Santa himself. Finn had loved it, taking it down and rocking it across the coffee table, making *clop-clop* noises.

She hung them all, loading the branches with the baubles and lights, wooden carvings and felted characters, designs pressed in clay that still bore the trace of her son's finger-prints. There was tinsel and a tiny stuffed reindeer and little cross-stitched stockings and fake candles made of plastic. They'd always had an angel at the top of their tree, but this year she set that aside. At the bottom of the box was a star that Finn had made, a simple thing of gold card with smaller star shapes cut out of it. She'd always hung it somewhere in the house but this year she reached up, caught hold of the tree's topmost point and bent it downwards so she could wrap the string securely around it. It sprang back into place and there it was, a star at the top, just as her ancestors had had in years past.

She closed her eyes, wondering if Finn would have liked

the result. He always trimmed the tree himself, taking each decoration in his hand, deciding carefully and seriously where each would go. For the higher branches he pointed out where he wanted each precious ornament and bauble to sit. Only when it was completed to his satisfaction were they allowed to stand back to admire their work.

Doing this now made her son feel closer than ever – and reminded her how very far away he was.

The box wasn't quite empty; there should be one more thing. She reached in to the very bottom until her fingers touched a little parcel of soft material. She pulled out the swathe of bright red ribbon, knelt on the hard flagstones and ducked under the lowest branches, ignoring the needles prickling the back of her neck. She wrapped the ribbon around the trunk, seeing as she did the way it had been hacked through in broad strokes by an axe: perhaps the same one that had stolen a child's life.

Leah shivered and stood, brushing fragments of bark from her collar. It didn't matter what had been used to cut it. The tree was hers now.

Finally, she picked up the pieces of holly and ivy she'd swept from the mantelpiece and replaced them, thinking of the old carol. Almost without thinking, she started singing softly,

> *'The holly and the ivy,*
> *When they are both full grown,*
> *Of all the trees that are in the wood*
> *The holly bears the crown.'*

The holly, she thought, *not the mistletoe*. She had heard once that, long ago, holly was considered male and ivy female, but if Martha's country lore was correct, the mistletoe represented both together; conspirators, perhaps.

After a moment she set the mistletoe back into place too, threading it in among the rest. The tradition of bringing evergreens inside at this time of year was far older than Christmas: the Romans had done it at Saturnalia, but mistletoe had been considered special even longer than that. Leah pictured the druids cutting it with golden sickles by the light of the full moon and never allowing it to touch the ground. Perhaps they hadn't even needed such precautions; after all, her mistletoe had held its spell without them.

She sat down, straightening her back against the hard settle, and looked at what she had done. It looked just as it had when Martha had arranged it.

Suddenly she looked down at her own hands. She was a Maitland, wasn't she? And Martha had been *pregnant*. She imagined that baby growing up over the years, and its baby, and the next, forming the line that led to her. She had known that Ellis must be her ancestor but it only struck her now that Martha must be, too.

The idea made her feel nauseated and she tried to push away the thought. She didn't want to think of that woman's blood running in her veins; that was something she could never be rid of. And what about Ellis? He was a murderer—

Leah raised her gaze and almost as if she had summoned him, Ellis was standing in front of her. With a sickening lurch in her stomach, she thought of the leaf in her pocket and reached for it, but it was too late. He was looking directly at her, his eyes intense – looking *into* her.

'I am so glad,' he said, 'that you could be here.'

Fear iced her veins, until he glanced around, his eyes taking in the whole room, resting on nothing. Ellis stood in front of the hearth, a fire blazing at his back, but he didn't appear to feel the heat. He held a tiny glass of some dark liquid, port, maybe, and he tilted it, catching the fire's light in a well of ruby.

He was wearing a black cravat and black gloves. A black band wrapped the sleeve of his shirt. His countenance was rueful, as if he shared Leah's sadness and dismay.

'In times like these, it is only with the help of our friends and neighbours that such a thing becomes bearable. And for it to happen in such a way, so unexpectedly, and in this very place – indeed, with friends and family all around! Truly, when we are called, it is God's will. Not one of us can see what lies in wait for us – and yet we may stand together now.'

God's will? Leah pictured him pushing the berry between Isobel's lips.

'I shall stand with you. I want you all to know that. I shall take up the burden I have been asked to carry and I shall carry it. My late cousin was interested in local traditions and legends, as many of you will know; he often spoke of the stories he uncovered. I shall endeavour to follow where he led. His son still lives. Samuel's past is here at Maitland Farm and his future lies here also. I shall nurture it as best I may, so that when I pass it on, it will be all the better for him. That is my wish and I hope you will pray for me that

I may succeed, for as many of you know, the farm is not without its troubles.'

Ellis looked around the room again, his expression the very image of humility.

'And Samuel will continue to be loved as he is now,' he said, 'by all of us, from master to the youngest servant. All that he requires shall be his. Martha is sewing a Christmas gift for the boy even now, I believe, and Jack had already fashioned something for him – allow me to show you; he must have learned the way of it from my cousin and his histories. It will look somewhat primitive to your eyes—'

Leah started as he stepped forward, but he didn't even look at her, just strode across the room and the door swung closed behind him. She already knew what he was going to show them – she had seen it before. But Ellis didn't return. His footsteps faded in the hall and the house remained silent.

That couldn't be all. There must be more to the story. She wondered if Ellis had been speaking at Isobel's funeral, painting a happy picture of a family holding together in the face of adversity, doing everything they could to serve the needs of the farm.

Leah strode to the door and into the hall. Ellis had spoken of nurturing the farm and it always returned to that: to the land. So she would look outside. She would go in search of whatever came next.

The first thing she saw when she opened the front door was not the fields stretching away around her, but the snowman: the simple thing they had made together, she, Andrew and Charlie, the image of a family that wasn't a family at all.

It stared out at her from the blaze of glittering white. The snowman's face had partially melted, softening before freezing once more, making it look hollow-eyed, its mouth twisted in grief.

Before she could think, she placed both hands against it and pushed. The snow didn't so much break into pieces as disintegrate, falling into powder, larger pieces rolling away. The head came to rest against the wall, half buried in a drift.

Suddenly, Leah wanted to laugh. What had she done? At least Charlie would never see it.

She stepped past the broken thing, pushing aside the thought of how happy they had been that day, at least until Charlie had found the axe. She turned towards the barn. If she sought answers, that was surely where she would find them.

The barn looked as if no one had disturbed it in a hundred years or more. There remained all the inexplicable tangle of metal and wood, the blades, the spikes, the teeth; and there was the Charlie doll, just where she'd left it. She had placed it in the hole in the wall by the slaughtering bench, but it would not swallow the thing; it must still be demanding something of her.

She stared down at her hands, remembering the way she had once walked across the yard and sensed another set of footsteps tracking her own, not quite in time with hers. She did not feel alone now. She felt as if someone was near, someone with a will reaching out to subsume hers, someone who desired, who needed – *what?* She was not certain, she could only feel their sense of purpose wrapping itself about her, like mistletoe growing around a branch.

No longer certain if she was following a ghost or leading one, Leah's fingers tightened about the heavy, warm neck of the little figure on the bench. The hunger she felt was as real as if it were her own. A succession of faces passed before her: Charlie, his eyes full of doubt; Samuel, proud and unsuspecting, and that of another doll in another time, one she didn't know – then many of them, wax effigies, sacrifices, each one created in the image of a child.

Leah fought the images back, trying to rid herself of that sense of terrible intent, but she couldn't move. Her hand was fixed in place about the doll's neck, but it wasn't fabric she could feel under her fingers: it was frail skin and beneath, bones, slender and fragile; and the warm pulse of blood.

No. This wasn't the vision she had sought. This was nothing to do with her. Her life was removed from the past, she was years distant from any of it—

Something flashed at the edge of Leah's vision and she thought suddenly of Charlie's words. He'd said the axe had moved all by itself – except it hadn't, had it? It was *Jack's* axe. Now he had come for what he craved.

She closed her eyes, but she heard the sound of the axe landing, the wet crunch it made, the splintering as it was pulled loose again from the thirsty wood of the bench.

They would have used it for slaughtering . . .

Was this the offering that was demanded – by the land, or by a mere man? Was it Jack's strength of purpose she felt, lending iron to her fingers? Could it be his actions she sensed, not images on a screen, not an echo, but here, in her blood and her bones?

It had to be him. These couldn't be her feelings, her desires. It couldn't be anything inside *her* . . .

In her mind's eye, blood seeped from the gash the axe had made, spilling over her hand, sticky, like—

Like mistletoe juice, she thought, remembering how she'd crushed the berries between her fingers in the orchard, the goddess moon shining down on it all. And her brother was the sun: the dying sun that needed sacrifice, hungering to be reborn . . .

Still Leah couldn't open her eyes. She pictured the doll in front of her, its eyes wide with horror, its mouth open in a scream – except it wasn't a doll any longer; it wasn't even Charlie. It was Samuel Maitland, and she knew she could no longer be in the present. The past was gathering all around her, building in the silence that was broken when the axe rushed past her again and fell – and fell once more.

Leah held the boy down, her fingers pressing into his throat, though she had no need to do so, not now, for Samuel had fallen still. He no longer struggled against her; his ribs no longer flexed with his breath. She envisioned his blood, however, could hear it slowly dripping from the bench.

Suddenly she could move again.

Leah snatched her hand away and as she did, that strange sense of purpose drained from her, leaving her shaky and sickened. At last, she opened her eyes to see the doll, nothing but fabric, nothing but wax, but cracked and shattered. An ugly rent had cleaved its skull; another had almost parted its arm from its shoulder. She slipped her fingers into another rent in its blue coat and felt a cut in the body beneath, but it was dry, not sticky as she had expected. Her touch met with nothing but sand.

Its face too had changed, the wax discoloured to the colour of a bruise. Its hair was still red, though; it wasn't Samuel's doll, but it no longer looked quite like Charlie's either. It looked like both of them together, and she realised it was: it represented all the sacrifices that had been made to the soil, all the sacrifices that could still be made.

From outside the barn came the scrape of boots against stone. Leah turned to stare after it. The image that came to her was a broad-shouldered man standing in the yard, an axe held casually over one shoulder. He was almost handsome, his hair black, his sharp eyes staring straight at Leah.

Jack Hirst. She found herself forming his name, though she didn't say it aloud.

There was another crunch of snow, then a long dragging sound.

Leah drew in a ragged breath. She wished she were miles away from here, in another life, but she knew the vision wouldn't let her go, not yet.

She walked towards the yard, leaving the ruined doll behind her. In this strange day that belonged only to the past, the moon hung low in the sky, though the sun had yet to fail. Shadows had turned to indigo, twisting and distorting every familiar shape. The scent was of clarity, of cold. And the snow fell, almost hiding the shadow that detached itself from the farmhouse wall and struck out towards the field.

Leah followed, though she wasn't sure she could still see the shape at all – then she heard another long dragging sound. Was that a shadow walking ahead of her? She had the impression there was someone standing there, moving awkwardly, taking slow steps as they struggled to pick up something that was lying on the ground.

Then they were gone. She glanced up at the farmhouse windows, which were dark, their diamond panes glittering back only the image of the moon: a thousand milky berries of mistletoe.

A louder crunch sounded from the gate leading into the field, as if something had been thrown over it, and she hurried to follow. Had the shadow she'd seen slipped over the top – was that a darker form crumpled at its feet?

She didn't know how it could have moved so quickly, and by the time she had scaled the gate herself, it was gone, but there was another scraping sound, longer, more pained, ahead of her. She peered into the whirling snow, but couldn't make out its source.

She looked down to see the trail they'd left behind: a hollow about a foot wide, as if someone had been making a snowman, or a sack had been dragged across the snow. To the side were footprints, a man's, it looked like. And there was something else, something dark spilled across the clean surface.

The scraping noise had faded, but it hadn't stopped; now it was coming from the far side of the field, and somehow she knew that it would not stop, because he was giving the land what it needed, wasn't he? Jack Hirst was giving it the blood it craved.

This was the offering he'd wanted to make.

Leah half closed her eyes and watched the light shift across the land, the last dying gleams of the sun catching at the field, liquid shadows meeting and joining. Soon they would cover everything, swallowing the world, turning it not to gold, but to crimson.

The snow that had been falling all around Leah suddenly stopped. She stared around her, seeing it hanging there, not drifting or spiralling on some breeze, but poised motionless. The world was silent; she couldn't even hear her own breath.

Slowly, almost in a dream, she reached out and plucked a snowflake from the air.

As if she had broken the spell, the snow fell to the ground and was gone. The flake on the palm of her hand had already disappeared.

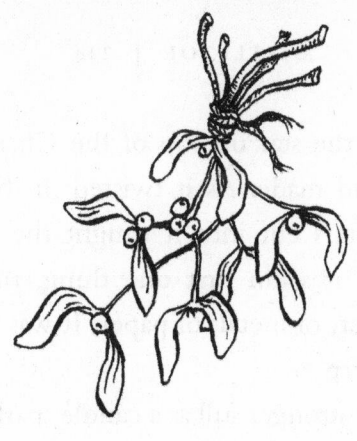

Chapter Fifteen

It was Christmas Day.

Leah shifted uncomfortably on the settle in the living room, hardly knowing where she was. She twisted her neck to loosen it, feeling a sharp pain down her back from sleeping here, the thin cushion doing nothing to soften the hard surface. She began to remember the dreamlike night, the doll, the yard, Jack Hirst, shifting before her eyes, but now she saw only the room that had become so familiar to her: its walls still waiting to be filled with pictures, its spaces to be filled with furniture. At least the hearth was heaped with firewood; and there was the Christmas tree, its lights waiting to be lit, today of all days.

She shuddered, still feeling the fragility of a child's bones beneath her fingers. When she looked down at her hands, she was somehow surprised to find them clean.

Leah stared at the star on top of the Christmas tree, the one that Finn had made. As it twisted in the draught, the host of smaller stars cut into it caught the light from the window, making it seem first one thing, then another: it was made of paper; of metal; of paper. It was made of metal, gleaming and sharp.

The light grew stronger still as a candle sparked into life – a real wax candle, attached to one of the branches with wire, and another flame appeared, and another; it was Christmas after all, time to set lights against the encroaching darkness. They sent shadows wavering about the room, the needles of the tree magnified against the wall, lengthening into spikes.

All of Finn's beloved decorations were gone and instead the tree was weighed down with objects Leah had seen once before: delicate globes of hand-silvered glass; paper roses; gilded sweets; painted pine cones; gingerbread and sugar and shiny red apples. Candles warmed them all, filling the air with the scents of pine and ginger and cinnamon, melting wax and smoke.

'You see, it was never really a Christmas gift.'

Leah was unsurprised to hear Ellis Maitland, but when she turned he wasn't there; she realised his voice was coming from outside the room. She put a hand to her shirt pocket, felt the mistletoe within.

In the hall, the front door was open and the snow that had drifted inside was dusting the flagstones with white. A dead cold was rising from the ground.

'How could it have been?' Ellis' voice sounded as if it was close to breaking. 'It was not even the right day of the year for a gift, was it? It was approaching the shortest day, the very depths of the year, when he put the doll into the boy's hands. And what man of his rank would give a gift to the master, however young he might be? Such things are not given upwards but passed down, are they not? The doll was not a gift but a sign, all part of his heathen belief that the land demands a life. I should have seen it at once. I blame myself utterly.'

Although she had not been surprised to hear Ellis, the answering murmur gave Leah pause, for it was not the sound of a single person, but many.

Ellis was still speaking to his unseen audience. 'The effigy even resembled the boy. It was dressed in a canary-yellow waistcoat, just like the one Samuel so delighted in, a gift from his loving mama. Ah, God – and after his mother passed, the way the boy looked, his eyes so hollow – it was as if Jack had planned it all along. He made the thing for the boy's burial doll, but more than that, it was obviously meant for some unholy ritual – one he has now carried out.'

Leah went to the door, but she couldn't see Ellis for a crowd of men surrounded her, all of them in workers' clothing: fustian waistcoats and jackets that were repaired and patched, worn at the sleeves, sun-faded across the shoulders. Some wore gaiters of sacking to protect their trouser-legs, as if in expectation of dirty work. The only colour was in the kerchiefs wrapped tightly about their necks. They clutched their hats in one hand, heavy walking sticks in the other, all except for one man who instead carried a gleaming sickle.

Once again, the mistletoe had drawn her into the past and immersed her in it.

The tallest worker had old-fashioned whiskers and a thick moustache. The man standing next to him had a thin, pinched face that reminded Leah of the woman who owned the village shop; another sported hair the same auburn shade as Andrew's. There were others, too, standing together, shoulder to shoulder.

Leah stepped fully into the doorway and found herself at Ellis' side, almost as if she was his accomplice. She wondered what his audience would do if they knew that Ellis too had blood on his hands?

'Soon we must prepare ourselves for church,' he went on. 'This is a blessed day and this is not man's business, but God's. We protect our own.'

Leah started at those words, the echo of Cath's – and yet he hadn't protected his own, had he? He had murdered Isobel, the woman he had professed to love, and he had failed to take care of his cousin's son.

The men shifted, murmuring agreement. Ellis bowed his head, pinching the bridge of his nose between his fingers as if it pained him to speak.

At last he said, 'Even if it is too late, blood cries out from the ground.' He pointed, not towards the men but beyond them, at the first field. 'We should not stop our ears to it, and we shall not.'

Leah followed his gaze. The snowy surface was scarred with blood.

'We're ready.' One of the men stepped forward, the one with red hair. He spoke with a slight Scottish accent. This must be Cath's and Andrew's ancestor, the one Andrew hadn't wished to be reminded of. She supposed he was acting in good faith, taking revenge on a child-murderer – but there had been no trial, nor any semblance of law here. Would all their hands be stained with blood?

Some of the folk from round about got together and took it into their own hands . . . rough justice, I suppose they'd call it now. Nothing to be proud of—

Leah glanced over her shoulder, as if seeking a place to retreat, and saw Martha standing behind her, hidden in the shade of the hall. A secretive smile was playing about the maid's lips.

A shout went up from the men, followed by angry cries and the stamping of feet. Almost without making any decision, Leah found herself following Ellis across the yard as he led the way in silence.

She knew where they were going even before they stopped outside the barn doors, which were smartly painted, not rotten and sagging from their hinges. She couldn't see inside; there were too many people blocking her view and in any case, she wasn't sure she wanted to look.

She glanced at the white sky. It was Christmas Day. Surely they couldn't think of administering their 'justice' on such a day?

But it appeared they would. The crowd parted and she saw Jack Hirst at last.

He looked just as she'd pictured him. Despite his muscular strength, he was kneeling on the ground, peering up at his accusers through his tousled black hair. His shirt had been torn, his face bruised, and blood trickled from the corner of his lip. His hands drew her gaze: well-made, with short, strong fingers: these hands had wielded the axe. There was blood on the knuckles – his, or someone else's?

She looked into his eyes. Was there any mercy in them? Was there any in hers? Just as it had the last time she stood in this place, a sense of purpose gripped her, this time emanating from the men who stood around her. Leah looked at Jack with contempt, thinking of Samuel accepting his gift with genuine pleasure, the way he had invited his murderer to a Christmas party – just as Isobel had with Ellis. And was it Jack who had come to Leah in the dead of night, sliding into bed beside her, reaching for her with those hands?

She shrank from him even as he looked up at her, his eyes widening as if he had seen her. But that couldn't be possible – except that it was Christmas Day and the past and the present were so deeply entwined they might never be separated.

The red-haired man stepped forward, obscuring her view, but Leah heard the sound of a blow. 'He deserves no better,' he said. 'Let him die like a pig.'

'Aye,' said someone else, 'go on, Drew – give him his own fate. It was his axe that killed the boy. Well, his turn to feel it now.'

Drew. His name ran in the family too then. Leah's gaze went to the slaughtering bench, which stood where it had always been, looking as it always had. The axe leaning next to it, its blade gleaming, looked just the same too. She thought of Jack's hands smoothing it to his grip with years of work, and she thought of him sharpening that blade, caring for it so that it was always ready, so that it was sharp.

Hatred rose within her. She too had lost a son; she knew what that loss felt like. She had held her precious boy's head in her hands, willing him to be well – but he wouldn't ever be well again and now he was gone, his bones turned to ash that she had tried to grasp in her fingers, willing it to take on his form again. Would Jack have held *her* boy down so mercilessly, killing him as if he were nothing but an animal?

Leah willed the men around her to act, but none did. No one reached for the axe. Instead, they looked uncertainly at Ellis, the undisputed master of this place, waiting for him to do something; to lead them. Only one man could wield an axe, she realised. And Ellis could surely have no scruples, not after what he had already done.

But it was Andrew's ancestor who moved at last, to aim a kick into Jack's ribs. The labourer bent double, his forehead almost touching the ground. A murmur ran through the gathering, something like satisfaction, and Leah sensed the hunger for more moving among them.

'Tradition,' Ellis said. 'We shall do what Jack himself would have wanted.' His gaze rested for a moment on each of the men's faces, as if to make each person complicit. 'He wanted a sacrifice, did he not? He believed that to be what the farm needs.'

Jack tried to shake his head, but Drew caught his hair, holding him still.

'There,' Ellis said, pointing at one corner. Leah didn't understand what he meant, but the men must have, for they moved to obey.

One of them returned carrying a rope and began twisting

it in his hands as if making a wreath – but it was not a wreath. Jack pulled free of his captor's grip but he remained kneeling, watching dully, his eyes glazing over as if he had been hypnotised – or maybe he was just resigned to his fate.

He opened his mouth. His voice was nothing but a whisper, but Leah thought she could make out the words that were on his lips.

Ellis did move, then, striding forward and grasping Jack around his neck, silencing him. 'You'll not speak. Not to me.'

The noose was almost finished. Leah stared at it, fascinated by the way it had been formed so easily, a simple rope turned into an instrument of death. Josh must have done exactly this, formed a noose of his own – she had been so caught up in the fact of his loss she had not thought of it before but now she wondered how long it had taken him, how long he had spent planning it. Had his eyes been full of concentration on his task, or were they blank? She wished it was Josh she was seeing now, that he might feel her presence too, hear the things she wanted to say to him, the things she should have said . . .

It wasn't Josh kneeling before her, however, but Jack, the man who had killed a child. Their gaze met and a cold finger traced a line down her back.

The rope went snaking upwards, thrown over one of the beams that latticed the roof. More hands caught the other end as it fell towards them.

'Tradition,' Ellis repeated. He still hadn't moved to help the others; he looked content to stand by while they did his work. 'The hanged man will soon be buried. Perhaps the land will feast on your bones, Jack Hirst. Perhaps something new will come of it. Whatever happens, you will be forgotten.'

As if only now realising what they intended, Jack struggled. One of the men pushed him onto his side and the others closed in on him.

'Curse you all.' He jerked away from them as they dragged him to his feet, speaking clearly at last. 'Curse this whole damned place.'

'You've done that already,' Ellis said, 'with the blood you spilled, the unholy spells you wielded.'

He gestured to his followers. They dragged Jack to the waiting noose and Drew pulled it over his head, tightening it about his throat. Jack did not look at Leah again. His eyes were closed. He must have heard their jeering and mockery as they made the rope fast about his neck, then vied with each other to hoist him into the air.

Only Ellis did not help. Leah watched: bearing witness was the only thing she could do. The man surely deserved to die – and yet so did Ellis, and all she could think of was blood, tainting them all until they were steeped in it.

Curse this whole damned place.

It was so slow. That was somehow worse than anything else. Leah could not bear to see Jack being lifted from his feet so she squeezed her own eyes closed, but still she could hear the rope creaking like the straining branches of a dying tree.

When she opened them again, Jack was staring straight at her. His eyes bulged but he did not blink, nor did he look away. The veins stood out on his neck and his mouth twisted in an effort to draw in air, but he made no sound, nor did he appear to be asking for her help; he knew that none would be given. Leah could see no accusation in his eyes, but neither was there any acknowledgement that this was what he deserved. She could not have said for certain that he even saw her at all.

Leah had to look away. She fixed her gaze on the floor, but she could not escape Jack Hirst's presence. The shadows of his feet turned a little one way, then swung back the other, accompanied by that endless creaking, while his neighbours watched without a word. There was nothing left to say.

After what felt like an age, she heard a slashing sound, followed by a heavy thump. Ellis had taken up a weapon after all, not an axe but a sickle. Jack Hirst lay dead at his feet.

Justice, Leah thought, but she could not feel any triumph over the empty shell lying in front of her. His eyes were blank. His past, his memories, his loves and cares, his ideas and his deeds: all of them had gone.

Still the scene did not vanish, nor did the men. They stood around her as if she was one of them, staring down at this thing they had done together.

We protect our own. And she knew that she would have helped them, if she could; she would have done it a hundred times over if, in doing so, she could have protected her son.

All their bravado had gone, dissipated into the air along with the man's life. Now the men looked chastened.

'The orchard.' Ellis said it like a command, but not one of them moved.

'He thought he owed the land blood – well, let it drink. The boy shall have a proper burial, but Jack Hirst shall have none. He shall not lie in hallowed ground, for surely it would not hold him. And it is the time of year when some would wassail the trees and make them an offering, is it not? Well, we shall give him to the trees and see how they fruit.'

Ellis started to pick up tools from around the barn, thrusting them into their hands. The men took them, but then stood there like mannequins. Ellis passed the last a pick for breaking the cold ground and still they waited, until he lost patience and began pushing them towards the door.

One stumbled over the body and fell, landing half across it with his fingers on the dead man's face. He pulled away with a cry, wiping his hand on his trousers.

'There's no use in trying to wash your hands of it.' Ellis dragged him to his feet. 'Look – see what you've all done! There is no taking any of this back, my friends. What did you think would happen? We must stand together now, unless you wish to suffer a similar fate. Do you wish to hang? Or you' – he pointed, and again – 'or you?'

See what *you've* all done: that was what he'd said, and still not one of them spoke; no one dared to cross him. How could they? It was their hands that had fashioned the noose, that had hoisted Jack to his death. They hadn't done anything to stop Ellis, not even questioned him. There wasn't a man among them who could ever accuse him.

They walked ahead of Leah out of the barn and towards the orchard, two grasping the dead man's arms and dragging him with them. Ellis walked behind and Leah followed last of all. There was nothing else they could do.

They were a community.

The day was cold, the sun shining down indifferently, warming nothing. The orchard, though, was changed: the trees were smaller, younger, straight and sprightly, despite the snow weighing down their branches. They hadn't yet failed; they hadn't begun to rot. Would Jack's blood really make the orchard flourish? Leah wondered who would eat the fruit that might grow there.

The way Ellis stood, his eyes gleaming defiantly, provided her answer.

They left Jack lying face-down in the snow where they'd dropped him. Leah flinched at the sight, even though the cold could not trouble him any more. A dull scraping sound drew her attention to the nearest tree, where one of the men was rapidly shovelling the drifts aside.

He stood back and a grey-whiskered fellow took his place, swinging his pick at the hard ground. The clods he dislodged were hard as rock and others stepped in to kick them out of the way.

Ellis stood by and watched. It was his orchard now; it was his farm.

Leah watched too, wondering if she should be horrified to see the grave that was being dug, here on what was also *her* farm. She thought of the times she had walked here, the way she had grasped the mistletoe in her hands. This ought to have come as a shock to her – but she had sensed it, hadn't she: not new life springing from beneath the ground, but death.

She pictured her trees, winding their roots around the murderer's body, finding their way beneath his skin, twining about his bones. Little wonder the land was uneasy; little wonder restless spirits walked these hills.

She was helpless to change it. She covered her face, but she could not prevent herself from hearing the thud and scrape of their work. When she looked up, one of the men was standing thigh-deep in the hole they had hacked out of the unwilling ground. The tree spreading its branches above his head trembled as if they had unbalanced it with their digging, but soon enough the hole would be filled and the tree would have new sustenance to help it grow.

The sounds began to fade at last and when next Leah looked, most of the men had vanished from her sight, leaving only two shovelling earth into the hole. She was glad she could not see into it. Then they too were fading, merging with the shadows of the trees.

Ellis remained, a black crow at a funeral, watching the aftermath of the death he had orchestrated. There was no sign of triumph on his face but Leah could feel it all the same.

And she saw someone was coming to join him: a slight figure picking its way across the snow. Her face was veiled, but she knew it was Martha.

When the maid reached Ellis' side, she lifted the veil. Her expression betrayed nothing. Neither turned to the other; they simply regarded the pitiful mound of earth.

Eventually, Martha spoke. 'You've managed it all just right,' she said.

'Have I?' Ellis stirred at last. 'I believe you give me credit for too much cleverness, Mistress Martha.'

Leah suddenly remembered the words she had heard from a

dead man's lips, the words Jack Hirst had repeated, mouthing them at her from his knees as he awaited the rope.

You paint me a cleverer man than I am.

And she saw it again: standing in snow that whirled in front of her face, disguising the figures she half glimpsed in its midst. But Ellis had been there – she had heard him speaking of the doll, of traditions that went back for centuries, of Jack's choice of Christmas gift: the thing that had secured the noose about his neck.

It is part of a quite ancient tradition. My cousin had an interest in such things. He wrote a monograph once, did you know of it? I dare say they must have discussed it between them.

But *had* they discussed it? Or had the gift been nothing but that – a gift to a well-loved child?

As if in answer, Martha replied. 'Well, it was clever of you to tell them all those things about the doll. It was a fine story. I never would have thought of the half of it, even if I did show him how to make it. Not that he knew he were stitchin' a *burial* doll.' She giggled.

Leah closed her eyes. She remembered the doll, not as it had been in her world, but when she'd seen it in Samuel's hands, its waistcoat a new, bright yellow, its skin smooth and fresh. What had he called it? *A kind of portrait.* She imagined Jack's hands making it, his strong fingers wielding a needle and thread; the only gift, perhaps, that a poor man could make to the boy who would be his master. And Martha had been his guide.

'Would you not, you vixen?' Ellis laughed in return, though his look was strangely distant. 'The mistress stood in our way;

the mistress is dead. The boy stood in our way; the boy is dead, and the man has paid for the sin. It strikes me that *you* have arranged it all remarkably well. I scarcely know how you have done it.'

'I, sir?' She sounded shocked, and yet she caught hold of her skirts and bobbed a mocking curtsey.

'Aye, you.' He caught hold of her shoulders and spinning her around, said, 'What witchery did you work? I said once that I ought to watch you, and so I should.' His smile faded. 'What is it you have made of me, Martha? What have you made of us all?'

She shook him off. 'I have made you a master,' she said, her voice hard. 'Do you not like it?'

He stared into her eyes, then broke his gaze and looked around as if to take in his farm, his land, his trees. Yet he did not appear to see the thing that was growing there even as Leah watched: the mistletoe creeping along the dark, leafless branches, new life springing from death.

As if caught in its spell, he turned to Martha and put his hands to her cheeks before he leaned in and kissed her.

The holly and the ivy, Leah thought. *The holly bears the crown – although it was the ivy that won it for him.*

And now here was the mistletoe itself, twining more strongly about each stem by the moment: mistletoe that was male and the female together – and both of them feeding on death.

Some even thought it carried the soul of the tree.

But this mistletoe wasn't springing from the trees, for it was rooted in a new source: the one Ellis had ordered buried there. It had sprung from Jack's bones. This was the new life Ellis had given to the farm. Leah asked herself, *What if it wasn't carrying the soul of the tree at all – what if it was carrying Jack's soul?*

She watched, alone and unseen and cold to her bones, until they broke their kiss.

Then Martha threw back her head and laughed. 'If they only knew it was never Jack's hands that wielded the axe, but yours,' she crowed.

Ellis did not laugh. He flinched and looked grave as he replied, 'If they only knew mine were not the hands that held the boy down, but yours.'

Leah looked down at her own hands, feeling again the doll's neck under them – except it hadn't been a doll's neck, had it? And it hadn't been her hands. She had felt the axe rushing by her face, had seen in her mind's eye what they had done to Samuel – together. They had used Jack's axe, but Ellis had wielded it. And it was not Jack who held the boy down on the slaughtering bench, but Martha. It was her sense of purpose that had filled Leah's mind, urging her to tighten her grip; it was the maid's hands that had taken possession of her own.

There was no trace of guilt on the girl's face as she touched her belly and smoothed down her dress, revealing the growing mound of her pregnancy.

And Leah saw it all. Martha's path was now clear before her. Isobel Maitland had been in the way of Ellis gaining possession of the farm, so they had rid themselves of her. But until Samuel was dead, Ellis was not truly the master – and

Martha's child would never be the heir – so she had needed to be rid of him too. The notion of tradition and sacrifice was nothing but a story they had turned to their purpose: it had served well to put Jack Hirst in the ground.

And Leah supposed he *was* a sacrifice, of a kind; one to their desires. He had taken their place, had been punished for their crime. Were these really her ancestors? *Is it their blood that runs in my veins?*

She looked around at the mistletoe, which was continuing to spread. This was Jack's legacy, wrapping itself about the apple trees, leaching the life out of the orchard. This is what had been haunting her: not the curse of a murderer, but of the murdered. Here was Jack's gift, in memory of all the kisses he would never have, all the Christmases he would never see.

Leah turned back to Ellis and Martha again, but they had vanished, leaving nothing but the barren, snow-covered ground and the knowledge of what had happened here. She stood a little longer, looking at the place where an innocent man had been buried, but there was nothing else to see.

Now she knew the truth. The story had been told; her haunting had reached its end.

Eventually, she turned and walked back towards the house. How strange it was, to realise that it was still Christmas Day. As she shook the snow from her boots and hung her coat over the acorn she was surprised to find she was eager to see the tree with her own decorations hanging there, her own life restored to her.

As she opened the door, there they were, all the things

she and Josh had chosen together, the ones Finn had made, with his crooked star above it all.

Leah's smile faded when she turned to the fireplace.

She did not remember there being quite so much mistletoe. The mantelpiece was laden with it, not just a few sprigs woven into the holly and the ivy, but heavy clumps of the stuff, thick with berries. When she went closer and took hold of one of the stems, intending to pull it away, her puzzlement increased. It wouldn't come free. The stems hadn't been cut and arranged; they had sprung from the ancient beam that formed the mantelpiece. They were rooted into her house.

The mistletoe emerging from the cracks in the desiccated wood had not just taken possession of the mantelpiece but were spreading across the walls. The leaves were fresh and healthy and green, the translucent berries ripe to bursting. The plant was thriving.

How can the living grow from the dead? she wondered. But she thought perhaps she knew.

She grasped another stem and tried to yank it away, fighting it with all her weight – but it only snapped, spattering her hand with sap and leaving the root embedded in the beam.

She tried another piece, more slender than the last, wrapping it about her fingers before tugging. This one eventually burst from the wood, scattering rotten fragments across the floor.

The mistletoe wasn't just Jack's curse, she was certain of it now. It carried his soul; it *was* his soul. And it hadn't finished with her. It wouldn't let her go.

She had watched him die, never questioning what was being

done to him, feeling that he *should* die, that he deserved his fate. *We protect our own*, they had said. And she was one of them, wasn't she? She was a *Maitland*.

Would he haunt her always? Would he never leave her, but come to her in her waking hours – in her dreams – in the coldest of nights? Would he sleep in her bed beside her?

A new year, she thought. *A new start*. The words were nothing but mockery now. She shook her head as if to be rid of them, to be rid of it all, then heard, as at a great distance, the chiming of bells.

It was Christmas, of course. Was the sound coming from the church in the village? And yet it wasn't a Christmas service she thought of but a wedding, the lych-gate strewn not with snow but with garlands of flowers. She imagined Martha's pleasure when she cast off her mourning black, worn for the mistress she'd seen into her grave, instead donning the white gown she had so desired. She would take Ellis' arm and smile up at him as the sun shone high in the sky, burnishing the green slopes and warming all who stood in its light.

The bells were still ringing. Leah closed her eyes, thinking that the wedding scene didn't feel so much like a vision as a dream—

—and when she opened them again she was standing in the kitchen, *her* kitchen, except that the worktops were laden with food: there were dishes heaped with goose and pheasant, a large pie, tongue and other cold meats; boiled potatoes, boiled onions and braised cabbage; jellies, custards, blancmanges and mince pies. At the centre of it all was a fat roast turkey, golden and sizzling, fresh from the oven.

The ringing sounded once more, this time much nearer, jangling and insistent, drawing her attention to the wall where a row of little bells were hanging. One of them was jerking on its wire.

It wasn't a wedding but a summoning.

What had Martha said? *Don't forget the roasts, Martha, turkey and fowls, get them basted, get the puddings boiling, and always, her little bell ringing—*

Leah pulled her apron over her head, wiped her hands and threw it aside. Then she stared at the soiled, discarded thing on the floor. She had surely not been wearing an apron; she hadn't even seen it before, at least, not in the present. This belonged to the past; it was Martha's apron.

She looked down at her scalded and roughened hands. She was no longer seeing into Martha's life. She *was* Martha.

She strode out of the kitchen, leaving the food she'd been slaving over, all of her hard work, and burst through the door to the living room to see Ellis standing by the hearth, warming himself by the steadily crackling fire. He held out his hands to her as if he'd not noticed her expression, or perhaps ignoring it.

'Is everything ready, my little dove? Time yet for a kiss before our friends come back again for the feast.'

'A kiss!' She found herself scowling, hardly knowing what words she spoke. 'You think I've got time for such things? Don't you think I'm busy working my hands red for your precious friends?'

He tilted his head and looked at her. '*Your* hands, red—' He let the word hang in the air before he went on, 'And do you think I have an appetite to see them all here, to sit at the head of the table and smile while we all pretend that nothing has happened? Indeed, I wish I could withdraw the invitation. I would do so, out of respect for Isobel and the boy, but—'

'But you have to reward the hands that did your work.'

'*My* work?' His voice faded. 'But come now, Martha: we must all forget the past, must we not, and as quickly as we are able. Besides, this is tradition, and our tenants would surely think it a dreadful rudeness if we were to fail in our duty.'

'"Dreadful rudeness"?' Martha glared. 'Do you not think it rude to use me like this, as if I were nothing to you but cook, cleaner and scullery maid? I see to *every* need of yours, and yet you summon me with a bell like a common servant?'

His expression became thoughtful. 'But you *are* a servant, Martha.'

Everything stilled. She stared up at him and she did not blink.

Ellis looked away, shrugging his shoulders, almost as if he could brush her off, but when he next spoke, his tone was softer, appeasing. 'Things must be done as they have always been done – do you not see that? We are yet in danger. We do not wish to alert anyone to anything strange at Maitland Farm, do we? *Especially* now. I need you, my dove, truly. There is a masque to be performed and we must all don our guises.' He laughed and added, 'Besides, I have no other servant.'

'I can do owt that's needed, Ellis,' Martha said. 'By your side.'

He tossed his head. 'For shame, Martha! So soon? And your mistress barely dead, not even cold in her grave? They think I was paying suit to her, that I truly cared for her. Would you give us both away?'

'You'll dance with me, then. Call me into the room and dance with me in front of them all. It'll be like the party should have been. Even the mistress said it was for everyone together, servants as well as the gentlefolk.'

'To what purpose?' he said quietly. 'The mingling of society is only for a season; only for Christmas, when we celebrate together, as well you know. It cannot be so always.' He looked around the room and added wryly, 'Besides, it was easier for the master to mix with the servants when there was more than one of them left alive.'

It was her turn to fall silent. Then she rushed to him and threw her arms around his waist. 'Oh, Ellis, don't let us quarrel. They can't do owt to us – they made sure of that when they put their hands to the rope. They can't stand against us and they'll not keep us apart, not any longer. An' if they try it – why, I'll make more dolls! Burial dolls, that look like their own children. That'll rattle 'em. There's nowt I won't do.'

His expression darkened.

Dismay crept over her as she stared up at Ellis, wrapping her arms more tightly about him, pulling him closer.

Ellis stood taller, as if reminding himself that he was a gentleman and she a maid.

She said, 'They'll know better anyhow, when we are married.'

'*Married?*' Ellis echoed the word, his astonishment plain.

'Aye, married. Have you forgot the promise you made me?

You'd not have the other, you said, not for worlds. It was me you wanted. And – and I threw over an honest man for you an' all! Don't start making me think I chose the wrong one, Ellis Maitland.'

'An honest man – you, Martha?' He sounded incredulous. 'You do not mean Jack Hirst? You did a little more than jilt him, did you not? If he were offered the choice now, you or the rope, I dare say he'd prefer the rope.'

By his expression, if he could have made his choice a second time, it appeared he too might have chosen differently.

Her cheeks reddened under the scald of his words. She opened her mouth to speak, not knowing what she would say, but he raised a hand to stop her.

'There will always be a place for you here, Martha. As you said yourself, do not let us quarrel. After everything – well, some would cast you off, but I will always take care of you. I thought that much was clear. But to think it could be more than that—'

She met his incredulity with bitter fury. She did not shout; she did not need to. 'You are *nothing*, Ellis Maitland, nothing but what I made you. Are you forgetting how close you were to ruin? Drowning in debt, you were, and no means of holding your head up, not unless you did as I said. Cast off, you say? It's you would have been cast off, by Isobel Maitland and everybody else, all your fancy friends, if they'd known how badly you needed coin. Different now your pockets are full, is it? Well, not a single one of them would sit down with you if they knew how you went about getting it. They might be the ones who held the rope, but it's you what put it in their hand – and as for my poor mistress, it'd be different if they knew the truth of that an' all, wouldn't it? A killing kiss – they'd be talking of that from here to Lunnon Town.'

'Do not jest of such things with me, Martha.'

'Jest?' Her eyes narrowed and her hands cradled her full belly once more. 'Do you laugh at this, Ellis?'

'Laugh? Not at all. You were very obliging to me, were you not? And now I am the master I shall have the means of looking after it . . .' He paused and looked at her speculatively, before going on, 'Although from the way you speak of Jack Hirst, I wonder if that isn't his child in your belly, not mine.'

She stared, speechless, then curled her fingers into claws and flew at him. Ellis didn't give way before her but stepped forward and grasped her shoulders, then thrust her away from him.

She stumbled and fell at the foot of the Christmas tree, her expression disbelieving, then enraged. '*Jack's* bairn?' she said. 'Is that what you think?' She pushed herself to her feet, strode to the fire and caught up the poker, but she never had the chance to wield it. Ellis snatched it from her and swung it through the air, missing her ear by a hair's breadth.

She flinched at the rush of air and cried, 'You dare do that to—'

'Do I dare?' He reached out with his free hand and caught hold of her neck. 'Are you surprised at what I wouldn't dare, Martha? This is who I am: this is what you made me. I do not suppose either of us like it very much.'

She tried to step away, but he held her firmly, his hands clamped so tight around her neck that she couldn't move

– she couldn't even breathe. Leah dimly realised that it was she who was being strangled. She clawed at his fingers – and suddenly she was released.

She opened her mouth and heard Martha's voice emerge in a raspy croak. 'I chose wrong. He would have *never*—'

'Aye, well, perhaps you did at that. I believe you are right: Jack Hirst would never have listened to you. He would never have put a rope around an innocent man's neck. He would never have been driven to such madness – he would *never* have buried an axe in the child's—' Ellis' voice broke and his gaze dropped.

'What of it? You'll have your own son now.'

'I don't deserve a son. Do you think I could hold a son in these hands?'

Leah's head was suddenly yanked upwards, grabbed by her hair. Her vision blurred with tears.

'I dare say it is his brat growing in your belly, come for revenge on me,' Ellis spat. 'Will he have his father's eyes, do you think?'

The next moment Leah was thrown to the floor, striking her elbow on the stone hearth, sending a jagged bolt of pain shooting to her shoulder. It was no use telling herself this wasn't real, that it was in the past, like images on a screen, or that she was safe – that it wasn't even happening to her. She wasn't safe. She was no longer an unseen observer. The boundaries were failing; the past and the present were here together, in this room. What was happening to Martha was happening to her too.

A slap across her cheek rocked her head back. She heard

Martha's cry on her lips even as she felt a new pain, a sharp stab that started deep in her belly and reached even deeper into her, and then it jagged through her again, so bad that she could not stop a second cry. This time the sound was lower, wordless.

She reached to wrap her arms protectively around her belly and felt a kick into her side. Someone was sobbing like a child; she realised it was her. Then the blows ceased and there was silence.

At last someone spoke. Ellis asked, 'What *are* you?'

She tried to roll over, peering up through her hair to see his face staring into hers. His eyes were narrowed, as if he might be able to see past the surface of her to whatever lay beneath. Was he seeing Martha – or her?

Another gripe tore through her belly and curling into a ball, she clutched at it. What had he done to her?

His hands grabbed her shoulders, pressing her down, and he said, '*Who* are you?'

She no longer knew. She let out a moan, one that didn't sound like her, couldn't possibly be her. She could feel the heat of the fire at her back, too close and too intense, but it was nothing to the heat inside her.

She twisted under Ellis, trying to get loose, as a warm, liquid rush went through her. She felt it leaving her body, dampening her thighs.

But Ellis' face was drawing away – he was letting her go – he was rising to his feet. He hadn't finished with her, she knew that, but for now he grasped the poker and began to strike the great beam over the fireplace, over and over again, lost to his rage.

She grasped blindly at her shirt, praying to feel its touch rather than Martha's faded print dress, and she found there the edge of a pocket. Reaching into it, she touched a familiar shape and pulled free the leaf of mistletoe that had somehow created a doorway between them, a withered berry still clinging to its stem. The pinpricks forming Ellis' initials were like Braille under her fingers.

Ellis had stopped attacking the mantelpiece. He loomed over her, staring down at her hands, looking at the leaf she had once presented to him as the symbol of their union.

No: not *their* union. That was Martha—

Leah twisted away from him, ignoring the pain still tearing through her belly. Now she couldn't see his eyes. There was only the fire, its flames licking towards her, its heat blossoming against her cheek. She jerked her hand towards it, thinking for a moment that the leaf was too light. Surely it would dance away from the warmth, drifting on the rising air, and for an instant it did – but then, with a rush, it was drawn in and the flames took it. The desiccated thing ignited at once. With absolute clarity, she saw the black rot at the heart of each pinprick start to spread – and in the next moment, the leaf had gone.

Leah looked around at a silent room. Ellis – and Martha – had vanished. There was only dust spiralling to the floor where they had been. The walls were crumbling, the furnishings gone, all but the settle and the threadbare armchair. There was no sign that anybody lived here at all, save for the Christmas tree standing in the corner. It had no lights and its branches were dark, but there were decorations hanging from them and they were her own.

She pushed herself up, half expecting to see blood pouring from her, spreading across the floor. She pressed a hand to her belly, then tested her arm, but there was nothing: no blood, no bruises, no tender skin, no discomfort. The pain had gone. But then, the pain had not been hers.

Leah had been so afraid – of the ghosts and what this place had to show her, but most of all of the thought that it was inside her too: that she was descended from Martha and Ellis' child. But there had been no child, of that she was certain. She had felt it slipping from her as if from her own body.

Leah stared into the silence. Should she be glad? But she could feel no triumph; only sadness remained. She wondered if the maid, long in the past, was still lying by the hearth, still clinging to her leaf of mistletoe, young and vibrant, yet entirely useless.

All Martha's efforts had been for nothing after all. She would never be the mistress here; her child would never be the heir. She had not even been able to keep hold of Ellis. She might have won his kisses but his love had been less easy to hold on to.

'Ellis must have started again,' she whispered to the empty room. Once the farm was his, he would easily have found someone of his own station to marry him, for he would have been a man of means – and a tragic figure, having lost his first love and her son. He must have had more children, for Leah carried his blood in her veins.

But not Martha's.

It might only be half a reprieve, but a little hope was better than none at all, wasn't it?

As she sat there, she felt the chill of winter rising from the stone flags, through her spine and into her bones. Even the air had turned cold. There were no cheering Christmas lights, no orange glow in the hearth. The heat coming from behind her had faded; the fire looked as if it had long since gone out.

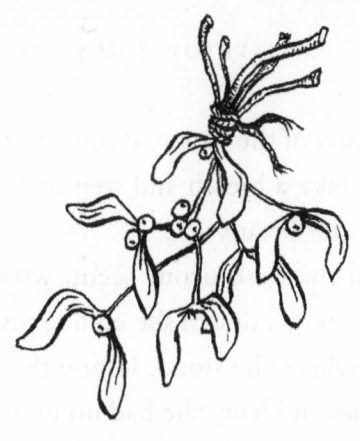

Chapter Sixteen

In the afternoon of Christmas Day, Leah stepped outside to see a world transformed. It was snowing again, but not as she had seen it before. These were no grudging pinprick flakes, nor the thick white drift so beloved of children, nor even wet, driving sleet. This was entirely magical.

The sun's rays shimmered everywhere, the light seeming to rise from the ground rather than falling from the sky. The flakes were fine but the air was so full of them they created a glowing mist, drawing veils that shifted and re-formed in a moment, obscuring everything. Forms danced within, becoming almost distinct before being hidden once more, so that it looked like there were figures out there in the snow, but Leah knew there was no one; her ghosts had been banished at last.

She walked into the field, wondering if she would vanish

too, becoming a part of the dance. If only everything were so easy; if she could take a breath and step out and lose herself in it, seeing only the beauty . . .

She breathed in the fresh ozone scent, wondering if there was some message in it, a design she could sense but not quite see. She stopped where she stood, letting the flakes settle on her skin and clothes and hair. She had no idea where she was. She'd been aiming for the exact centre of the field, but she realised it didn't matter – it might be better if she didn't see, if she could never again stand in the same spot and think, *here*.

But the snow was kind. It would keep its secrets. When it melted, the past would finally be gone, along with everyone who had lived within it.

She took hold of the larger object she had been carrying so carefully. It was the urn which belonged to Josh. Leah wanted to picture his face, but no matter how she tried, he was still as she had found him: suspended in the air, his eyes turned away from her.

She let go of a long, unsteady breath. It felt as if she'd been holding it for weeks, months.

Slowly, she unscrewed the lid. A tendril of ash escaped from it, snatched at once by the snow, as if it had been waiting. Leah felt she should say something, perhaps a prayer, but there were no words left in her. Instead, she remembered another day when she had been swathed in white: not snow, but a lace wedding gown. She remembered the way he had smiled when she put her hand in his. And, a few years later, how he looked when she told him Finn was growing inside her. Finn had been a stranger then; she hadn't yet seen his face, but she had known him more intimately than she had ever known herself.

She tilted the urn and let the wind take her husband. She had imagined the ash settling on the snow, something to blank out the memory of the blood that had been spilled, but it was gone at once.

She unzipped her jacket and took out the smaller urn she had been carrying next to her heart. She didn't think of Finn's face or the last time she had seen him or the smell of his skin and hair, nor did she think of his unfathomable absence. What she thought of was the teddy bear they had both so loved, looking out of the window as if awaiting his master's return. But she knew now that Finn would not return. He was never coming back.

Leah bowed her head. Now that the moment had come, she couldn't do it. It had been so easy in her mind's eye – opening the lid, shedding a tear as she spread his ashes over the field. She had pictured him standing out there watching, perhaps alongside Samuel Maitland; the two boys even playing together, throwing snowballs at each other and laughing.

In her memory, Finn was always laughing.

Leah stood still as the wind rose and buffeted her. She couldn't see Finn in the shapes it made of the falling snow; of course she didn't. Whatever spirits had walked in this place had left her and now she had to allow her own ghosts to rest. She had seen enough of the past. She had to let go.

It was almost New Year. The days were growing longer, the sun returning to the earth.

Leah mouthed words that were only for her son as she tilted

the urn and released Finn's ashes. They flowed away from her, a new shape borne on the wind; then he too was gone.

Maybe they all belonged here, now: Josh and Finn and her, together. Maybe that would allow this place to be renewed: not a sacrifice, but a gift.

Would the land take what she had given and burst into new life? Would fresh green emerge from the earth, new blossom from the trees? Now that the past had been laid to rest, would the place entrusted with their memories recover?

Would she?

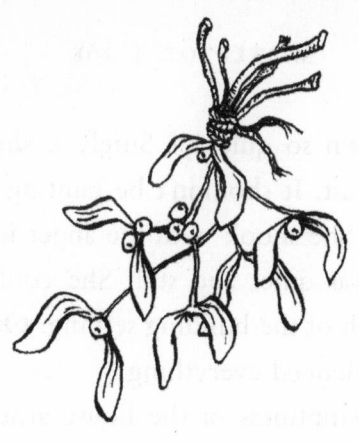

Chapter Seventeen

And yet when Leah went inside, the mistletoe had spread. It had gripped the mantelpiece even more tightly and was inching across the walls, like the branches of an espaliered tree. The plaster was cracking where it was thrusting its roots into the house – into *her* house. It had twined about the mirror, penetrating each carved loop and whorl in the frame. She could no longer see the holly and ivy; they were already drowned.

And it had found its way to the Christmas tree. Pale stems had pierced the trunk and wrapped about its branches, choking the lights. Leah began pulling it away from her ornaments, freeing the little snowman, the rocking horse her son had so loved: it had no right to touch these things. They were *hers*.

She let the broken strands of mistletoe fall to the floor.

How had it grown so quickly? Surely it should have died along with the past. It shouldn't be tainting her life or her things, not now. She shook with the anger inside her – and yet everything was quiet and still. She couldn't even hear the rustle and sigh of the building settling. Outside, no birds sang; the snow silenced everything.

Leah felt the emptiness of the house around her. There were no ghosts left, but their absence hadn't brought the place to life – and nor had Leah, because she wasn't living, was she? She had cut herself off from the life she'd had, from her work and her friends, the people who had cared for her, and from the beginnings of the new life she'd planned to build. She'd even banished her new friends, rejecting the living for the dead, and now the dead had abandoned her too. A Maitland had returned to the farm, the cursed branch of a cursed family, and there could be no life, no colour, nothing that might turn this place into a home.

For a moment, she almost wished she hadn't destroyed Ellis' leaf. Wasn't the company of ghosts preferable to nothing at all?

She went to the window and looked out across the frozen field. She had finally laid her husband and son to rest. They couldn't be closer than that, but they had never felt so distant. Now it didn't feel so much a gift as a surrendering, giving to the land the last precious thing she had. But it hadn't been enough, and here was the proof, for only mistletoe could find nourishment in such a place.

Leah took a sprig in her hand and turned it, letting the light shine through the milky berries. The leaves were soft and new against her hands, so unlike the dried-out remnants from the past she had found. What had Martha suggested? That the leaves were for the man: they were like a woman, their almost ovarian shape ready to receive him – and the berries were meant for the woman, carrying his potency. The woman must eat one for every kiss she had received.

Leah swallowed, tasting bitterness on her tongue. How many kisses had she received in her lifetime? There had been so many – Josh meeting her at the door, pulling her into a hug made all the warmer by his thick woollen sweater, or stealing a moment, putting his arms around her while Finn was occupied elsewhere. Josh, holding a sprig of mistletoe over their heads and laughing. Josh in their bed, sliding his hand along her back, his touch so light it made her shiver . . .

And Leah *did* shiver, feeling another touch, one that had come to her in the night, but this one so cold. Could that really have been Jack Hirst, seeking all the kisses he could no longer have? Had he come for revenge against the last of the Maitland line – or had it been Ellis, climbing into bed next to her, as he would with his wife? He must have married again, after all; perhaps that was where he'd slept, not wishing to take Isobel's room, where he'd been hoping to lie with her: the woman he had murdered, mother of a dead son. And always cold, so cold . . .

Leah swallowed again, the back of her throat clogging as she did, and she forced herself not to cough. Isobel had only eaten one berry – surely not sufficient to end anyone else's life, but with her *aversion*, her allergy, it had been enough. Did that mean she had only ever received one kiss, the one meant to kill her?

She let the sprig fall and reached up to pluck another. This too was laden with berries, full and ripe, each one a lost kiss. She pulled one from the stem and raised it before her face. She opened her lips – and realised what she was doing.

Had she been *eating* the berries? She cast the sprig away. How many had she swallowed?

She glanced around the room. Nothing had changed – but somehow *everything* had.

The house was no longer empty.

Leah had told herself that her ghosts were gone, but someone was here. She could feel them watching her.

She searched once more, expecting at any moment to feel a breath on the back of her neck, to hear the whisper of a voice, but still she couldn't see them.

Her hand went to her pocket, although she didn't know why, for the leaves she had found a lifetime ago were gone: one crumbled into dust, the other consumed in a fire that had burned more than a hundred years ago. Their story had been told; there was nothing left.

And yet she slipped her fingers inside and felt – not the dry curve of a leaf, but caught in the very corner, a small rounded object, hard as a pebble.

She pulled it out and held it up before her eyes. It was withered and dried and long since dead, but she knew what it was. This berry had been plucked and discarded so very long ago but she knew whose hand had taken it, whose lips had received all the kisses it represented.

She remembered finding it in the wardrobe. This berry must have parted from its stem – and she had forgotten it.

The berries – well, they're meant for the woman.

It was *Martha's* berry – and she had been wearing it next to her heart this whole time.

She thought about all the visions she had seen. The boy had been called back to her by the doll. Jack had come in answer to the leaf bearing his initials and Ellis had been close by, connected to her by the second leaf. But Isobel had been there too – and Martha, closer than any of them: two berries; two women. She must have burned Isobel's berry along with the leaf the woman had marked with Ellis' initials, but Martha's had remained.

And Martha had orchestrated everything. She had encouraged Ellis to court her mistress, and to slip the fatal berry between her lips. Her hands had held Samuel down on a bench meant for slaughtering while Ellis took his life. And she had set up an innocent man and watched as he suffered the punishment meant for her and her lover.

Leah looked down at her own hands, sensing again the touch of a child's frail neck under her fingers, remembering how it had felt as if she had been strangling him herself. How could she have done such a thing? She grimaced. It had felt as if Martha had been there, not with her or watching her, but *inside* her. And she remembered the pain in her belly as Ellis had kicked her, as if she in turn had been inside Martha.

She had always been so *close*.

Leah shut her eyes, still tasting the berries on her tongue. Had that been Martha too, making her take them one by one? She hadn't even realised what she was doing. And the berries were a conduit, opening the doorway between them; that was how Martha's ghost had come to her – but how many times? Had Martha in turn been watching her while she slept and ate and worked? Was she there even when Leah thought herself alone?

What is it you have made of me, Martha? That's what Ellis had asked her.

What had she made of them all? Leah remembered Isobel's words: she had said, '*See how you carry your point, Martha.*' For the girl had prevailed on her mistress too, persuading her to bring mistletoe into the house, to take part in her ritual using its leaves. And Ellis had succumbed to her charms, but had it been more than that?

You little witch, he'd said. *Did you cast a spell on me?*

Perhaps she had.

Moving as if she was still lost in a dream, unable to stop herself, Leah raised her hand and looked at the ancient withered berry before placing it between her lips. She waited as the taste of dust spread slowly across her tongue.

Then she walked over to the fireplace, but she did not touch the mistletoe. Instead, she reached up for the mirror. Dragging leaf and stem along with it, she lifted it away from the wall. It was heavy, but she managed to turn it and hung it again, this time face outwards.

That was the way it had been, the way she always remembered it, though the once-spotless surface was dull and grimed with dirt, the glass scarred where the silvering had peeled away. The front of the frame was ornate, with a carved design of twisting leaves, not of mistletoe, but of apples.

She stared for a moment at her own reflection.

Then someone knocked at the door.

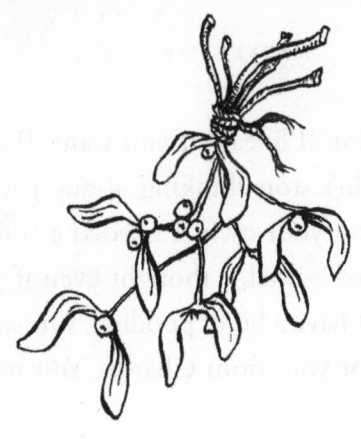

Chapter Eighteen

A man was standing on the step, holding his coat tightly around his neck against the snow. She did not need to delve deep to find a name, for she could see it in his face, in the prominent bones of his cheeks, the auburn hair darkened with damp: *Drew.*

He wore a tentative, almost foolish expression as he stood there clutching something in one hand. He held it out to her like an offering: a bowl of plum pudding, or at least a slice of it, the domed crust half covered in custard long since gone cold.

The snow falling all around him feathered the man's – *Drew's* – hair and coat. It swept into the hall, the flakes briefly bright against the dull stone.

'I know you've made your mind up.' He spoke rapidly, as if he had a speech prepared and wanted to say it all before she could stop him. 'I'll leave if you want. But it's Christmas Day and I couldn't stop thinking about you. I mean, you being out here, on your own. I needed a walk so I thought I'd come over, and – well, I thought even if you don't want dinner you might have a bit of pudding. Oh, and I've brought something else for you, from Charlie. You never did get his present.'

She did not speak, only opened the door wider and gestured for him to come inside. He did, and as he stamped his feet, sending more snow scattering across the floor, she felt a stab of irritation: no one ever gave any thought to the person who'd have to sweep it all up, then polish the stains away, did they? But then she smiled. *She* didn't have to, did she? She was the mistress now.

She took the bowl from him while he took off his coat, sending more droplets to the floor. 'Sorry,' he said as he hung it over the newel post. She continued to watch him in silence while he rummaged in his pocket, then held out something else: a piece of paper.

She took it and unfolded it. He'd given her a picture, clumsily drawn and crumpled at the edges. It showed a man, a woman and a boy building a snowman. The boy was frozen in the act of reaching up to put something around its neck. She supposed it was a scarf, though it looked a little like a twist of rope.

She smiled, folding it again, and nodded her thanks.

'So,' he said, 'what did Santa bring you? Did you get many presents?'

'Oh, yes,' she replied after a moment. 'Many.'

She gave him a warm smile, then gestured towards the living room. She followed him inside and as he perched on the settle, she glimpsed that figure in the mirror again – her own reflection. Her lips twisted.

'Are you all right?' the man – *Andrew*, that was it, not Drew; she must remember that – asked.

'Yes.' She stared into his face, recognising the features that ran in his family; she had known them at once, though this man's cheekbones were even more prominent, his eyes softer. He shifted under her stare and she forced herself to look away, saying, 'I'm better than I've been for a long time.'

He didn't answer her but he looked awkward as he pinned his hands between his knees and glanced around. He took in the Christmas tree, tilting back his head to see the star, then frowned at the mistletoe around the fireplace. Had he noticed that it was actually growing there, where nothing should grow? But all he said was, 'You've trimmed up, I see.'

She nodded. He had large hands, she noticed, lightly freckled on the back, the fingers neat and well-formed. He was a tall man, taller than his predecessor, and broad across the shoulders, although the way he held himself diminished that. She should have him stand straighter. She pulled her own spine straight, feeling the weakness in muscles that were unused to such a rigid posture. But then, she wore no corsets – she would change that, too; she could change everything.

She shook her head to clear it. Then she looked at the bowl of plum pudding in her hand.

'Wait here,' she said, and walked over to the fireplace. She set the bowl down before reaching out to the mistletoe and choosing a sprig, which she ran between her fingers. It took only a moment to select a large leaf and pluck it. A plump berry fell and rolled across the floor, but that didn't matter, not now; she didn't need it.

Andrew looked alarmed – did he expect her to lean across and hold the leaf over his head? – but she cast another smile in his direction, picked up the bowl and walked out of the door.

The kitchen was all wrong. She stared in shock at the broken wall that had once been the pantry. The range, so good for boiling and baking, had gone too, along with the welcome heat it had given. There were no shining copper saucepans hanging from the rack, nor bright dish-covers; there was no china on the shelves. At least the old deal table remained, so she set down the pudding after pausing to run her finger over the scars in the wooden surface. She recognised some of them, recalling the knife strokes that had caused them. But the wood had been allowed to dry and crack, the stains now spreading through the grain beyond anything that scrubbing with salt and water might do.

She pulled open drawers until she found what she sought: a narrow-bladed paring knife ending in a sharp point. She set down the leaf and tilted her head, considering where to begin, before holding the knife against the flesh and pressing down. Sap oozed from the wound she had made, viscous as blood. As she repositioned the knife the first mark was already turning black. A second joined it, then another. A short horizontal bar was followed by a longer vertical, then a curve: the letter J.

J was for Jack. J was for the man she should have chosen, the one who would have cared for her, who would have done anything for her. He might not have been able to turn her head with riches or hold out the promise of a life of ease – though in time, perhaps she would have been able to change all of that too – and he could never have made her the mistress of Maitland Farm. But with Jack, the child in her belly could have lived. And he had been a handsome man, a strong man, a man who would have loved her always. He would never have spilled the blood of a child: not Isobel's son, and not her own.

She closed her eyes, remembering, and her lip twitched, as if dismissing some small confusion.

Her berry had called her back to this place; it had given her another chance to live, but she had plucked that berry with her own hand, when she was young and strong, long ago. Would this leaf – a new leaf – really be the same? She reached inside herself, seeing memories rise before her like pictures in a book: her, curtseying to her mistress, telling her of the old stories, about the spell she wished to weave. She'd selected a hatpin tipped with a lustrous pearl, and saw her hands pricking out the initials – not those of Ellis, who had spurned her, but those of the man who should have been hers.

Then she'd stitched the two little bags from scraps of material, slipped a leaf into one – and cast the other aside, concealing it at the very back of her mistress' wardrobe. Later, in her despair, her plan to take Isobel Maitland's place in ruin, she had returned. Her hands had been shaking with pain, clinging to another leaf – and she had relinquished that too, knowing it had never been hers. She had put it in place with the first, nothing now but a symbol of lost love, entwined with its twin.

And new memories came: soft, unworked hands tearing out old wood, ripping up floor coverings, scrubbing away the dirt ingrained over so many years; delving into the wardrobe and finding the leaf, the one she had fashioned when she still had all her hopes and poured them into it: the one that had always been meant for Jack.

She slipped the new, useless leaf into her pocket, abandoned the knife and looked around for other tools. She recognised the heavy crowbar Jack had always kept in the barn, not only out of place in her kitchen but misshapen and filthy, looking as if it had been used to chip away at something hard as iron. She picked it up and walked into the hall.

'I shan't be a minute,' she called out, and without waiting for an answer she walked upstairs, running her hand along the balustrade. It felt so different, grime embedded in the grain instead of smooth with polish as it had been.

She was no longer surprised to find Isobel's bedchamber different too. She opened the door to reveal nothing but an empty shell, the light from the window falling across exposed floorboards greyed with time. The rag rugs she had so laboured over were gone, as was the bed. How many times had she removed its heavy draperies and beaten them until the dust was flying and her arms aching? The washstand was missing too, also the cause of so much labour: hauling fresh water upstairs to fill the ewer, removing the slops and scrubbing out the chamber pot, carefully cleaning all those little bowls. Even the dresser she had spent long hours polishing until the good dark mahogany shone had vanished.

She had thought that dresser would pass from Isobel to her, along with all her trinkets: the silver-backed brush and mirror she had so coveted every time she dusted them, the little jar of fragrant ointment, the pretty pins and ivory combs. Whenever the mistress wasn't there to chide her she would spend a moment running her fingers over her things, waiting for the day when she would have the right to open the carved jewellery box and choose between the garnets and the opals. But that was never to happen now, for she had been betrayed.

Her eyes hardened, but she waved that thought away. Those weren't the things she needed; bitter memories and dust were not what she had come for.

She strode to the place where these hands – *her* hands now – had crumbled Jack's leaf into dust. When she peered down through the floorboards, she half expected to see his dark eyes looking back at her, but of course there was nothing . . . not yet.

She set the iron crowbar to a gap in the boards and leaned on the metal, trying to prise one of them up, but the wood gave all at once with a sharp crack as a piece broke away. She slipped the edge into the wider gap and started again, and now she was no longer troubling to be careful, it took only a minute more.

A short while later she entered the living room again, carrying two bowls in front of her, a smile written across her features. Andrew twisted towards her, his face creased with concern. 'Are you all right? I thought I heard a noise.'

'It's quite all right. Forgive me. I just 'ad a little task to carry out, but it's done now.' She smiled brightly as she passed him one of the bowls and he took it from her.

'I've already had some.' He looked rueful. 'I'm stuffed. What did you have for dinner? Cath did us the works. I don't think Charlie's going to move for a month.'

Her smile widened. 'Charlie.' She nodded towards the folded paper she'd left on the table. 'The one who did that. How old is 'e?'

'He's eleven.' Andrew looked surprised by her question. 'He doesn't like drawing that much these days, not really. You're lucky.'

'Yes, I am.' She spooned pudding into her mouth as if showing him what to do, smiling broadly, although she was thinking about the boy. No doubt he would resemble Andrew and all his line: rough, red-haired men, bred to the land, the son of a son of a son, and all carrying the blood of one of them who had gathered that day to murder Jack Hirst. They might have done it in response to the story she had told, she and Ellis, but *they* had done it, not her. Jack Hirst was their friend, their neighbour, and yet they had killed him without a thought, without any heed for the law or the justice they so claimed to crave.

And here was Drew's descendant: Drew, who had placed the rope about Jack Hirst's neck. What could be more fitting?

Only herself, perhaps, since she had already taken Ellis Maitland's descendant; the last remnant of his line. She bit back the laughter that rose to her lips at the thought of Ellis, the man who had so willingly taken her body and her counsel, who, acting on her will, had become a master – and who had then so brutally rejected her, not just spurning her love, but destroying the life she carried in her belly. Well, now she possessed the life belonging to Ellis' seed – surely the perfect revenge.

She tightened her fingers about the bowl, bowing her head as if to sniff the plum pudding, concealing her mirth. All of a sudden she could see these same fingers wrapped around a young boy's neck. For an instant his face changed: he was no longer Samuel Maitland but a younger version of this man sitting opposite her. *Charlie.* The little artist was a Slater, too, wasn't he?

She blinked away the image and instead focused on her fingers. Her hands were only a little chapped, as if they had been doused in freezing water or frozen in the snow. They were not so red and rough as she was accustomed to seeing; already, she had the hands of a mistress, not a maid. For now, she pushed that thought aside and softened the smile she wore.

'This is delicious,' she said. 'Go on, have some with me, please. Just a mouthful to keep me company – I never did like to eat alone.'

Obedient to her word, Andrew bent his head to the bowl and started on the pudding. It was stone cold and she had stirred it into a nondescript mess, the only way to conceal what she had mixed in among the dried fruit and spices: the fragments of Jack Hirst's leaf, recovered as best she could from the dust beneath the floorboards of Isobel Maitland's room.

He didn't appear at first to notice anything amiss, until he went to speak and instead found himself stopping short, staring blankly as a puzzled expression spread across his face.

She said, 'There always used to be tokens in the Twelfth Night cake – that's what we used to have when we were little. Do you remember that?'

He shook his head, looking even more confused.

'We had a pea for the queen, a clove for a knave, a rag for a slut, a forked stick for a cuckold, and a bean – whoever found that was king of 'em all for the day.' She leaned towards him. His expression still hadn't changed. 'I don't know if there were ever a token for the hanged man. Do you – *Jack*?'

He shifted as if something was troubling him, then bent over the bowl again and started rapidly spooning the pudding into his mouth. His neck muscles bulged, as if he was having to force it down. He didn't speak, didn't look at her.

She could *feel* him; she thought she could almost see him, walking across the snow, his dark figure emerging from under the apple trees, just as he had always been: his hair hanging in his face, his gait slouching, almost awkward, but with such strength in his limbs – such *life*.

Jack Hirst: emerging from the orchard that had become his grave. The mistletoe, the only thing that would grow in such ground, had whispered his secrets and preserved his strength until it was his time to return, life giving way to death and death once more to life. It had carried his soul.

Would he come to her draped in its leaves, ready to take back everything that should have been his – ready to receive her kiss?

He had never known the part she had played in what had happened, and of course he never would know – only that she had loved him enough to call him to her down the years.

Andrew, still sitting on the settle, raised his head from his bowl, which he had scraped clean. He looked dazed, but a new expression was beginning to form somewhere deep in his eyes. He opened his lips, flinching as he spoke, as if the voice didn't quite belong to him, and said, 'Martha?'

She smiled and took his hand, pressing it to her cheek. She drew him to his feet so that he was standing beside her in front of the fireplace. This was the very place where Ellis had turned on her, where she had lost everything. Now she would regain it all.

They had come home. Maitland Farm belonged to that family no more. It was theirs now.

She gestured at the mirror and they stood there caught within its frame: two figures, one sure and smiling, the other just beginning to understand. There was little wonder if he was awed by the mystery of it. He had been sleeping so long, and both of them were entirely changed from who they had once been.

They had travelled so very far to be together.

For a moment she thought she glimpsed something else in the depths of the mirror, another form that coalesced before dissolving and slipping away from her, shifting and elusive like snow forming and re-forming on the breeze.

She peered into it, trying to make out what was hidden there, but it was nothing. No one else was near. No one would come to trouble them.

She reached out and picked up the boy's drawing. She saw again what was pictured there, a man, woman and child: *a family*. She had already replaced the woman in the picture, and so easily. Jack would stand in the place of the man. And the boy too could be replaced in time, or got rid of if need be; for certain he would never be the heir to Maitland Farm.

She put a hand to her belly. It was empty now but it had borne fruit before and it would again – it might even be that her own child could also live again, life following from death, if the right sacrifice were made.

She looked at the unnatural growth of mistletoe wrapping the mirror that framed their faces. Jack's eyes shone from Andrew's features. He had swallowed down the ancient fragments without murmur or complaint, as if he had known what was meant to be. Now she would present him with the leaf she had made just for him.

She took the fresh mistletoe marked with the letter J from her pocket. When she held it up she could see how vibrantly alive it was. It had rooted here, in their home, growing in spite of everything that stood against it. She held it over their heads and he leaned in towards her, obedient to its call. Other than to pronounce her name, he still hadn't spoken – he hadn't yet proclaimed his love – but there would be time enough for that. For now, she only wanted his kiss.

Then something made her draw away from him. Her gaze snapped back to the mirror, but there was nothing there; only the dull shifting of veils in its white gleam, and the sense of a presence – then it was gone. She peered over her own reflection's shoulder, but she realised it wasn't behind her but *in* her. She could sense it flickering there, feel it like an itch under her skin.

Someone was watching her from her own eyes.

She stared down at the leaf. The letter she had marked on its surface was familiar to her, of course it was – and yet somehow strange memories rose, moments that did not belong to her. The man reaching out for her, kissing her, was not Ellis, nor Jack. She could not place him. She closed her eyes, trying to *remember*, once again feeling that itch at the back of her mind, but what she saw was a body hanging from a rope, turning a little one way, then the other. But the hanged man was not in the barn; this was somewhere strange to her.

She felt there was something she should know, something she must see. Another memory came: her hands carving the letter into the mistletoe leaf, using the knife she'd found in the kitchen. But then she'd stopped, overwhelmed with the sudden certainty that it wouldn't work, because this wasn't Jack's leaf at all.

Josh.

The name on her lips was strange and yet familiar, like a taste she had known as a child and hadn't experienced in a long time – like the Twelfth Night cake her mother had used to make, so redolent of Christmas, of hearty dinners in wavering candlelight, everyone safe and happy, everyone together.

Family: a man, a woman and a child.

She wondered why that clumsy drawing kept coming back to her; why it seemed to mean everything to her, although when she tried to read its meaning it was a different man she saw, another child.

Suddenly she pushed Jack away from her, Jack in the body that belonged to Drew – no, *Andrew*, that was his name, wasn't it?

For a moment he shook his head as if waking, but he didn't awaken, not really. He only stared at her as if he didn't know who she was.

Did *she* even know?

The light had grown uncertain and strange. Outside, the snow had become a whirling torrent, no longer a mist of delicate flakes but a violent mob hurling itself against the glass.

There was something in the snow.

She didn't know where the thought had come from but she turned from Andrew and strode into the hall. She grasped the door handle, but when she pulled it open, snow flew into her face and she was enveloped by a rush of icy air that flurried around her, covering her hair with feathery flakes. She welcomed it, reaching out her arms, closing her eyes.

Finn.

That was the name she had sought – the one that was like home. And J – that was for *Josh.*

Family.

The names rose easily to her lips but they were immediately snatched away. She could see only a short distance before the world was drowned in the cascade of snowflakes. They glowed with a light coming from everywhere and nowhere at once, not from the sun or the moon or reflected from the ground, but from *within* the snow, or beyond it; perhaps from some other world entirely.

It grew brighter, each particle illuminated with sudden clarity, and something moved: a figure that seemed to dissolve when she peered directly at it, only to take form again a little closer than before.

No: *two* figures.

Her heart faltered. She couldn't catch her breath. She heard footsteps behind her, Jack or Andrew, she didn't know which, and anyway, she wasn't looking for him.

Feeling detached from everything, she grasped at the doorframe as if she could hold on to it – the farm, the land, her very presence here – just as if it all couldn't be swept away in a moment. She sensed the earth's turning, the clock's hand ticking inexorably forward, one season passing into the next. She was floating in the storm of snowflakes, no longer anchored to anything. She never really had been, had she?

But she felt the tie connecting her to the shapes that were walking towards her from out of the snow.

She remembered stepping into the white field, such a short time before, carrying all she had left of them; watching their ashes mingle with the snowflakes.

Is that why they have returned to me? Is that what called them back?

But no, she didn't think so. They needed no physical thing to draw them to her for she had tried so many times, running her fingers through those very ashes, clinging to Finn's toys, holding Finn's bear close to her – and none of that had worked. But they were here now, when she needed them.

And suddenly she knew they had been with her all along, in each breath, in every step she took, in every memory – in every thought that entered her mind, for they were a family.

Josh, Finn and her: Leah.

Leah. That was her name, nothing else. She was not Martha; that was a name that belonged only to the past.

Leah stepped into the snow. She could almost see their faces, for all it had been so long since she last looked into them. Finn's had always stayed with her, vivid in every detail, clear as a photograph; but of Josh she had seen nothing and she was suddenly afraid. It had been turned away from her even in her dreams. Now she shrank at the thought of what she might see in his eyes.

Still she reached out towards her husband and son, who had not abandoned her or left her entirely alone. They burned more brightly with each moment, burning *them* away, Martha and Jack, the remnants of a past that was long buried and would soon be forgotten.

Then she did see his face, though she no longer knew if her eyes were open or closed, or if the moisture on her skin was tears or melting snow.

His expression was full of love. There was nothing else hidden there: no fear, no anger, no hurt, no blame. His eyes were as warm as she had always known them. He'd smiled down at her that same way when they gave themselves to each other, when they declared their love, when they made their son . . .

And finally, something tore free inside her, some last clinging connection with what had gone before. There was no pain, only lightness; she was warm to her fingertips. She hadn't known how deeply the cold had rooted in her, twining about her bones, until it began to let her go. It could not last, not with the warmth of her family near her, their kisses in the snowflakes that moulded themselves to her eyelids and cheeks and lips. For an instant she felt fingers wrapped around her own, the clutch of a little hand; then it was gone.

She realised she was still holding the mistletoe leaf just as it was whipped from her fingers, taken by the wind. Snow was flying everywhere, into her eyes and mouth, and she couldn't see anything at all. When her vision cleared, only the snow remained.

She put her hands to her face as if in memory of a kiss. She would always have that; even when nothing but snow touched her cheek, it could never be taken from her. Letting go of the past had not been enough. She had needed to remember what *life* was – and she *had* remembered. The love they had shared would remain. It had been there all along, if only she could have seen it, and she knew that it would be enough: not even ghosts could fight it.

She had thought Martha strong, but she was not; her feelings were weak. Her love had meant nothing, its roots shallow and quickly uprooted. Martha could never reach out to Leah again. She couldn't steal her breath or her warmth or a single minute more of her life if Leah did not let her – and she would not, because Leah hadn't finished living it.

A hand reached out and closed about her arm, drawing her back into the hall before pushing the door closed against the freezing wind. As if they had been suspended in the air

by some thread that had suddenly been cut, the snowflakes
billowing inside fell to the floor.

Leah turned to Andrew. There was an odd light shining
in his eyes, one she didn't like, but he didn't say a word.
She put her hands to his cheeks to find they were bitterly
cold, like the hall, her whole house. Why had she let it
grow so cold?

She said his name – and again, softly, as if trying to wake
him, and he stirred but still did not reply. She called to him
again, more forcefully, wanting to draw him back from wherever Martha had sent him, and this time he put out a hand
and steadied himself against the wall. His gaze sharpened and
he glanced about, recognition returning to his eyes.

He looked bewildered when he gazed at her and she
realised her hands were still clasped about his face. Another
memory rushed upon her: the kiss he had given her when
they'd stood beneath the mistletoe, and his sister's words: *Did
he have that effect?*

She let her hands fall.

He opened his mouth but still didn't speak; it seemed
he didn't know what to say. He looked around again, as if
trying to remember what had happened. His gaze took in
the snow that had blown into the house and around the hall,
the shadows darkening each corner.

Finally, he said, 'This is a strange place.'

'It was,' Leah said softly, 'but I think all of that's done now,
Andrew. It's only a house.'

'A home?' He raised his eyebrows with a wry smile, but
there were other meanings hidden in his gaze, as if he was

wondering if that was what Leah would make of it; if that was what she even wanted. Whether she would stay.

These were questions she couldn't answer, not yet, but she reached out and caught his arm and led him back into the living room. Even with the Christmas tree it was a little dismal, although she could soon build the fire and have its glow darting about the walls. She would turn on the Christmas lights too. She had half expected – or hoped – that the mistletoe would have vanished, but it was still there, although she saw that it was already dying. It was wilting away from the holly and ivy, both of which gleamed through it, verdant and bright. Tendrils had fallen to the mantelpiece and more lay withering on the floor.

Leah wondered if it was retreating from the orchard too, returning to Jack's grave. Come the spring, the apple trees might blossom. She pictured the branches growing strong, laden with white flowers that would fall, billowing in the breeze like snow.

Everything passes. Everything is renewed. She could feel new life beneath her feet beginning to stir, rising like sap rushing into the trees. Life would come back; it would start again.

Jack's story had been told.

She would not disturb his bones, she decided. They had already become a part of this place, a part of the land, and she thought he would be content with that.

She stooped to the table and retrieved the gift she had been given, seeing the picture with fresh eyes. It had been drawn just for her: the man, the woman and the child, building a snowman.

She pushed the mistletoe aside to make room for the drawing on the mantelpiece, ignoring the berries that dropped to the floor. They were already turning brown, decaying on the stem.

I won't have it in my house again, she decided. *It might be tradition, but it's not one I need to continue.* The past would not dictate her future. Her family might have done terrible things – their blood might run in her veins – but no one could decide anything for her any longer. No one could direct her hands or guide her thoughts. After all, Martha had controlled Ellis, but he had allowed her to do it, overcome by his greed and envy, blinded by lust. Now, with the help of her true family, the one she had chosen, Leah had broken whatever spell Martha had held over her. She could try to build something better.

'You know, you don't have to stay here.' Andrew was peering out of the window. Behind him, through the glass, she could see that the snow had thinned, the flakes shrinking, as if winter had decided to loosen its grip. What remained drifted slowly, at peace. Over the field, a bright moon was rising.

'Not tonight, I mean,' he went on. 'You don't have to be on your own. You could grab an overnight bag and walk back with me. It isn't far, not really. It is still Christmas Day, after all. Spend it with me and Cath and Charlie. We could be there in no time – back in the land of the living.'

And he held out his hand towards her.

A short time later, Leah stepped out once more into the snow. This time she didn't peer into it, trying to make out the forms hidden in its depths, for there were none. She could feel the years settled into the land all about her, but no one else walked its paths, not now.

The farm had been transformed into a scene of beauty. The slopes were silvered by the moonlight, the sky lit by an astonishing array of stars. For a moment, they stood and looked at the perfect stillness and Leah wondered when she had ever seen anything so lovely.

She stirred, realising that Andrew had stopped staring at the sky; instead, his gaze was fixed upon her. She answered his look with a smile and they set out, creating new footprints in the snow. This time, when she crossed the hill, she would pick up the little sentinel Charlie had set to watch over her farm and return it to him. It didn't need to stand guard any longer. It wasn't much of a gift, but it was something.

Leah turned to look back. She couldn't see the orchard, but she could see the way the house nestled into its little hollow and from here, it didn't appear dark or ruinous. It looked as if it belonged. Each window shone back the snow's light so that it almost seemed that someone was already at home, warm and cosy, really living there.

She turned from the sight and went on. She didn't know if she had caught a glimpse of her own future or someone else's, and it didn't matter; time would reveal its secrets.

For now, whatever the future held was something only the snow could tell.

Acknowledgements

A book is a labour of love, and not just by the author. Thanks and festive greetings to the lovely team at Jo Fletcher Books and Quercus, particularly Jo Fletcher herself, and to my agent, Oli Munson of AM Heath. A big 'ho ho ho' also goes to my web guru, Wayne McManus.

Christmas quaffs to my crazy, funny, talented writing buddies and the convention crews of wonderful events like Sledge. Lit, Edge.Lit and of course Fantasycon. You keep me sane (or perhaps the opposite – who can tell?).

Sherries and indeed snowballs (nicer than it sounds) to my fabulous parents Ann and Trevor, and a mistletoe smooch to my partner, Fergus Beadle.

Most of all, heartfelt thanks, Dear Reader, to you. May you find comfort and joy, not only in the bleak midwinter, but all year round.

THE
HIDDEN
PEOPLE

ALISON
LITTLEWOOD

IN HALFOAK, TRAGEDY IS ONLY
HALF-A-STEP AWAY . . .

Pretty Lizzie Higgs is gone, burned to dead on her own hearth - but was she really a changeling, as her husband insists? Albie Mirralls met his cousin only once, in 1851, within the grand glass arches of the Crystal Palace, but unable to countenance the rumours that surround her murder, he leaves his young wife in London and travels to Halfoak, a village steeped in superstition.

Albie begins to look into Lizzie's death, but in this place where the old tales hold sway and the 'Hidden People' supposedly roam, answers are slippery and further tragedy is just a step away . . .

Jo Fletcher
BOOKS